YOU HOLD THIS YEAR'S THIRTEENTH ISSUE OF *ANALOG* IN YOUR HANDS!

For more than forty years ASTOUNDING/ ANALOG Magazine has been perhaps *the* premier magazine of the science fiction field. ANALOG was the magazine that gave us Asimov, Clarke, and Heinlein in the Golden Age of science fiction, and continues that tradition today, producing such bright new talents as Orson Scott Card and George R.R. Martin.

But it's never been enough. To the devoted readers of ANALOG, twelve issues a year just can't provide enough of the incisive fiction and fact they demand.

So: The ANALOG Yearbook, Volume II, an entirely new collection of never-before-published work selected by the editor of ANALOG: *Science Fiction/Science Fact,* tailored specifically to the discriminating tastes of his readers, filled from cover to cover with the crisp writing and meticulous extrapolation the public has come to expect from the Grand Old Mag of science fiction. Enjoy!

analog yearbook II

analog
yearbook II

EDITED BY
STANLEY
SCHMIDT

SF
ace books

A Division of Charter Communications Inc.
A GROSSET & DUNLAP COMPANY
51 Madison Avenue
New York, New York 10010

ANALOG YEARBOOK II
Copyright © 1981 by Davis Publications, Inc.

An ACE Book by arrangement with
Baronet Publishing Company

First Ace printing: March 1981
Published Simultaneously in Canada

2 4 6 8 0 9 7 5 3 1
Manufactured in the United States of America

CONTENTS

Introduction
Stanley Schmidt

To be strictly accurate, the cover of this book should list not one editor, but two.

Ben Bova, editor of *Analog Science Fiction/Science Fact* from 1971 to 1978 (during which time he won five Hugo awards as Best Professional Editor), conceived and originated the *Analog Yearbook* as a sort of thirteenth issue of *Analog*. This served two purposes. First, to provide an extra helping of the unique blend of fiction and fact *Analog* has long been famous for, for the enjoyment of readers both old and new. Second, to get a sample of this unique blend—a sample of what *Analog* offers in magazine form every month—into the hands of people who might not be familiar with the magazine itself.

With the hope, it must be cheerfully confessed, that such readers, with their appetites once whetted, might seek out the magazine to find more.

Noble goals, and still valid.

Late in 1978, Ben left the editorship of *Analog* to go on to other things—in which we wish him the very best of success. Before he left, he had already bought some of the stories and articles and art destined for this new *Yearbook*. Through a set of singular and surprising circumstances, I found myself in the chair Ben had vacated. As the new editor of *Analog* (though not new to the magazine in all respects, as it had been publishing

1

stories of mine for some years), I bought the rest of the contents of this book.

So who's the editor?

Well . . . it's true that I did the final putting together. Since Ben had selected a very significant part of the contents, though, it seemed to me that he should share the byline.

But he, modest fellow that he is, said, "*Analog* has but one editor, and that's whose name should be on the *Yearbook*. And that's you, now."

So there you have it—but I thought you ought to know. If you find something in these pages that especially strikes your fancy (as I hope you will), there's a good chance that you have Ben, and not me, to thank for it.

I'm not going to tell you who picked which pieces. If it matters to you, you can try to guess. But I speak for both of us when I say that we sincerely hope you enjoy all of them.

And if you like what you see here, and you're not already familiar with *Analog,* the magazine, please do pick up a copy—or, better yet, a subscription.

There's lots more where this came from.

New York
April 1979

When cultures give way to new ones, things are lost and things are gained. Recapturing even a taste of what's been lost is no small task.

Première
Tony Rothman

The name of my company is MRP. I've never been sure if MRP means anything in particular, which might be considered strange as I run the place. It has been called the Music Recording Project. Others say that name is too limited and call it Miscellaneous Research Projects. Still others feel either title misses the true flavor of the enterprise and would say instead Megalomania Recapitulates Paranoia. It is best to ignore such slogans; they tend only to confuse the issue. The issue is what MRP does. Basically, we are in the entertainment business: movies, music, holoporns, video games, subliminal seduction, the usual.

I like to keep a tight rein on things and that day I was down in the studio listening over a tape just produced by the computer. We planned to market the recording under the name of a new hit group called the Electric Cinder Block but I was not, as yet, satisfied with the performance. Something bothered me about the computer's selection of tone colors. The Fourier analyses chosen for the vocals were too gentle and the upper harmonics for the guitars did not grate harshly enough on the ear. I requested additional passion; the volume increased, as well as the grating, and I was satisfied.

As far as real emotion goes, that mysterious thing injected into a composition called "inspiration," no computer has ever been able to produce it. But since the public has never recognized inspiration anyway, no one notices its absence any more than they noticed its presence. After all, the definition of an ordinary man is one who does not distinguish the ordinary from the extraordinary. And, by definition, the public is composed of ordinary men. Maybe that's being a little harsh. In any case, inspiration isn't a marketable quantity so we don't deal in it.

As I completed the adjustments, the phone light started flashing.

"Someone to see you, Roger. Should I let him in?"

"Sure, I'm just about finished in here."

The heavy, padded studio door swung open and a tall man, slightly hunched over, stepped inside. He was taller than I, a little, probably thirty years older, with hair that immediately reminded me of fallen snow. I flinched. I hate metaphor. When he held out his hand, I at once noticed the incredibly long, spatulated fingers which completely enclosed my own when we shook.

"Roger Talfin," I said. "What can I do for you?"

"My name is Herbert Seckslonger," he said, and I almost laughed. He continued: "I have been informed that you are rather influential in the world of music. Can you tell me if this is so?"

Normally, I would have immediately answered, "I am *the* most influential person in the music world." But I didn't. There was something about the way Seckslonger was looking at me, or rather beyond me, that made me uncomfortable. It was the kind of gaze that said he wasn't really concerned with what I answered, that perhaps a third of his concentration was focused on me at the moment and that, try as I might, I never could be as intelligent as he so I might as well not try at all. Those thoughts flashed by in an instant and I got angry. "I am *the* most influential person in the music world," I said.

Seckslonger smiled. "Excellent! Formidable!" he said with a voice twenty years younger than his hair. "I have a proposal to talk over with you. Tell me, are you an adventurous man?"

"Not for bad business risks—"

"Mr. Talfin, I think you are an adventurous man. Excellent. Why don't you join me at my place for lunch? It's not too far from here."

I cocked my head and nodded. Something about Seckslonger struck me as anachronistic. Perhaps it was his slightly formal way of speaking. Perhaps it was the lavender shirt whose ruffles peaked out from beyond his jacket cuffs and above his black vest. Such styles were usually reserved for weddings, funerals, and barroom brawls; to see them on the street was distinctly unusual. "Why not?" I said after my examination. "You caught me with a free hour."

"Well, what do you want?" I asked later as Seckslonger sat me down at a table, suspiciously already set for lunch. "I'd like to know who I am getting involved with." I didn't appreciate being out-maneuvered.

"With whom you are getting involved, I believe you wished to say. That is easily explained." Seckslonger sat down and poured some wine as I regarded his apartment.

It was a world of shimmering crystal and sumptuous carpeting. Lining the walnut walls were mineral specimens from around the world, lighted from hidden sources. Green malachite slabs glowed luminescently, as did nested tourmaline and fire opal. A small stream of water cascaded down a rose quartz fountain into a small pool of jasmine which occupied one corner of the living room. It was clearly the home of an unadulterated romantic. I flinched. I hate romantics. I refuse to deal with them. And if they deal with me, they do not remain romantics for long.

"At present," Seckslonger was saying, "I am in a state of active retirement. Formerly, like yourself, I was in advertising—"

"You're putting me on."

"No, quite the contrary. I was so good that I bought all my own products."

Could Seckslonger really be a man after my own heart? It was hard to believe. "Then why did you leave the business?" I asked.

Seckslonger sighed. "It was after the campaign for the Ultramatic camera which, as you know, takes photos without any assistance from the owner whatsoever. It roves around on its electric wheels and snaps pictures of anything which satisfies certain programmed criteria. A colossal success. Look to the streets; they're swarming with Ultramatics. After the campaign, the realization gradually came to me that I had swindled millions, that I had convinced these people an electronic eye could perceive what they could not, focus on what was to them indistinct and unfelt, what they were incapable of feeling. It was a wonderful revalation—until I realized I had also been swindling myself. I don't mind swindling others so much, but myself . . . that is another matter.

"So I left. Occasionally, the 'advertising urge' returns. It is a deeply rooted urge; the advertising mentality, I fear, is one well-disposed toward self-deception. However, I have thus far relented and remained in retirement, doing as I please—"

"And now?"

"I want to play some music for you."

I spilled my wine. "Do you mean you dragged one of the busiest men in the world away from a heavy schedule just to play some music for me?"

"That's precisely what I mean. Now attend to your wine and listen."

I was getting very annoyed, I have to admit. "And, damnit, why do you always talk like you have a board rammed down your throat?"

Seckslonger smiled. "Rather than guillotine my sentences both fore and aft, I prefer to obfuscate with distinction."

I think I hated Seckslonger at that instant, but Seckslonger, in his hideously superior way, didn't even deign to notice my anger and began rummaging through his obviously extensive musical collection. He selected one of the nickle-sized holodiscs and popped it into the player. The room was filled with a glorious march theme that every music lover knew by heart. "Tell me what you think it is," said Seckslonger.

"Finale from Beethoven's 10th symphony," I replied unhesitatingly. "But I can't place the synthesizer. It's not one of ours."

"Beethoven's 9th," Seckslonger smiled. "And it's not a synthesizer; it's an orchestra."

I think I was startled. After all, orchestras, next to

opera, were the most economically unfeasible artistic institutions ever devised and died out sometime in the last fifty or sixty years. They just didn't exist any longer. As one of my college-day colleagues once said, "Art, in the face of cost accounting, is impotent."

"Well, let's try another, shall we?" Seckslonger asked as he put on a second piece.

I listened. I did not hear anything that struck me as extraordinary. The sounds were mildly rhythmical but could not compare with anything I could generate at MRP given the proper voltage-controlled oscillators and filters. So that indicated something old. "Bach?" I asked.

"No. Try again."

I listened a second time. Perhaps Bach, living in the nineteenth century, did not have such large orchestras at his disposal, although my chronology was a little weak, so I couldn't be sure. "Brahms?" I asked on a hunch.

"You're getting warmer. A third try. Listen carefully."

This time I brought forth all my concentration. I listened to what I took for a savage ostinato of the strings, jagged outbursts of the brass, general cacophony of the woodwinds. Still, it was pretty tame. "Tchaikovsky," I concluded.

"Sorry. It's Stravinsky: *Le Sacre du Printemps, The Rite of Spring.*"

I shrugged. "Another one of those early romantics. They all sound the same to me." Actually, I didn't think Seckslonger was being quite fair. He couldn't really expect me to be able to distinguish 400 years of composers from one another when synthesizing the so-called classics is only a minute part of MRP's operations. Still one thing impressed me, the same thing that impressed me with all classics, both ancient and modern: For the larger public, which is not interested in such things, we usually settle on a simple rhythmic pattern that repeats itself over and over again every four or eight bars for the duration of the piece. It has been that way for the last 100 years. I am always impressed by the classical composer's delusion that he will be able to market a piece of any greater complexity. I am always impressed.

Seckslonger, at my response, threw up his arms in despair. "Can't you *hear*? Can't you hear the near riot this piece caused the first time it was performed?"

"No."

"Wouldn't you love to hear this piece for the first time, fresh? It would startle you."

"I am hearing this piece for the first time, fresh, and it doesn't startle me."

Seckslonger regarded me keenly. "You are really being very ordinary, you know, not being able to perceive the extraordinary."

That was below the belt. I immediately went on the defensive. "Or the piece has lost its impact over the years. That happens to them all, you know. If you want, I can beef it up for you at the labs."

Seckslonger sat down on the floor and ran his outstretched fingers through the carpet. I thought I saw white tears glistening in his eyes. "Yes," he nodded, "you're right. I was being harsh on you. 'Early romantic.' A good way of putting it. Bach merges with Brahms; Stravinsky and Tchaikovsky are indistinguishable. Yes, even to me. There has been so much music written over the intervening centuries that once great stylistic innovations have lost their identity. And then the synthesizer. What can compete with the synthesizer in cost benefits, in convenience? Composers write only for synthesizer; the Beethoven symphonies are reissued only on synthesizer. Everything is One. Out of Unity, all things.

"We must cut out those intervening years. We must bring the piece back in its original form. It must be premièred all over again."

"How can you première a piece that had its première more than 150 years ago?"

"That's where I thought you might be of assistance. How would you make an audience forget a century or two?"

I began to see what Seckslonger was getting at. My mind raced. "Hypnosis. It would have to be hypnosis."

"Exactly my thought. Can it be done? Can you dress an audience in period clothing, hypnotize them, and make them believe it is 1913?"

I cocked my head and thought quickly. I didn't really give a damn about the music end of this but the general scheme was devious enough to capture my imagination. "Yes, technically I think it could be done."

"How?"

"Well, a variety of techniques would necessarily be employed. For instance, we might use a tachistoscope, a device which premièred in the 1950's. It's basically just a movie projector which flashes messages on a screen too fast for the eye to perceive. But the *brain* perceives the messages. Flash 'Drink Coca-Cola' to an audience tachistoscopically over a feature film and Coca-Cola sales skyrocket afterwards. We use the technique all the time now; it's good for keeping an audience in the state you want them. Nowadays, we also have drugs which act on specific brain centers that can make people feel or act in a certain way, even experience induced hallucinations. They would be useful. Also, let's not forget the sub-sonic sound waves and powerful alpha-wave generators that can influence the victim without him knowing it—"

"Please clarify 'without him knowing it.' "

"You didn't expect to *tell them,* did you? Nobody sits still for having his mind tampered with knowingly."

"Yes, I hadn't thought of that. A good point."

"But give me half an hour of preparation and I should be able to have him in any state you want. I think, though, that the process will be slightly more involved than the one you had in mind. We will have to not only hypnotize an audience into forgetting nearly two centuries, but add what has been forgotten."

"That sounds impossible."

"Not really. There have been documented cases of people becoming proficient artists after an hour of training under hypnosis. They were literally fed high-speed art courses in the space of one hour. We will have to inject an entire culture, more information than an art course, but less specific. No skills to build up, which will make the process easier."

Seckslonger shook his head sadly. "My hopes are dampened. The human mind is complex. I am sure it cannot be a success."

I began to wonder what kind of success Herbert had in mind. If he thought I was getting into this just for an evening's worth of music, he had a revalation coming. But for the moment, it might serve to allow him to remain his romantic self, as long as it would get the ball rolling. "But certainly it is worth trying for the experience of hearing *Le Sacre* fresh."

Seckslonger's eyes brightened again. "Yes, it is worth the risk!" he said, jumping up from the floor.

A new difficulty suddenly occurred to my business mentality. Now my hopes were dampened. "Where are you going to get the musicians? They are rarer than camels in needles' eyes."

Herbert was not to be daunted. "I will scourge the entire world to find them if I must."

"And where will you find a concert hall to stage this?"

"The Théâtre des Champs-Elysées, where the first première was held, if possible. If not, I will build a replica."

"Costumes?"

"A trifle, *mon cher,* Roger. Seamstresses may be in no more abundance than rich men in heaven but they can be found."

"And who is going to pay for all this? You are talking about a multi-million dollar venture."

Seckslonger smiled wearily. "Mr. Talfin, I am not a poor man. I am prepared to stake my entire fortune on this 'venture,' as you call it."

I paused for another moment and thought out the plan again. "No, it won't work."

"It won't?"

"No. There is no way you are going to get an audience to dress up in antique clothing, go to a specially built concert hall to listen to the only orchestra in existence, selected painstakingly from around the world, and hypnotize them into believing they are at the first performance of a work that premièred in 1913, and which no one has bothered listening to for decades."

"Why not?"

"You need a gimmick."

Seckslonger put his head in hand. "Forgive me; I am stupid. I hadn't thought of that."

"The answer," I said after a moment of silence, "is Celebrity. The common man is attracted to celebrity like a moth to the flame. The thought that a celebrity may be a real person with feelings and, perhaps, a worthwhile fellow at that, is exorcised from the fan's mind. After all, if the fan realized the celebrity was real, that would be the end of the fantasy. But, as it stands, you could introduce him to a rock and say, 'This is the King of Siam,' and he would fall to pieces with happiness. Invite two hundred actors, diplomats, royalty, and the rest of the tickets will sell out in a flash."

Herbert grinned. "The idea is simplicity itself. I knew I had chosen the right partner. Excellent! Formidable! The truth is always blinding. I leave that end of the affair in your hands totally. And, if your philosophy is correct, it should be an easy matter to put the audience in the state of mind we wish them. Give them royalty, give them clothes to dress up in, give them a fairy-tale event, and they will hypnotize themselves. All of your tachistoscopes are probably not even necessary."

"To some extent you may be right but we can't bank on that. The average man does not have enough imagination to hypnotize himself. Yes, they can delude themselves about celebrities from now until doomsday, but to convince themselves that *they* should become magical for an evening, that *they* should be part of the fantasy, that is asking too much. We'd better rely on mechanical methods."

"Yes, your words have the weight of Truth behind them. Where do you suggest we begin?"

I was hoping Herbert was beginning to view this event in the correct light. "We should see about the concert hall first. If the Theater des . . . whatever-you-called-it is available, that will save a lot of work. If it isn't, to ready another will take the bulk of the time. So work on that should begin at once. Where is this Theater des . . . des—"

"The Théâtre des Champs-Elysées is in Paris."

"Let's go."

The next day Herbert and I were strolling down the once tree-lined boulevard known as the Champs-Elysées. Our excitement rose as we approached the theater where *Le Sacre* originally premiered. Seckslonger almost ran the entire last block, nearly being run over three times by American-hating French drivers. How they knew he was American—if he was—with his ruffled shirt, I chalk up to Gallic pride which divides the world into Parisian, French, and American. When we got close to the site, I could see his shoulders droop. I took a few more steps and stifled a chuckle. No Théâtre des Champs-Elysées. A soda fountain and hamburger stand instead. Well, as I always say, "Where there's Life, there's Coke."

Seckslonger remained undaunted and his disappointment evaporated immediately. "We will have to build a replica," he said with his unflagging exuberance. "The question I put to you, my wonderful colleague is: where?"

We began strolling back the way we came and in a flash I had the answer. It was a stroke of genius, if I may say so myself. "Texas. We'll do it in Texas."

"Texas? Why Texas?"

When we arrived in Austin, Texas, it was clear that my choice was the perfect one. The atmosphere was as nearly Parisian as one could get without being in Paris. Here, as in Paris, no building was less than monumental; the kinship between the French and Texans showed up plainly in their grandiosity. Admittedly, there was a slight difference in the matter of style: The Parisians could not construct an edifice which left a square meter unadorned with intricate baroque flourishes while, in Texas, the architectural style was more or less a cross between paleo-monolithic and neo-cube.

But those were just details, superficialities. At bottom, it was really just the same old provincialism which bound Texas and France into *fraternité*. Just as Paris viewed itself as the center of the known Universe, so did Texas. Texas had always prided itself on its "anti-culture," a culture based on that which the rest of the civilized world regarded as nonessential: a worship of Coors Beer, football, armadillos, wet t-shirt contests, the Gutenberg Bible, and the ROTC. Indeed, when the armadillo became extinct (due mostly to the unique Texan driving habits), a giant 15-meter tall, stainless-steel statue of the beloved *Dasypus novemcinctus* was erected in front of the university library, whose own floor plan had been designed in the shape of Texas.

The Texans did not stop there. After the many

energy crises of the last century, during which precious Texas oil had often been called upon to rescue the rest of the country, the Texans finally stood their ground and seceded from the Union. Now Texas, or Lone Star as it is called there, is an independent country, complete with its own defense budget and Joint Chiefs of Staff. Furthermore, as a result of these energy crises, the rest of the world had been forced to abandon large automobiles. Rather than undergo such extreme hardships, the Texans set up their own Cadillac manufacturing plant. Texas is now the only place on earth where such dinosaurs can be found.

Of course, money attracts money, and Texas soon became a center of true culture. Holoporns now flourish there, as well as all branches of synthergistics. Video-football, computer recording companies, ersatz beer, all have their bases in Texas. A "Made in Lone Star" label on an import is always a sign of quality merchandise. Yes, Texas is to be admired for doing an about-face from being the center of anti-culture to the hub of civilization.

And naturally, because it was the hub of civilization, that is where we would hold our concert.

Within a few days we had located an old tenement block which we could afford to buy as the site for the Champs II. It wasn't in the best part of town but we were too impatient for anything else to open up. Several weeks after then, we contracted a construction company and showed them the plans for the hall, painstakingly retrieved from the Paris archives. When Seckslonger pointed out all the details, the elaborate woodwork, the handpainted murals, gold filligree, the sculptured cherubim which would adorn the proscenium arches, the builders said it couldn't be done in less than five years.

"We'll have to go plastic," I told Herbert. "And styrofoam cherubs."

"No. I refuse. But we shall worry about those details later. We must proceed with all haste."

There was Herbert's romanticism surfacing again. I would have to act surreptitiously.

As the building began, under a clamp of "top secret," we tackled the next problem, which was to round up the musicians. One evening, Herbert and I sat in his living room studying a rare copy of the score to *Le Sacre* in order to determine what we needed.

"An orchestra of 110, strings fairly standard—"

"What do you mean, 'standard'? Strings don't exist anymore."

"I meant standard for the day, of course. The winds are heavy. Look at this: 3 flutes, two doubling on piccolo, 4 clarinets, 3 oboes, two doubling on English horn . . . Oboists were hard enough to find when they existed, yet alone now. Also: a conductor, a choreographer, lead dancers, and corps de ballet. This will be a formidable hunt, I am afraid. Do you have any suggestions?"

I almost laughed. "I'm afraid this is your department, Herbert. Naturally, the entire resources of MRP are at your disposal but I doubt they will help much."

"Well then, I suggest we start in the simplest manner possible with advertisements over the telenews and in the plastics . . . How about something along these lines: 'Musicians needed. Expertise on real instruments required. Only classically trained instrumentalists wanted. Computer experts need not apply. Also needed: ballet dancers, choreographer, and conductor.' "

"I'm a little worried about that," I said. "The word 'musician' is fast disappearing from the language. It has already reached the status of a technical term. I might have to reword that, but the idea is O.K."

"Good. We should place the ad immediately and see what results it brings."

The results it brought were disasterous. We had not been careful enough in regards to the words "classically trained." The overwhelming majority of respondents thought that the classical period was synonymous with "before 1990." We got hundreds of electric guitarists, balefuls of drummers, dozens of harmonica players, some saxophonists, and a few trumpeters. We did pick up one or two violinists along the way, fiddlers from Appalachia, found one drummer who could play tympani, and two trumpeters who would service if nothing better came along. Still, we had a long way to go. We replaced the ad, being more explicit about what we wanted.

The second round brought encouraging results and within a month we had recruited some dancers, a handful of woodwinds, and more than a dozen string players. We immediately had them begin rehearsals on any available music, just to start building a sense of ensemble, but all it brought was civil war. The winds complained the strings were too sharp; the strings complained the winds were too flat. A violinist grumbled that brass should be seen and not heard and, as a reply, received a shattered eardrum which took no less than three weeks in the hospital to mend. A clarinetist remarked off-handedly that the only thing worse than one flute was two flutes. The flutist smashed all the clarinetist's reeds.

It was clear that we needed a conductor. As Herbert once sagely observed, a good conductor was one of two types. Either he was an expert funambulator, a diplomat who could assiduously smooth out the continual, ego-bruising squabble among musicians, or he was a martinet who solved the same problem by directing everyone's hatred at himself, thus causing them to forget the internecine strife. The reason most of the famous conductors of the past had been of the latter type was simply because that was, by far, the easier way out.

Thus began our world-wide search for a conductor, as well as a choreographer and the remaining musicians. We still needed many more strings, especially violists, who were always the rarest of that breed and seemed to be found mainly in convents praying to the Lord to supply them with more interesting parts. We would find a cellist deep in the jungles of Brazil playing for the macaws. A violinist would be found sitting on a rooftop in Tel-Aviv. Tracing the records of the now-defunct Tuba Players of America brought to light the needed master of that instrument. The manhunt stretched from weeks to months and had Herbert and me jetting around the world in opposite directions, often coming no closer to one another than in the near collisions between our planes. I began to think we would never pull it off. To find a musician became an occasion as rare as a solar eclipse and was cause for great celebration.

The two of us happened to be together when we found our first legendary oboist. We were in Togo sitting at a Togoland munching on a couple of Togoburgers. It was Seckslonger who first noticed him. The man was young, middle twenties, and was sitting beneath the large, flashing "Togoland" sign, hunched over and busily wielding a knife on something in his hands that was too small to be seen.

"What are you doing, if I may ask?" Herbert asked.

"Making a reed," replied the young man without looking up. I had yet to see his face beneath a tangled mass of dark, curly hair, but I did manage to make out a long Fu-Manchu moustache trailing off his chin.

"What for?"

"One must do something with one's time, musn't one?"

"But what is the reed for?"

"For? The reed is an end in itself." The man held a small object up to the bright African sun and scrutinized the tip from one angle and then another. "I believe that somewhere exists a perfect reed and all physical reeds partake of its form. The better reed partakes a fraction of the perfection and the poor reed a lesser fraction. I have not yet found the path to the one, true reed. My quest is never ending." The young man put the reed to his lips and blew into it. It squawked. "This is not the perfect reed," he pronounced and threw it over his shoulder.

"Surely," said Herbert, "at one time or another you must have made reeds for something, an instrument perhaps?"

"Oh yes, that," said the reedmaker gazing into the

nostalgic past. "That was a long time ago when I was young and idealistic. Then I was an oboist and under the delusion that reeds were for the oboe."

"Don't you still play?"

"There is not time."

"Why not?"

"I spend all my time working on reeds in order that I should be able to play."

Seckslonger yanked him to his feet and brought him with us.

The search continued. By ones and by twos we rounded up the musicians and dancers and shipped them back to Austin. Most were willing to go as they had nothing better to do with their time. Naturally, the two most crucial persons, the conductor and the choreographer, were the two last to be found.

We excavated our choreographer in a Swiss sanatorium. He claimed to be a faun and pranced about like one. Nonetheless, Herbert was not convinced of his choreographic ability until we saw his ikebana. Herbert exclaimed, "This reminds me of the Dance of the Semi-Precious Stones from Prokofiev's *Kameny Tzvetok*. The faun replied, "That's exactly what it is." I said, "Opacity is the virtue of mankind, but will it sell?" Herbert nodded and the three of us cheerfully departed.

Our conductor was found in similar circumstances. We were walking through a small Latin American village whose streets were lined with almond trees and whose houses were made of adobe brick, when we happened across a squad of soldiers dressed in sweat-stained khaki, carrying ancient single-shot rifles.

"Halt!" they shouted as we approached.

Seckslonger and I exchanged glances. After all, soldiers were as obsolete as musicians and neither of us had ever seen one before except in photographs and parades.

"Do you support the Liberal or Conservative party?" one of them demanded.

"I . . . I . . ."

"Come, the Colonel will see you now."

They bound our wrists and marched us into the largest house in town. We entered to see a man with a swarthy face, also dressed in khaki, pacing the room. He sported a black, waxed moustache and large puffs of smoke from the cigar he was waving about would periodically obscure his face as he stalked back and forth, attention riveted on a large map covering the floor.

"No, no!" he shouted, oblivious to our entrance. "We need more from the right flank. The entrance must not be delayed. The precision is in the waiting. If you wait precisely the right amount, the attack will be on time." An orderly moved some markers on the map. "No! Imbecile! Have you no sense of line? The movement must flow from the lower parts to the higher. You have destroyed the line. And look here, the second company is advancing too quickly. One must not force climaxes prematurely. The final push must be reserved for the last moment. Do you understand? Imbecile!" He kicked the orderly out of the way and the toy soldiers scattered throughout the room.

Finally he turned to us and threw up his arms. "These peons have no sense of orchestration. How can one win a revolution without a sense of orchestration, will you tell me that? Bah."

"Sir," interrupted Herbert. "Tell me, have you ever conducted a symphony orchestra before?"

"Ah," replied the Colonel, hand on heart. "My first love. I was trained as a conductor but never realized my dreams as orchestras died out in my youth. What I would give for the opportunity!"

"If you are willing to trade one war for another, we will give you that opportunity."

The Colonel's eye lit up and he threw down his pistol. "Do you think I give a picayune to your revolution? Imbeciles. Who cares whether the Liberal or Conservative party wins? Do you think it will make a difference in the end? Politics is for amusement only."

Now that we had just about finished collecting all the needed personnel, I had time to turn my attention to what I viewed as the actual guts of the project: the devices that would hypnotize the audience into forgetting almost two hundred years of recent history and adding two hundred years of a forgotten history. Since the technology was available, the problem was simply to find the best way of implementing it.

The day before the first scheduled rehearsal, Herbert approached me. "And how are your 'mechanics' proceeding?"

"I think everything is set. As the patrons arrive, we provide them with drinks on the house. This should help put them in a forgetful frame of mind. That's the first step. The lobby is lined with specially adjusted alpha, beta, and theta generators which should help the process along. We also have added soft background noise which contains encoded instructions to be subliminally assimilated, as well as speeded up variations of seventeenth, eighteenth, and nineteenth century music to provide the correct cultural framework. That's the second step. Thirdly, I've arranged a projection booth which will flash messages tachistoscopically over the sets at the rear of the stage. This will be used to more firmly implant the suggestions and reintroduce more ancient cultural concepts. We should try it out at the rehearsal tomorrow."

"What do you mean?"

"You claim to desire authenticity. You have named musicians after their original counterparts. Certainly, for true authenticity, you want the musicians to be drugged and hypnotized into believing they are living in the early twentieth century."

"But for the entire six months, or however long the preparations take?"

"Why not?" I shrugged. "Most people spend their entire lives drugged, so what difference does it make?"

Herbert acceded and I prepared my magic potions and ray guns.

The next day, the orchestra members wandered into the lobby and, one by one, I handed them a drink. The effects were remarkable. I think everyone began speaking like Herbert almost immediately.

The moment of the first rehearsal was at hand. Pierre Monteux, the conductor, stood on the podium of the still unfinished hall as workmen hammered and sawed away on the construction of the first tier of balconies. He raised his baton but did not give the downbeat, as if he were waiting for something to happen. While he stood in that expectant pose, the last straggling musicians walked onstage and took their places. Monteux smiled. "Now we can proceed with Art."

He raised his baton again and softly began counting in four. The bassoon started its solo in the extreme high register, soon joined by the other woodwinds. After six bars of varying meter, the clarinetist missed his cue, and a totally misplaced flute chirped in the wrong place.

"You call this music?" one of the orchestra members shouted. "What do you take us for anyway?"

"I think you have answered that question yourself," replied Monteux. "Now again, from the beginning."

At the end of the three hours, indicated to the second by the large union clock, which was displayed prominently next to the podium, the orchestra stopped playing in the midst of a bar, rose as a man, and walked offstage.

"In the name of Art, come back!" cried Monteux.

"In the name of Overtime, we won't!"

Herbert sighed and paid them overtime.

Preparations went on for the next year. Vaslav Nijinsky, the choreographer, determined to overcome the incredibly complex rhythms which Stravinsky had provided him, required more than 130 rehearsals to begin to get the piece in shape. And he was still worried. During those rehearsals I would go backstage and see him shouting, "One! two! three! four! One! two! three! four! five! One! One! two! . . ."

I became vaguely impressed with the amount of effort needed to mount this single performance. A composer writes a piece; a choreographer studies it and maps out a dance equivalent; an orchestra and ballet are assembled. By now, it may be two years after the composer has originally conceived the work. Each of 110 musicians spends his days perfecting his tiny part, blistering his hands on one finger of the statue. The orchestra as a whole and dozens of dancers struggle with the music as a whole for a whole year. But the struggle is necessarily waged in a piecemeal fashion; the musicians are only able to see one flake at a time, rarely the full statue which they are carving. At the end, only several glimpses of the whole have been attained. The musicians and dancers still have not yet stepped back to see the full height of the colossus. They do not yet have it right. But can they ever? Perhaps only a synthesizer is given that privilege. Battles rage, spirits sink. The conflict is immense, though an audience is never privilege to that struggle either. At the end, everyone has had enough. Even Seckslonger, Monteux, and Nijinsky, who are known for their enthusiasm, have had enough. The outlook is grim.

"Will it succeed?" I asked Seckslonger. "What do you think?"

Herbert put down the score he had been studying and the mass of bills he had been paying. He rubbed his eyes. It was very late. "Will it succeed? No. People will listen, shrug their shoulders, and that will be the end of it. I will have spent 20 million dollars for . . . for an interesting experience."

"And where had your riot gone, your glorious riot? You expect this to be just an interesting experience. It had damn well pay more than that."

"Riot. No. Look at these musicians who spend all their time grumbling and arguing with one another. Why do they do it? Because they are bored. Because the music is boring and not interesting enough to spend a year rehearsing. They are bored; the dancers are bored, all as bored as the day you first heard the piece. There is not enough energy in this music to cause a riot. We should 'beef it up at the labs.' " Herbert got up slowly. "Now I think it is time to get some sleep."

Exhausted, I watched Herbert leave. I began to see that I understood him no better now than I did two years ago. His motivations were as unclear to me now as then. Perhaps he really did just want to hear a piece of music fresh. I didn't know. His mind, from another age it seemed, would be forever blocked from my view.

But I was so persuaded by Herbert's gloomy forecast that for the first dress rehearsal I corraled one hundred unsuspecting victims off the street and had them listen to the run-through. I carefully watched for any reaction whatsoever. Twenty-three people walked out, five had severe coughing fits, three old ladies spent the entire time knitting, thirty-eight laughed, the rest just sat there. That was truly the end of it, I decided. Unless it was a problem of being below critical mass or temperature. I thought desperately for a surefire method of ignition, one that would bypass all uncertainties. There had to be a way.

Inexorably, the day arrived. Both Herbert and I had spent the last night sleepless. What would happen, neither of us was sure. All I could do was make checks on my apparatus to make sure it was in working order.

The concert hall, Champs II, had barely been finished on time. As it turned out, the rush did force us to use the styrofoam cherubim and Atlases after all. We also had the workmen spray on the gold paint just to get the job done on time. Still, with all the corners cut, the place looked magnificent. I gazed at the corinthian columns flanking the stage, the giant, plastic chandelier, sparkling and glimmering red as it reflected the lush carpeting which covered the aisles and seats. I smiled at the angels embracing the vaulted ceiling and the great Atlases holding up the heavens. I marveled at the gold trim which surrounded each proscenium box and the entire parquet. I wondered at the concealed lamps which cast long shadows of all the smaller columns whose capitals, garlanded with flowers, supported the balconies. Indeed, there was not another place like it in all the world.

And indeed, we had paid dearly for it. Seckslonger was broke now; he was no longer a rich man. The entire fortune he had made as a successful advertiser was invested in what would take place this evening. And, as it stood, it looked as if nothing would take place whatsoever. We would see.

Even though it was still morning, some of the invited guests and curious onlookers had come to take a peek. The switchboard at the hotel was busy all day confirming the VIP arrivals. Tickets, as I had predicted, sold out in a flash, within hours after the names on the VIP list were made public. The sell-out was doubly impressive as the exorbitant price of the tickets was largely to cover the cost of appropriately tailored clothing to be worn at the concert. Well, that's the magic of celebrity. At least we would have a full house.

By seven in the evening, both Herbert and I were in such a state of agitation that neither of us could refrain from pacing up and down the length of his hotel room. My starched collar itched dreadfully and I found myself adjusting it every few minutes. Seckslonger, too, would stop his pacing suddenly, stare into the dressing mirror and brush off his lapels, then begin his nervous stalking once more.

We jumped when the phone rang. "Your cab is here, Sir."

Acting as a pair of twins, we grabbed our top hats and headed for the lobby. Even after all the preparations, I was surprised to see a liveried coachman waiting for us beside a magnificent antique: a two-horse carriage. Seckslonger tipped his hat and we climbed in.

At the snap of the driver's whip, the horses trotted off down the road. I imagined their hooves clacking lightly against the cobblestones of ancient Paris. For a fleeting instant, I thought I understood Seckslonger a bit more. Perhaps he had been telling the truth all this time. Then I discarded the thought as an impossibility. Nonetheless, I once again put to Herbert the question which he had so unsatisfactorily answered so often before: "How will it go? What do you say this time?"

Seckslonger took a monogrammed gold cigarette case out of his breast pocket and flipped it open. He leaned back and grinned, tapping a cigarette on the side of the case. "The smart audience will be there in all its glory, tails, tulle, diamonds, and osprey. The younger aesthetic crowd will be present in regalia befitting their view of themselves and will applaud novelty simply to show their contempt for those in the boxes. The affair will be a painting by Monet, but the shades of color which, in his work, merge indistinguishably into one another will be replaced by shades of snobbery, super-snobbery, and inverted snobbery. The audience will play the part that is written for it."

I was pleased to hear that Herbert had a rather deep streak of cynicism rooted beneath his omnipresent beatitude. Nonetheless, I was not optimistic. The dress rehearsal still weighed on my mind.

The early evening air was oppressively heavy, laden with the probability of rain. It suited my mood that night as the cab trotted past the old library built in the shape of Texas which had turned from white to grey in years. I smiled as we passed the giant armadillo forever immortalized in stainless-steel which stood on the library's great brick plaza.

I think I could hear Seckslonger's heart beating as the cab turned the final corner to the theater. The crowd which had already formed parted and the driver was able to pull up to the curbside. A footman opened the door and waited for us to get out. Herbert and I stared long at each other. There was nothing to be said now, if there ever was. We shook hands and stepped onto the red-carpeted sidewalk.

"Will seven francs be enough?" Herbert asked the driver and paid him as the coachman tipped his hat.

The crowd pressed in on us and the holovision crews traced our every step.

"What do you expect to happen tonight, Mr. Seckslonger?" called one of the reporters as he shoved a microphone in Herbert's face.

"I expect to hear a good piece of music."

I laughed to myself. We shoved the rest out of our way and quickly gained entrance to the lobby.

Just as we entered via the front door, a silver-haired woman and a younger version of herself began descending the grand staircase.

"Who are they?" I whispered to Herbert.

"The Comtesse van Kness and her daughter, Christina, I believe."

We stood there enchanted as the Comtesse and her daughter gracefully floated across each step of the lushly carpeted marble staircase. The Comtesse herself was about Seckslonger's age and wore a deep black gown which barely touched the floor and was trimmed in satin. A triple-chained necklace of the finest pearls, which matched her hair in whiteness, encircled her throat and tangled themselves amid her nervous fingers. Her aquiline nose turned up as she nodded regally to each person she passed.

But it was upon her daughter that my attention was fixed. Her coiffeur, intricately arranged and secured at the nape, was crowned by a cluster of pomegranate blossoms. Her cornflower blue decollétage served to accent her ivory white shoulders and bosom, while the delicate green embroidery that rimmed the dress matched perfectly the color of her eyes. A diamond brooch fastened over her breast glistened as she walked.

Herbert was introducing me although I hardly heard a word he said. I bowed at the waist, taking first the Comtesse's gloved hand and then that of her daughter. My lips lingered on her slender fingers for as long as I dared and my eyes shyly rose past her golden bracelet and bare arm to receive the blessing of her sparkling gaze.

"I hope I may have the honor of the first mazurka at the ball."

"It would be my great pleasure," replied Christina, staring after me as her mother pulled her off for more introductions.

My own gaze followed her throughout the room. "Enchanting," I said to Herbert as he handed me a cocktail.

"Ah, Talfin, good to see you!"

"Good to see you too, Steinberg," I said, pressing a five hundred dollar bill into his hand. Steinberg tipped his hat and was off. Seckslonger cocked an eyebrow. "The country's most influential music critic," I said. "He's in our camp now."

Finally, I had a chance to take a good look around me. The magnificent floor-to-ceiling mirrors convinced one that the lobby was twice as large as in reality one knew it to be. The gasoline lanterns' flickering light provided just the right touch of intimacy. And the crystal chandeliers in the lobby refracted the lamps' elongated flames into a spectrum of colors and refracted the great crowd around me into its component parts.

From one corner of the room came the cultured laughter of the rich society damsels whose furs and diamonds were displayed with tasteless conspicuousness. Skirts rustled and artificial dewdrops glistened on artificial corsages. They daintily sipped cordials provided for them by liveried servants who deftly darted in and out of the crowd carrying their silver trays.

Nearby, their husbands clustered around the bar, gulping liquor in thirsty mouthfuls. These men had the complexion of wealth. Their long sideburns fell over low-turned collars as they wiped their lips with large, monogrammed handkerchiefs. The looks they wore on their faces as they chatted idly about the day's races were so calm, so indifferent, so satisfied, that they might as well have been dead for all the passion they exuded.

~~In the opposite corner of the lobby were the young Bohemians, in ill-fitting suits rented for the occasion. They talked of Truth as if it were their property and of the New Order which, naturally, they would bring about. A disagreement over a political issue would raise an eyebrow, while a disagreement over a brushstroke would provoke a fistfight. Yes, they would not lose the opportunity to battle with established society under the banner of Art.

Soon, the lights dimmed and waxed again, signaling that it was time to enter the concert hall. I found Herbert with the Comtesse and Cristina and together we took our box. The orchestra was already in place and through my opera glasses I spied the oboists bent over their reeds. I quickly surveyed the hall, glancing over the shoulders and tight chignons to see who might be attending the ball afterwards, although I was careful in my manner for Christina was at my side. I still dared not hope that she would honor me with her attention that evening and thought it best to make contingency plans. I looked up at the primeval forest scene painted on the slats at the rear of the stage and sat back eagerly anticipating the première of this new and unknown piece of music.

"Tell me, Herbert, what do you know of this Stravinsky fellow?"

"One of those young Turks who, I am told, is out to overturn the music world. It is rumored that this ballet has taken almost 150 rehearsals and that the dancers still cannot follow the music."

"Nijinsky did the choreography?"

"Yes, exactly."

"Then there's no telling what we might expect. He runs hot and cold that one."

Now the house lights went down and the conductor, Pierre Monteux, took his position to the audience's light applause. Monteux slowly raised his arms and the silence was absolute. I glanced down at my program to see the words *Première Partie: L'adoration de la Terre,* just as an eerie melody, produced from somewhere deep in the bowels of the orchestra, floated up to the balconies.

"What is that instrument?" I heard from the next box.

"It's an oboe."

"No, it's a muted trumpet," came the sharp retort.

"Shh," said Herbert brusquely, leaning over. "It's a bassoon."

During most of *L'adoration de la Terre,* the audience remained relatively quiet, pacified to some extent by the neo-Debussyisms of the opening. There was some shuffling and fidgeting which was due mostly to the old ladies, who were always fifty years out of date anyway. Towards the end, where the sonorities were becoming complex, whispers began shooting around the auditorium, questioning in the dark the sanity of such a composer.

But at the opening of the *Danses des Adolescentes,* whose violent, jagged outbursts must have sounded more like roaring volcanoes or dinosaurs than young boys jumping up and down in white smocks, the audience began to erupt. Laughter and booing broke

out in the boxes which was countered by applause
from the young Bohemians stationed in the peanut
gallery. It was becoming difficult to hear the music.
For a moment, order was restored when the house
lights were brought up. Everyone froze as if they had
been caught stark naked and the percussive thunder-
ing of the brass burst through the air undiminished.
But the moment the lights went down again, the hissing and howling started anew. Insults richocheted
around the hall, countered each time by sharp cries of
"Quiet!" from the young Bohemians.

Now one of the dancers lost his footing and slipped
on stage.

"Un docteur!" called a voice from the darkness.

"Un dentiste!"

"Deux dentistes!"

Then the female dancers entered for *Jeu de Rapt,*
the *Ritual of Abduction.* The music whipped the dancers into a sexual frenzy and, as the stylized rape began
onstage, so did it in the audience when a nearby
dignitary hoisted his wife over his shoulder and began
storming out of the hall.

The Comtesse stood up. "Well, I'm 60 years old
and this is the first time anyone has dared to make
fun of me."

A young man in the box behind us rose to his feet
and began to beat rhythmically on top of my head. I
hardly even noticed, so great was my own agitation
which was displayed by shaking the shoulders of the
woman in front of me.

A lady in a nearby orchestra box stood up and
slapped the face of the man in the box-next-door who
had been hissing loudly. The man slapped her in return. Her escort rose and cards were exchanged be-

tween the two men. I am sure a duel was fought the next day.

By this time the audience was in a total uproar and the concert hall was shaking as if it had been struck by an earthquake. The music was totally inaudible. Herbert was leaning over shouting orders to the dancers onstage but I have no doubts that they could not hear anything he said. And there was Monteux, still beating away, rigid as a crocodile, at the center of the maelstrom, impervious to everything going on around him. How he managed to keep the musicians playing and the dancers dancing in the center of that cyclone, I shall never know.

"Come on," said Herbert suddenly. "Let's get backstage."

We left our box to cries of "Bolshevik!" from the boxes and *"Taisez-vous les garces du seizieme!"* from the Bohemians.

Backstage we found Nijinsky. He was still in practice costume, not yet having dressed for *Le Spectre de la Rose* which was supposed to follow. He was standing there, quivering, beating out the rhythm with both fists and, having lapsed into his native language, was shouting to his dancers in Russian, "Raz! dva! tri! chetyri! Raz! dva! tri! chetyri! pyat! Raz! Raz! dva!. . ." The dancers could not understand anything he said. His wife was there also, trying to keep these same dancers from bursting into tears. We could not hear anything now other than the shouting and the stamping but I peeked out from behind the curtains and saw Monteux still standing, rigid as a crocodile, pounding away. I felt sorry for them all.

Now a large part of the audience began to stamp their feet in rhythm. The wave amplified and spread throughout the hall as more and more people joined in. The chandelier started rattling and the balconies shuddered. If before was an earthquake, this was Ragnarok. I was afraid the entire building would collapse at any moment. As it happened, one of our styrofoam cherubs got unpinned, fell from its position of grace, and bounced off the Comtesse's head.

The cherub was immediately snatched up from the floor and hurled into the orchestra where it smashed an angry oboist's reed. The Bohemians were standing in the ampitheatre cheering. A group of men in the parquet put shoulder and arm together and began ramming the columns which supported the balconies. Suddenly, the men in the parquet succeeded in overturning one of the columns and the balcony above them creaked and swayed. People jumped off to avoid the collapse. I turned my head just in time to miss the crash. When I looked up again, I saw a young man putting a flame to the curtains. This was the end. Before the first whiffs of smoke reached my nostrils, the dancers, as one man, stampeded off the stage.

I do not remember anything else until I found myself standing on the street. I assume I wandered there or was swept outside by the crowd. By this time, the flames could be seen shooting through the roof. The building, made largely of perishable materials, would go up quickly. There was a lot of screaming and milling about. I found Herbert. Together we sat down on the curbside at the end of the block where an occasional spark would land at our feet to keep us company.

Herbert was exuberant. "Ah," he sighed heartily. "So, a proper riot. You see what a fresh hearing will do. And I am sure you see the commercial possibilities here—"

I nodded. "I'm glad commercialism got the better part of romanticism in the end."

"This is truly wonderful," he went on. "This is Renaissance! Orchestras will be reborn, ballet, opera . . . It's extraordinary. The music was reignited once again. We cut out the intervening years . . ." As Herbert finished his soliloquy, he suddenly put his hands over his ears and began shaking his head. "I'm feeling very d . . . dizzy."

I was also. As per program, the hypnosis was wearing off.

Herbert shook his head again and glanced around at the crowd, each person also shaking his head in confusion. We both glanced at the theater. No flames were pouring from the roof, no sparks were fluttering to our feet. I smiled. My plan had worked.

"What is going on here?" muttered Herbert.

I shrugged. "I forgot to tell you: After that disasterous dress rehearsal, I decided on a surefire approach; I hypnotized the audience into *believing* the riot was real."

"Do you mean to tell me it was an hallucination?"

"Exactly," I smiled. "Within my strictly programmed limits, everyone imagined his own riot. Yours, no doubt, was slightly different than mine."

I could see Herbert was not amused. "Why you . . . you *fraud!*"

"Hold on!" I said, raising my arm. "Not only did it work this way, after we had both given up hope, but think about the cost benefits."

"What are you talking about?"

"Do you think we can afford to repair a theater after a riot every week? We'd go bankrupt. This way, everyone imagines a riot, it's as good as real, so who cares?"

"Then why stage it at all?" cried Herbert. "You might as well have hypnotized each person in his own home."

I passed the suggestion off with a wave of my hand. "Just as an ordinary concert produces a much better effect with an audience than without one, so here the hypnosis worked immeasurably better *en masse*. The pre-concert reception, the costumes, the physical presence of the performers, the live music, and, of course the audience, all were the basis, the kernel for the riot. Without that existing framework, to hallucinate a riot would have been impossible; with that framework it was a triviality. Much easier than producing a real riot."

Herbert slowly got to his feet and stared at me for a very long time. Then he said even more slowly, "Renaissance . . . An audience of drugged people watched a drugged concert and produced an imaginary riot . . . *Reducto ad absurdum, reductio ad finem* . . . Well done."

He turned from me then and began walking away. He glanced sidewards at me one last time with the faintest trace of a smile curled at the edge of his lips. A final recognition spread across his face. "Sometimes, it is the creator himself who is the last to see what he has done." He laughed, a crooked laugh if ever one was to be heard. "Yes, we've swindled ourselves once again, haven't we?" And then he walked into the darkness.

I have not seen him since that night, not at a one of the many concerts which have been held since that first première. Seckslonger is gone. I am richer.

Collision Orbit
David Andreissen

MEMO

Date: 2 Jan 1993

From: Director, Space Ordinance Development
      Center, American Sector Luna, M 10033.

To: Secretary of Internal Security, Washington,
     D.C. 20013.

Subj: Resignation

Dear Mr. Secretary:

I have received your directive of the 20th, requesting the Center to commence R&D on an air-dropped wide-area concussive-effect antipersonnel mine.

Given the trend of Party policies in the past few years, I suspect that the primary use of such a weapon would be the suppression of mounting internal dissent. After long consideration, I have concluded that I cannot in good conscience participate in the development of such a device.

I realize that this attitude may have the gravest personal consequences. . . .

          Dr. John Lake
          Director, SODC

Even the most comfortable acceleration couch is

confining for a prisoner.

Lake shifted against his seat restraints and, forgetting, flexed his wrists inside the handcuffs. The
movement triggered them and a high warning note
filled the cramped cockpit of the Moon-Station shuttle. There was a stir behind him and Lake tensed,
closing his eyes. The blow, landing square on the
back of his head, made him see a varicolored pattern
of brilliant flame.

"I told you not to do that, Lake," said Morock,
from behind him. "Just sit quietly and I won't have to
hit you again. How much longer to the Station, pilot?"

"About four hours more, Party Member Morock,"
said the pilot, tucking a curl of dark hair back under
her knit helmet cap. "Party Member . . . do you have
to treat him like that? I mean, it's not as if he were
dangerous. . . ."

"Disobedience of Party orders is the most dangerous crime of all," said the Party Member, a thin,
sandy-haired young man dressed in the drab DP cov-
eralls.

Lake twisted round in his seat and held up his man-
acled wrists. "Can't we at least dispense with these,
Morock? Or are you afraid I'll jump you and make
my getaway to Saturn through the air lock?"

"Remember your place, 'doctor' Lake," said Morock. "You're an enemy of the people and a prisoner
of the State, proceeding under arrest back to the Station for Party trial. And you call me 'sir!' "

As Lake opened his mouth to reply he caught
Brenda's eye, her slight warning shake of the head.
He bit back the words and turned abruptly round in
his seat, letting his fettered hands drift down to his

lap. He stared grimly forward, out of the shuttle's windows.

Earth was in sight, not ahead, but above. The Moon-Station shuttle ship was rotating slowly in free fall, two-thirds of the trip completed. Despite his situation, the sight of the blue-white swirled ball of Earth brought a slow smile to his face. *Down there,* he thought, *They're somewhere down there.* Martha, whom he hadn't seen for two years. And Jimmy, named ten years ago, when they had all still idolized the now aging Party Leader.

He bit at his lip as doubt wormed inside him. Should he have written the memo, refused the assignment?

So far as his own fate was concerned, his conscience was clear. He had run the Space Ordnance Development Center at Serenitatis for two years and had been commended for work on improved laser flux density and new weapons guidance systems. He'd believed in the work; he had believed in a strong defense against the Euro-Soviet bloc. But mines for use against American citizens—that was too much, too large a step to square with his conscience. The Party Leader was going too far in reacting to the riots and the increasingly common sabotage. 'Benevolent' tyranny was losing its benevolence, its only justification, and the only prop left to it now was naked force, naked terror.

But what will they do to my family? he thought, staring now past the Earth. *The kangaroo court they hold at the Station will terminate me, or at best give me a life sentence to Antarctica. But what will they do to my wife and son?*

"Morock?"

"What, Lake?"

"What will happen to my family?"

"The proper Party echelon will decide that at your trial."

"I know. But what usually happens in a case like this? Do you know?"

"Yes."

"What?"

There was a low *snap* just beside his ear and when Lake moved his head to see what it was he found himself looking into Morock's Party-issue Colt.

"So that's what you've been belting me with," he said.

"Shut up," said Morock, *"Shut up!* Or would you rather save us the expense and trouble of a trial?"

"I wouldn't shoot that thing in here if I were you," said Lake.

"Message," said Brenda suddenly, pressing her 'phones to her head. "Print it," she said to the ships-comp, and after a moment passed the slip of green paper back for Morock to read.

"Oh, hell," he said petulantly.

"What is it?" said Lake to Brenda in a low voice while the Party Senior, lips moving, read on.

"We've been diverted. They want us to alter course on the way in and check out a piece of inbound debris they have on their scopes, NAS-IDN K2006."

"Well, pilot? Aren't you going to change course?"

"Yes, Party Member. Seat restraints, please."

Brenda addressed her next few sentences to the ship's computer. Earth moved and relocated itself as the shipscomp reoriented the shuttle and finally reported ready for main engine burn.

"Burn," she said. The main engine vibrated to life

and they felt weight for a few seconds.

"Burn complete," said the shipscomp. "Intercept data: closing rate object K2006 point zero one kilometers per second. Intercept time forty-five minutes sixteen seconds."

"Recommend."

"Recommend reburn to slow closing rate in thirty-eight minutes forty point three seconds followed by a pilot-controlled visual approach."

"Analyze motion of K2006, Earth Reference."

"Analyzed. Object K2006 Earth Relative Velocity sixty point nine seven kilometers per second. Earth closest point of approach will be six thousand kilometers, with subsequent sun capture. Final orbit between Earth and Venus at an angle of forty-two point one degrees to plane of ecliptic."

"Not even close," said Morock. "It'll miss Earth by plenty."

Lake began to nod, and then the phrase 'six thousand kilometers' connected with something else in his brain and he said, "How far? The Station!"

"Good God, yes!" said Brenda. "Analyze motion K 2006 relative Station. Chances are against it, but—"

"Analyzed. Station Relative Velocity fifty-one point three two kilometers per second. Station closest point of approach between zero and one thousand meters."

Brenda and Lake stared at each other in shock for a second, and then the pilot reached for the transmit switch.

"That is within Collision Orbit parameters for the Station," said the shipscomp, as if just realizing that fact.

* * *

"I see it," said Brenda. "One o'clock, just above centerline."

Lake bent forward against the restraints to squint into the darkness. Brenda took one hand from the controls to point, and at last he saw it, a tiny white star moving very slowly against a background of a thousand other stars. Only now had it become visible with the naked eye, though they'd had it on the ship's radar for the last half hour.

Morock leaned over their shoulders to look out too. "Is that it? What are you planning to do, pilot?"

"We have plenty of line aboard, and magnetic grapples if it's a metallic body. We have just enough reserve fuel. If we can get a grip on it, I'll try to put another velocity vector on it—not a large one, but enough to make it miss the Station."

Several minutes passed as they watched. The moving star looked just as far away, but seemed to be growing brighter.

"How long till it intercepts the Station?" said Lake.

The computer picked up its cue before Brenda repeated the question and said, "Two hours, twenty-nine minutes seven seconds."

"How long till we're alongside?"

Silence. "Alongside K2006," said Brenda, supplying the referent the shipscomp needed to hear although all three of the humans had understood perfectly what Lake meant.

"With K2006, seven minutes, thirty-two seconds."

Clumsily, because of the handcuffs, Lake reached above his head, swung down the amplified light binoculars, and focused them on the tiny white spark ahead. Even in low power the size of the image surprised him as it swam into his field of view. "It's big," he said, the instrument still to his eyes. "Estimate, oh, twenty or thirty meters long."

"What would something like that do to the Station?" said Morock.

"Assuming it's as dense as your average stony meteoroid, at a striking velocity of fifty klicks it'll vaporize it."

The thought sobered them all for a moment. The Station—almost the symbol of Party America, first of the great structures in space, a kilometer long and with two thousand permanent inhabitants. It had been built for defense, and carried the heaviest missiles and space-to-space lasers.

"Couldn't they shoot it down before it hits them, Lake?"

Lake looked at him, not bothering to hide his irritation. The Party Member was no scientist. "Come on, Morock. With what? The missiles are designed to disrupt electronics, not blast rock. The lasers might boil a few tons of rock off it before it hit. As a matter of fact, maybe it would be best if it *did* hit the Station."

"What's that, Lake?"

"You know why. The Station takes more pictures of the States now than it does of EuroRussia. How many of those missiles and lasers are targeted on our own cities?"

"None!" Morock sounded genuinely shocked.

"Didn't they tell you that yet, Party Member? I wonder why not. How did I find out? Ordnance techs talk in bars, Morock. They won't set in the coordinates of American cities much longer."

"That's a lie! That's pure treason, Lake, counterParty propaganda!" Lake saw the gun butt from the corner of his eye and winced despite himself.

"If you hit him again, Party Member, I'm going to file a complaint," said Brenda.

Morock's arm halted in mid-air. "Complaint!" he said. "From—a *technician*—against a Party Member? By the Leader, pilot, don't you know what I can have done to you?"

But he didn't strike, and Lake, deciding to drop the matter, turned back to the binoculars, clicking them up to high power.

And froze. The speck had become a tiny, elongated cylinder. Abruptly, as he watched, he realized what he was seeing.

Lake swallowed slowly. The lines had been different, unfamiliar. The size was vast. The surface looked dulled by exposure and erosion. But he was an ordnance expert and there was no doubt in his mind of what he had just seen.

"Stop," he said.

"What, John?"

"Stop the approach. Quick."

Brenda triggered a series of attitude jets forward and the stars rolled in the windows, Earth above them now. Her fingers danced on the controls until the shuttle hung seemingly motionless, nose pointing toward the dot of light.

"Distance to K2006," said Brenda.

"Distance to K2006: four point two eight kilometers, constant," said the shipscomp.

"What was it John? What did you see?"

Lake released the binoculars and held out his fettered hands to Morock. "Take these off. Brenda, I need a suit and a tool kit. I'm going out."

"Out!" said Morock. "The hell you are, Lake. What is this?"

"Either I am or you are; the Station is going to want this investigated. And I think I'm a little more qualified. Because, you see, we don't have a meteoroid out there."

"Not a meteoroid! Then what is it?"

Lake stared at the point of light through the shuttle's windows, eyes narrowed in concentration.

"I think it's a weapon."

At four hundred meters and closing John Lake traded suspicion for certainty.

Size is hard to judge in space, but Object K2006 was, he estimated, about fifty meters long and four meters in diameter. One end of the dulled metal cylinder was rounded; the other end, obviously the stern to any being raised in atmosphere, flared outward in a conical skirt for perhaps a meter. As he closed, triggering his suit jets to slow his approach, the slow axial rotation of the object brought what looked like an air scoop into sight on its side.

"Well, Lake, what is it?" Morock's voice, heavy with suspicion, came over the short-ranged shuttle-to-suit circuit.

"It's an artifact, all right," said Lake. Oddly, he found himself whispering. "One-fifty feet long, seems streamlined, made of metal or something that shines like it. Looks in pretty good condition except for a jagged hole near the nose."

"Spacecraft?"

"Doubt it; no cockpit," he said. But that, he reflected, was not the only reason. It was something else, something that was also responsible for his urge to whisper. He knew weapons—had been involved with them in one way or another since the Jamaican War—and the tension in his facial muscles, the tight clamped feeling in his gut, meant that his body recognized it too.

Yes, it was a weapon, wherever it had been made, whoever made it. And this other sense told him more than that.

It might still be live.

"What's happening, John?"

"I'm touching down on it now. Very gently. There. Going to use a line and vacuum cement—don't want to turn on the magnets until I find out what it is."

"I can hardly hear you."

"I've got power out on my transceiver turned way down. Don't like to radiate more than I have to."

"Why? What do you mean, Lake?"

He didn't bother to explain. "Brenda, can you put a recorder on the suit circuit?"

He heard her talking to the ship in the background. In a moment she was back. "Recorder is on, John."

Lake's voice changed, became more detached, almost unconcerned. "I'm near the middle of this thing. Bigger than I thought; make it 50 or 60 long, five meters through. Surface is roughened, pitted metal, still bright though in spots. Looks like a ferrous alloy. Traces here and there of what might have been paint, or some form of surface plating. Not sure. I'm moving around its diameter now, using the suit jets and a length of suit line I cemented to the surface.

"What looks like an air intake is coming into view. No, it's not—shaped wrong. Odd. It's obviously an intake of some sort, but though the beginning of the opening is over a meter across, the throat is the diameter of a pencil. Can't see inside. Moving on.

"Looking at the surface as I go. No welds, rivets, or panels. Some of the pitting looks pretty deep—the skin must be thicker than on our ships. This thing is built heavy."

"I can give you a mass reading if I get in closer," said Brenda.

"No! Stay out there. If this is what I think it is, it may be set for something just like the shuttle."

"Lake, I order you to explain! What do you think this thing is? Some kind of bomb?" Morock, angry now.

"Order me?" Lake chuckled absently. "Sure, I'll tell you. Moving back up toward the tail. For want of an exact word, Morock, I think it's a torpedo. Or a missile. Or a mine. Whatever you call it, it's a weapon, an intact one, and therefore still to be considered dangerous. I don't want the shuttle here and I don't want to use a lot of power or magnetism around it because I don't know yet what it was designed to trigger on."

Morock did not respond. Brenda said, "John, it is one of ours? Or EuroRussian? Or . . .?"

"I think the 'or' covers it, Brenda. It's not American, and I know the other side's makes. I doubt if Earth technology could even boost something this massive."

He started aft again.

"All right, I'm at the tail now. It's self-propelled, all right. This is obviously an exhaust nozzle. Looks oddly straight-walled, though, not your conventional DeLaval bell inside. Must be an engine in there, but I'm not going to stick my head in it just yet. Going forward."

Silence followed on the circuit, broken only by the

crackling of radio stars in vacuum.

" . . .panel."

"What was that, John?"

"I said, there's a panel here, about five meters back from the nose. Not very well fitted, but looks heavy."

"Can you get it open, Lake?"

"That comes later, Morock. Ever worked on live ordnance? No? Then get off my back and let me do my job, all right?"

Morock didn't answer. Lake grinned to himself, despite his own tension. Even four kilometers away, Morock had sounded frightened.

"Here's the damaged area I mentioned. Lord!"

"What is it, John?"

"The edges of the hull are rolled up like tinfoil . . . looks like somebody used a hundred-ton can opener on it. This hull is twenty centimeters thick, and all steel, or what looks mighty like it. The edges, now that I'm closer, look melted rather than torn. Ah, got the suit light in there. Yeah. Electronics—smashed up bad. Bet you a fifty-buck piece this was the guidance and fuzing section."

"Then it's harmless?" Morock.

"Harmless, hell. I don't know anything about the fuzing circuits yet. It's just not going anywhere, that's all I know now."

"John," came Brenda's voice, sounding a little frightened, "ship says two hours to K2006-Station intersect."

Lake, looking down into the savaged hull, clenched his fists inside the bulky suit gloves. *This suit is malfunctioning,* he thought. Sweat was beading on his forehead, running into his eyes, condensing on the inside of the faceshield. *They can build a suit to last a month in space, but they can't make a decent air conditioner.* He reached back to the support pack and thumbed up the cooling. *Think,* he told himself savagely. *Two hours!*

If he defuzed it at all. His earlier thought came back to him. He pictured the Station, its garrison of Party bureaucrats, its reluctant technicians training its cameras and weapons on the restive American cities. With it destroyed, perhaps the Party could be overthrown without too great loss of life.

Life—yes, two thousand lives, the total complement of the Station, two thousand more or less innocent human beings. Could he make himself responsible for their deaths to strike a possibly fatal blow at the Party tyranny?

And if he did so—what of his family?

He shoved the question out of his mind and thought, *Whatever I decide to do, I'll have to know how this thing works. And whether it's still live.* He'd have to skip the slow, methodical investigation an ordnance engineer would ordinarily use. He had to get inside it—now.

"The panel's firm—can't pry it up with the suit multitool. No rivets or screws, no visible handles."

"Sealed from inside?" asked Brenda.

"Hate to think so. No, I don't think there's anyone inside, or ever was. It's for access from outside, all right."

"Is it round? Square?"

"Rectangular, curved to fit the hull . . . I'm pressing down on it . . . no luck, but I can't put much force on it before drifting away from the hull. Pressing each corner in turn . . . again, no luck. Heavy corrosion here . . . hey!"

"What is it, John?"

"This isn't all pitting. There's a design here, I think."

"Holes?"

"Yeah. Look deep. Wonder if they were meant for fingers?"

Lake tried his own, but the gloves made even his little fingers too bulky. Into the tool kit, then. He selected a screwdriver, a vacuum pen, and a length of steel rod. He inserted these into the holes and diddled.

There was a brilliant flash, and then the universe went black. Banshees howled in his ears, driving pain through his head. In agony, he cut off the radio, blinked, trying to restore his vision. Red and blue and yellow afterimages writhed in the blackness. *Blinded?* The suspicion had barely taken form before he realized he could see the readouts inside the helmet: O2, temperature, pressure, power, time. It was the helmet's sunshield that had turned dead black, and as he realized it he felt his face begin to smart.

Radiation—there must have been a terrific blast of it. Enough had gotten through in the microsecond before the shield darkened to burn his face. But the shield's protective opacity was already beginning to fade; evidently the flare, wherever it had come from, was already over. The outlines of the hull slowly became visible.

The cover of the access port was gone, leaving a rectangular hole in the hull. Lake raised his head slightly, keeping the rest of his body low.

Something shimmered above the open port. Nothing was really visible, yet *something shimmered,* making the calm points of the stars seen through it weave and twinkle as on a summer's night on Earth. Finding the steel rod still tightly clenched in his glove, Lake poked the end of it into the space above the opening.

Soundlessly, the solid steel blazed white, whipping outward in a tongue of varicolored flame, turning instantaneously from solid metal to incandescent plasma.

And that's it, he thought. *Radiation, with a capital R, in every wavelength.* Invisible in vacuum, of course, but the radio frequencies had all but deafened him, even outside the cone of radiation proper. And intense enough to cut tool steel like tissue paper in a blast furnace. No human technology could produce that kind of radiation flux, at least not for more than a millisecond.

Abruptly he tensed. The shuttle! Caught by that beam of destruction, sweeping slowly through space as K2006 rotated, even four kilometers away it would melt like a moth in flame. He glanced around, still keeping his head low to the hull; couldn't see it. *Maybe it's gone already,* he thought. He pulled himself away from the open port and around the curve of the hull, putting it between him and the beam, and cautiously turned up his suit radio.

" . . . Lake, I'm not joking. You're a prisoner and under my command. You'll answer me now, or you'll —you'll regret it! Lake!"

Morock's voice was cut off as Lake transmitted at full power. "Brenda! Move the shuttle aft of K2006! *Now!*"

"Moving," she said instantly. The shuttle came into view below him, absurdly tiny at such a distance, gas already glowing at the main and maneuvering engines. Relief flooded through him as he saw that she would pass clear of the sweep of radiation.

And his preconscious, the trained and thoroughly disciplined preconscious of a lifelong engineer, came through at the same moment. He saw clearly now what he was riding, intuited how it operated, *had* operated for untold years, centuries . . . millennia?

Call it a space mine, he thought. Purpose: destruction. Launched in anger once—other races, then, were not spared the scourge of war. After launch, missing its target or targets. Perhaps deflected from a homing course by whatever force had torn open five inches of metal like a popcorn bag. Speeding onward, wandering on between the stars, waiting mindlessly for its victim.

For any victim.

His mind sketched a diagram before his eyes. Any moving or maneuvering projectile had to be 'fueled' before launch with a given quantity of energy, both for motive power—the strange-looking nozzle aft— and for system operation. Chemically powered? Completely inadequate. Nuclear power? Neither fission nor fusion could account for the flood of radiation still pouring out from the hull where, evidently, it had been continuously generated since launch.

The only energy source that he could even postulate as adequate was the antimatter reaction. The missile must be powered by a reservoir of negative matter, contained within the hull in some manner he couldn't even guess at. From this reservoir—his mind sketched in lines in the diagram, 'pipes,' 'valves'— tiny amounts were fed, atom by atom, into a reaction chamber, directly under the access port he had opened. There it reacted with normal matter; interstellar hydrogen, perhaps, magnetically scavenged into the two intakes. The diagram grew denser, more complex. The reaction, a tiny fire many times hotter than the sun, produced a cacophonic scream of radiation from the dying atoms. He saw at once that this could be utilized for several functions within the missile. The radio frequencies could be screened out and used as a wideband radar for detection and guidance. The extremely high frequencies, light, X-ray, and so on, could be channeled—somehow!—to the rear for propulsion, a sort of light drive.

He saw at once that what he was riding was, in essence, a miniature starship. And another thought chilled him at the same time. What kind of war had been fought with ranges in light-years, with self-guiding weapons designed to operate for . . . how long?

And when they reached their targets?

Lake could design the systems for that himself. When the radar registered a suitable target within kill range, built-in explosive charges would rupture the 'container.' The remaining antimatter would react instantly with the vast mass of normal matter in the hull.

It would be, Lake thought, *very much like a short-term nova.* No ship could live within a radius of hundreds of miles, before the inverse-square law thinned the hail of radiation to bearable limits. It was the deadliest weapon he could imagine. He looked at the time readout inside his helmet. In an hour and forty-five minutes it would hit the Station.

Only six thousand kilometers from Earth.

An hour later Lake felt that he had the fuzing system fairly well doped out. His first speculations, he felt, were correct. The nose of the object was capped by a bubble of light-opaque material, but his faceshield had darkened and his skin warmed when he neared it. He was sure it was passing microwaves filtered from the maelstrom in the reaction chamber. The guidance and fuzing radar was still active.

He backed away from the tear in the hull, where he had been engaged for the past half hour, and spoke into the suit circuit. "I've got most of the wreckage cleared out of this section," he said. "I don't pretend to understand the electronics, but I think I understand the system. They use fairly standard cable forms, and I can pretty much tell what they're running to and from. I don't know how certain items work but I think I know what they're supposed to do.

"Basically, it's radar-fuzed and still active. I've got power right up to what I assume is the firing circuit. Whatever cut the skin open here also ripped hell out of one black box and associated wiring. Offhand I'd say it's a delay circuit, like we use in missiles to set the warhead off at the proper point for the fragments to intercept the target, and wired in series with the charge that starts the big blowup.

"Brenda, are you in touch with the Station?"

"Yes, John. The Party Member has been briefing them on the secure circuit."

"Can you put him on?"

"I'm here." Morock sounded less sure of himself, less the smug and self-important Party thug that he had been since picking Lake up in Serenitatis. *This may be good for him,* thought Lake fleetingly. *He's still young. He may come round yet, given time.*

"Morock? Here's the picture. You can relay it to the Station if you want. This bird is still live. I've analyzed the fuzing and I may be able, when the time comes, to hold the detonating circuit out by hand. But if this actually hits the Station the fuzing won't matter—the bang will be just as big when the anti-matter breaks loose. We've got to bump it out of this collision orbit."

"What do you want to do?"

"Doctor," said Lake. He could not help grinning, despite the fear in his own gut.

"What do you want to do . . . Doctor."

"Right. Brenda, bring the ship up to the stern of this thing. Carefully; and slowly. Have Morock suit up and bring me out the heaviest line we have aboard."

"Tow it?"

"Enough to clear the Station by a mile or so. The ship can tell us what kind of vector to put on it. It'll take most of our fuel, though, to get this monster moving."

"Right, John. Coming up on you in. . ." In the background noise Lake heard the shipscomp say, "Five minutes, zero eight seconds."

"Good. Standing by."

He watched the shuttle grow slowly larger 'below' him. Brenda's sure piloting was evident; the burns were very short, attitude nozzles beautifully angled to use every ounce of thrust to take pitch off and match roll to the slow roll of K2006. She let it drift in to a scant twenty meters, the ship looming over Lake like a planet about to fall, and took the last meter per second off with the briefest flare of the four forward jets. The ship and the mine now rode and rotated together, as if welded, amid a slowly wheeling universe of stars.

A suited figure emerged from the shuttle's airlock. Morock. He lurched toward Lake with badly coordinated jolts of gas, trailing coils of line behind him. It writhed slowly as trapped air escaped from the fibers.

"Lake?"

"Hear you fine. What did you tie the other end of the line to?"

"One of the structural members. It'll hold, the pilot said."

"Okay." Lake caught the end of the line, flipped a quick loop into it and looked around. What could he fasten it to?

"The nozzle, back here?" came Morock's voice. Lake pulled himself aft toward him. The younger man was pointing at the nozzle, which though straight inside was built with a slight flare in its outside diameter.

"Good thinking," said Lake. He fitted the loop to the nozzle and put a keeper knot on it. "Brenda? Calculations?"

"Right, John. It's close; we haven't much fuel left, and the mass reading on this thing is unbelievable. Over two thousand metric tons. Computer recommends a six-second 100% burn with main engine and comes up with a resultant half-kilometer miss distance to the Station."

"Half a kilometer!"

"That's the best I can do, John."

"Okay. It's close, but it'll have to do." He turned his attention to Morock. The man's face was pale through the faceshield. "Ready?"

"I suppose so."

"Brace yourself against the hull."

"Uh . . . right."

"Burn, Brenda!"

Two nose jets flared first, so close that Lake felt the push of their exhaust gas on his suit. The shuttle's nose swung away, then was stopped with a half-second burst. Lake eyed the rapidly tautening line, trying to gauge the way the mine would swing when Brenda applied thrust.

The main engine fired, and Lake began counting out loud. The shuttle's stern, hampered by the drag of the mine's mass, swung inward. They watched it as it swung, slowly at first, then faster. Acceleration dragged gently at them. "Four . . . five . . . six," counted Lake. The engine cut off just as the nozzle swung past them, the inner edges of the throat still glowing cherry-red.

"How's it look, Brenda?"

"Wait one . . . looks good, John. We put a nice outward vector on it and speeded it up too. Both actions will move the orbit outward. Shipscomp is giving me a combined miss distance now of seven point four—correction, *point* seven four kilometers. A little better than we thought."

"Close enough to scare them," said Lake. "And I hope that's all we do." With his understanding of what he rode now all thought of destroying the Station had gone. *Maybe,* he admitted to himself, *I could really have done it.*

But not if it could mean the destruction of Earth as well.

"Come on, Morock," he said. "Let's go forward."

As they crouched head to head over the opened electronics section, Lake pointed out the components of the fuzing circuit. "See this fat square cable, coming from the nose? Radar waveguide—can't be anything else. So this yellow thing here the size of an egg has to be the radar receiver. Since this black cable here runs to all the modules it has to be power. See how it's all grounded to the hull—I wouldn't do it that way, but it simplifies production. They must have fired these things off like bottle rockets."

"Who's they?" said Morock ungrammatically.

"Wish I knew. But I hope we don't meet them for a couple thousand more years. Back to the fuzing. The yellow egg is in series with these three cubes, the smashed-up box, and this tubular item here. I think the cubes are safety devices. This center one has a pipette leading to a small hole in the hull. That might be to detect atmosphere, in case a stray round heads into a planet." A nastier thought had occurred to him: that the bomb had been designed *for* a planet. Maybe even for Earth.

But he didn't want to think about that.

"So this tube here—see the upper end of it here?—has got to be the detonating assembly. This whole package is so simple it amazes me. All-modular, obviously designed for mass production and quick repair."

"Will it go off?"

"That's going to be the big question, my man," said Lake. "See these three buttons on the detonator? I don't know what they're for. I sure ain't gonna start pressing them at random. So we are going to ride this mother in, and watch things very closely. When something starts happening, well, we'll just play it by ear."

"And pray," said Morock.

"If you want to," said Lake. The Party, he remembered, was very big on prayer. He splayed his legs around the hull and tried to make himself comfortable. He glanced at the time readout.

Twenty minutes.

Earth was huge. The sharp line of the terminator curved away from him, over the swirled white and sere brown of Asia and the deep blue of the Indian Ocean. He watched it creeping onward, westward, and he could see the valleys and mountains of the Himalayas wrinkling its edge.

Which side would it be? he thought. *Sun side, night side?* The Earth was about two-thirds full; it would be mostly the sun side. If he failed, how many would die? There would be no blast transmitted through vacuum. It would be energy—an unimaginable blast of infrared and gamma and X-rays. The visible light would blind unsheltered millions in that short instant before death. It would be Hell in the sky for one endless instant.

After that the fires would complete the work.

"Ten minutes to intercept," said Brenda over the suit link.

The collision orbit, thought Lake, was not merely one of two celestial objects. It was a collision orbit of two cultures, two technologies. He remembered a story he had read as a child. Two Italian children, playing on a deserted beach, had come upon an unexploded bomb from World War Two. They had dug it out of the sand and dragged it in a toy wagon a mile inland to their home town, intending to frighten their playmates. They left the bomb in a vacant lot near their tenement. Late that night it had exploded, killing or maiming over twenty people.

Was this same accidental horror to be repeated, on a larger scale, to Man's home planet?

A minute tremor ran through his legs, making him start. The vibration passed, then returned. He looked around, puzzled. It grew stronger, becoming a rumble he could actually hear transmitted through skin and fabric and bone.

"John!" said Brenda. A climbing roar of static all but wiped out her transmission. "The port. It's glowing!"

He saw Morock point aft, his eyes wide. Lake twisted round, and blinked.

Space itself was shining. A long, pale, whitish-green beam licked out from the open port, shimmering, flickering, growing brighter by the second. *It can't be,* thought Lake, *light doesn't show in a vacuum. And we're 'way too far out from atmosphere for a glow discharge to show.* He stood up to see around the curve of the hull. And then he knew. Whitish-green flame glowed soundlessly around the edges of the port. The unimaginable stream of radiation pouring out was vaporizing the very material of the hull and whirling the bright-hot atoms of it out in a glowing, fluorescing beam. The rumble beneath him became louder, increasing steadily with the brightness of the glow.

"It's getting ready," he muttered to Morock. "Feeding in more antimatter. More power for maneuvering to catch an alerted enemy. A hotter reaction, to flash from end to end of this thing when the last switch closes. It's getting ready."

He was close enough to Morock to see the sweat on his forehead, to see his lips moving. He was praying. In that moment he even felt sorry for the Party Member.

He leaned forward and focused all his attention on the tube.

One of the buttons had lit. It glowed a pale yellow. Lake watched, clutching the multitool in his right hand, feeling the sweat creep down his back. *Should I push it? I don't know. Access to this thing was too easy. If I built something like this I'd have anti-disarm devices all over it. Still, this was originally under five inches of solid steel. They might not have expected a disarm attempt from here. Yeah, the booby traps would be up forward, in the radar dome. If they bothered to do it at all.* The relentless simplicity of the whole design seemed to speak against it.

The second light blinked and came on. At the same instant Morock said, "There's the Station, Lake— *Doctor* Lake."

A swift glance. Lake saw it—a bright shape, oval even at the great distance that still separated them.

"Twenty seconds to closest point of approach," came Brenda's voice faintly through the static.

Lake stared at the two palely glowing buttons. He had not the slightest doubt that shortly after the third button lit the detonator circuit would close. Whether this would trigger the firing circuit depended on the wiring in the smashed delay circuit module. *Jesus, Mary, Joseph,* he thought. He suddenly remembered that he had been a Catholic before the Great Revival in '85.

"Ten seconds."

"Lake! Do something!"

"Shut up, Morock." He poised the multitool, eyes darting frantically around the assemblage of components. No inspiration came to him. The terror closed his throat.

The third button flickered. Lake lunged for it, pressed it. It did not move. The Station loomed ahead on the edge of his vision, sunlight sharp on its great curved rim, its slow rotation bringing the letters U*S*A into view huge and black and divided by the sliding hatches that covered the muzzles of the lasers. He pulled up on the button. No good. The rumble beneath him increased, and a high whining buzz began to merge with it.

The last resort, then. With a half-curse, half-prayer Lake knocked Morock's frantically searching hands out of the hole and locked the multitool on the top of the tube. He stood up and gave a superhuman yank.

The tube pulled out smoothly. It was a little over two meters long and shone in the sunlight as it came up from the very guts of the mine. Lake did not pause to look at it. He threw it outward, hard, falling backward from the recoil.

It exploded in a soundless blast a second after he had released it. The multitool, which he had not bothered to unlock, came sailing back and caromed off the hull near him. The puncture alarm of Lake's suit went off and his hands went to the repair pocket and had begun the patch drill before he felt the pain in his left leg.

"Damn," said Lake. He found he already had the patch ready and he reached down to slap it on the hole, watching the plastic writhe and flow into the hole as it vacuum cured. The alarm stopped. The suit was airtight again. The warm wetness along his thigh could not be helped.

"John! Party Member!"

"We're okay," said Lake. "I got the detonator assembly out just before it went off. You can tell the Station they're safe now." He looked for it, found it already shrinking far behind them.

He looked around and saw Morock.

It was too late, far too late. Two fragments from the exploding tube had hit him, Lake saw. One in the neck, as he lay flat on the hull, and the other in the back. The worst place for a puncture. Even if he'd been skilled in a suit, which most Party people disdained as a 'technician's' skill, he couldn't have reached back there to patch himself. Lake lifted the helmet gently, saw the frozen red on the faceshield, and lowered it again to rest against the hull. He felt oddly swayed between joy and sorrow. Granted, Morock had been a bastard and a Party thug. But he had been brought up that way, Lake thought. And he was still young. Being young was reason enough to forgive many things. He hoped they would forgive his son for what his father was going to do.

At any rate, the Party Member's death made things much simpler.

"Correction," he said. "We're not both okay. Morock's dead. He was hit with two fragments from the detonator."

"Oh," said Brenda. "Do you need help bringing him aboard?"

"We're not coming aboard," said Lake, looking down at Morock.

"Not coming aboard," repeated Brenda.

"I can't go back, Brenda. I've got to ride it out."

"Ride . . . that?"

"It's going into a solar orbit now. Between Earth and Venus. It won't be all that hard to reach. A shuttle with extra fuel tanks should do it. The Party will have scientists crawling all over this thing inside of a month."

"Is that bad? I don't understand."

"You don't? This is a weapon, Brenda. It's also a

new source of energy. It's a starship, could be a starship—could take us Out. But can you see the Party using it for that? It's weapons they want, terror, power." A sudden horrible vision came over him, changing the blue and lovely Earth on which he looked into a bloody cinder. "Thirty years ago I'd have said, yes, bring it back, study it, learn from it. Maybe in thirty years more we could have. But not now. Not now."

"I don't agree, John. And what about me? I can't just let you go. No, I'm coming out."

Lake bent to the stiffening body and pulled at the suit pockets. Yes, Morock had brought it out with him. "You'll stay in the shuttle, Brenda, and you'll cast off. I've got Morock's gun and in sixty seconds I'm going to start putting bullets through the shuttle's pressure hull."

She did not answer and he went on, more softly, "Goodbye, Brenda. I'll last as long as I can, get this thing as far away from Earth as I can. I caught a fragment too and my radiation counter red-lined an hour ago."

"And what about your family, John?"

He looked out at Earth, blue and lovely and dwindling now as he left it behind forever at sixty kilometers per second. "At a certain point, Brenda, you realize . . . that they are all your family. But give my special love to Martha, if you ever can."

He lasted for two weeks, until the Party ship began its approach. Somehow he had improvised a way to trigger the main charge. And his wife, and his child, and every person on nightside Earth, trembled at the ring of fire in the sky.

Industry in space will need power. Where will it get it?
Here's one possible answer.

Telec
William Sheck
and
James Quinn

For the first time, scientists and businessmen are giving serious thought to the idea of manufacturing in space. When NASA's shuttle becomes operational, the weightless vacuum of space will be accessible to industry. The advantages of the space environment are well known: in space it is possible to make flawless crystals, perfectly spherical ball bearings, and exotic metal alloys. It is difficult to predict the impact space manufacturing will have on the industrial revolution, just as radio tube inventor Lee De Forest could not have predicted personal computers.

If the industrial revolution expands beyond the surface of the earth, it will because of the hardware that will make space business profitable. Before businessmen launch facilities into space for industry, they will want to know whether or not they can make a profit at it. NASA's most obvious contribution towards making space profitable is the reusable shuttle, which will lower costs. A less obvious contribution, however, is a new piece of hardware called TELEC, which may provide the energy space manufacturers will need.

There are many ways to get power in space. Past space missions have used fuel cells, solar panels, and nuclear isotopes to supply on-board power. These systems worked fine for small vehicles that have been launched to date, but they have serious limitations which make them less practical for larger energy requirements.

All these systems require bulky equipment that has to be hauled into space at great expense, used for a brief period of time, and then carried back to earth again. Large quantities of power require large power generators, and they in turn require even larger freight bills. Space manufacturers will not want to pay those bills because every added expense required in operating industry in space will lower profit. NASA recognized long ago that a cheap supply of energy was needed in space, so they began cost comparisons of different space power systems. The old systems—solar cells, isotope generators, and fuel cells—were compared to new systems—for instance, heat engines that run on sunshine.

But imagine for a moment that you could deliver energy in space as it is delivered on earth; by transmission lines. Then, you could boost power generating equipment into orbit permanently. When a shuttle load of ball-bearing-making machines achieved orbit, the workers inside could "plug in" to the space utility. Their power bill would be much lower than the cost of hauling their own generators.

Although power line transmission is not practical in space, the newly developed TELEC unit would permit the use of laser beams as extension cords to outer space. A TELEC, or thermo electronic laser energy converter, changes laser energy into electrical energy. Because of the very narrow divergence of a laser beam, it is practical for long distance transmission anywhere in the earth-moon system. Because of its relatively low weight, it is an attractive alternative for many applications.

Under a NASA contract, Dr. Edward Britt, technical director of the Direct Energy Department at Rasor Associates, helped develop the TELEC and test it at NASA's Lewis Research Center in Cleveland, Ohio, on the Center's 15 kilowatt laser. "The TELEC is an extremely power-hungry device," according to Britt. "It's one of the few devices that can take a 15 kilowatt laser beam right down its throat."

The heart of the TELEC unit is a solid machined-nickel cylinder, which is designated as the collector. The insulated emitters rest in two milled slots defining the 30 cm active cell length. The emitter blades are in opposing 180 degree eccentric positions. Depending on the collimated beam which will pass through the collector, the cylinder is bored along the center line, approximately 6 mm in diameter.

The pressurized cylinder (pressurized with inert Xenon) is then injected with a cesium vapor. The two emitters are given 100 volts for a few milliseconds to cause an arc. The arc in turn ignites the highly combustible cesium vapor and turns it into an active plasma which will interact with the laser beam in a nearly fully ionized state.

The two small emitters are heated by radiation from the plasma to a therminoic temperature of 2,000 degrees Kelvin (the emitters are machined to receive tungsten-rhenium thermo-couples to monitor temperature). The emitters are now emitting low energy electrons into the plasma. Due to this loss of electrons, the emitters become positively charged relative to the plasma.

Those low energy electrons shed by the emitters become high energy electrons due to the effect produced by the electro-magnetic field of the laser beam passing through the plasma. Increasing in velocity, the high energy electrons race out of the plasma in all directions. The electrons strike the largest neutral surface—the collector. Thus, the collector becomes negatively charged relative to the plasma.

When the collector and emitter are connected through an external load circuit, an electrical current will flow which will be proportional to the plasma electron temperature.

Cesium was chosen as the plasma because of its advantages of low ionization potential, large atomic mass, and durability. Although cesium, a liquid metal that burns on contact with air, is hard to handle, it could last up to five years before breaking down.

Some of the positively charged ions in the plasma strike the collector plate, too, reducing the current. However, heavier atoms in the plasma move slower, reducing the loss. "In cesium, the electrons are moving around like snowflakes and the ions are like boulders," says Britt.

Theoretical efficiencies of up to 48 per cent have been calculated for the TELEC, although laboratory prototypes have not reached this yet. The remaining energy is lost as waste heat, just as in any other power generating system.

In the TELEC, unlike other systems, the heat is shed at extremely high temperatures, a definite advantage when weight counts. The waste in TELEC is shed through its plasma to the collector, which operates at 1,000 degrees Kelvin. At that temperature, a small radiator will get rid of a lot of heat.

According to Donald Alger, project manager at Lewis Research Center, a TELEC conversion system could be launched along with a payload in the form of a collapsing mirror. Once in space, the system could unfold into an array of concentrating mirrors which would capture the laser beam. Collimating mirrors focus the beam into TELEC subunits. (See figure one.)

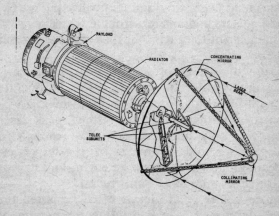

The beam, which could originate from an orbiting power satellite or a ground generator (the latter would have to be much more powerful to contend with atmospheric absorption) could be converted and used directly, or could charge on-board batteries. The most obvious use for this power is industrial, but it could also be used for ion propulsion, life support systems, and communications.

TELEC's usefulness for long distance transmission diminishes rapidly when leaving the earth-moon system. All laser beams have a natural divergence, which varies with the frequency of the laser light and the diameter of the laser apperature. The divergence varies as:

$$\frac{2.44 \times \text{wavelength}}{\text{aperture diameter}}$$

This divergence makes the TELEC an unlikely candidate for trips to the nearest planets. A Viking-like probe to Mars would need a collecting mirror 400,000 meters in diameter—roughly three per cent the diameter of the earth—at the closest approach to the red planet.

Testing of a TELEC prototype took place at Lewis Research Center July 23–31, 1978. To operate efficiently, the unit required an input of 15 to 20 kilowatts. During the actual testing, peak laser power was only nine kilowatts, just enough to break the threshold of conversion. "It was like getting enough power to crank an engine and have it idle for short intervals," said Alger.

Before higher power levels could be tested the TELEC developed a leak, causing the cesium to slowly oxidize. The chance for further testing will have to wait though. As of August 1978, Lewis Research Center has terminated all laser related projects.

One of the encouraging aspects of the project is, according to Britt and Alger, that TELEC does work. The efficiency ratings were anticipated. In the months to come over four thousand feet of magnetic tape will have to be decoded and analyzed. The computer tape recorded all relevant data at high speed during the short test periods. The final results may warrant future investigation into TELEC.

When peak efficiency has been attained, the conversion of a one megawatt of laser power would result in nearly a half a megawatt of electric power, enough to power fifty homes. In space, this electric power could be used for propulsion, communications, and life support systems.

The answer to long distance transmission of power in space doesn't seem so far off now. With the advent of a practical TELEC, the likelihood of industry in space will be one step closer.

Some things happen slowly—so slowly that their very slowness is a threat.

The Last Flute
Thomas A. Easton

New York: a city of barricaded streets and bridges, of unburied dead and desperate, panicked living.

New York: a portrait of the globe the year they announced immortality.

David Howell lived through it all. Caught between gigs by the announcement, he sat tight while the lines grew before the clinics and hospitals, while people responded to the inevitable shortages of the drug with the first riots, while paranoid minorities screamed for their share of the new miracle—NOW! He sat tight while the flames were whipped by rebellions around the world, rebellions against inadequate distribution and—sparked by news leaks—against rulers who tried to keep the news and the drug to themselves. He waited while the government hastily upped production and saturated the nation's cities with frightened medics, while the army stamped out the rebels and flew in food to the survivors.

He waited, and he survived. He and his wife had a room and a hot plate in a small hotel. Their window overlooked the street. From it, his Laura watched and waited for his return, for the information he might have gathered, the gossip and the rumors. He heard much, and he paid for it with his flute. The nightclubs were closed, and he could not work, but people still liked to hear his songs.

One day, near the end of the troubles, he returned with a frown. His flute still rode in the pocket of his boot, not at his lips, from where it usually heralded his approach.

"What is it, honey?" asked Laura. She was a small brunette, short and light and rounded. She belonged in a gypsy caravan, and now more than ever she looked as if she lived with one. Her clothes, like his, were grimy, and if her hair shone, it was with oil. They had been out of soap for a week. They both smelled.

He shrugged out of his shoulder bag. "I just found out the medics didn't tell us everything. Their circulars weren't very complete." He spilled packages of oatmeal, dried eggs, and raisins on a table. Small packages, but they were a day's rations.

"Doesn't it work the way they said?"

"Oh, that's plain enough."

"I never understood it." She pushed the eggs and raisins to one side and stacked the others on a shelf. "We can have these with some of that rice we had yesterday."

"The thymosin helps you fight off diseases," he said. "Jazzes up the immune system. Keeps the body from tearing itself apart. From attacking itself the way it does some bug. So we live longer. The other stuff in the shots helps the thymosin out."

"What's the problem, then?" Their single pan rattled on the hot plate as she began to heat the leftover rice. He stepped behind her and cupped her shoulders. He kissed the back of her neck.

"We're hardly immortal."

She stiffened and spun within the circle of his arms. "But that's what all the mess is about!"

"Oh, we might as well be, I suppose. We've got a while yet. But a fellow I met this afternoon told me we're dying all the time anyway, in places the thymosin can't reach."

He paused to reach behind her and take the pan off the hot plate before it burned. She heard the scrape and turned back to her task. "Go on."

"We're losing cells all the time. Like a hundred thousand brain cells every day."

"That sounds like a lot."

"But we have so many that it'll be about three thousand years before we lose a tenth of our brains. And we'd hardly notice that."

"Three thousand years!"

"And more," said David. He reached past her again, this time for a handful of raisins. "But not forever."

"We'll never see it, though. Or I never will. I couldn't stand it, I'm sure. I'd kill myself in three hundred."

"If you were all alone, maybe. But there're others around too, you know.

"There aren't as many as there were a month ago."

Laura needn't have worried. She died in the sights of a sniper the day before the barricades came down. David found her by the window, the book she had been reading spilled on the floor, her head spattered on the wall. The flies, fattened on carnage, were already strafing her.

He wept and he raged, and his music grew wild and mournful by turns, but he was spared the sight of his wife bloating and rotting. The next day's clean-up squads built pyres, and he carried her there himself to watch the greasy flames devour her. He wished he could pay her Charon-ride with a joyful tune that would turn away Lethe, but his happier songs were vanished in the emptiness within him. The only funeral song he could squeeze between his lips was a black and awful dirge, crowded with hate for the world, its living and its dead. He thought he must be mad.

But he lived. He saw the dead counted and the peace restored. He saw immortality spread across the civilized nations of Earth, and he saw a new, long view take over morality as well as politics. A quarter of the world's population was gone, but the growing seasons were shrinking too, and even this lesser number, the survivors of the upheavals that had cost him his Laura, could only be fed for a while. Marriage went out of style, for "till death do us part" was now meaningless, and divorce was a bother. Children became rare, and then extinct, for reproduction seemed both obsolete and dangerous when all could live forever. And as the world aged, progress slowed; it was no longer lubricated by the creative juices of youth.

He lived, but he wished he hadn't. He had loved his wife, and his music was now too furiously mournful to stand. No club, no group would hire him. The gift of life was now more than ever a thing of joy. The fear of death had been removed, and no one wished to be reminded of it.

He lived, but he mourned for a thousand years.

*   *   *

David had survived as truck driver, farmer, and student, as street-sweeper and teacher, mechanic and policeman. A millennium was more than time enough to learn and practice a dozen trades, and he had practiced many. His flute was no longer a living, but he had never let it go. At home or in an office, on the beat or in the field, it rode forever in the pocket of his boot, emerging only to mourn, loudly and intrusively. The few who paused to listen invariably scowled at his fury. Although, in truth, the scowls had been less in the past century or so. He was a government clerk now, and a finally mellowing climate was filling his knowledgeable colleagues and friends with a more tolerant optimism.

Now he struggled through the drifts of a late April snow toward the dome of Stanley and Martha Jimson. Married only three hundred years before, when it was briefly fashionable, they still found each other bulwark against the cold. They still shared home and love, as they shared an office down the hall from David. They had been three equals once, a long time before, when they had shared a farm. Though David now filed their reports and summaries of a dwindled world, they remained friends. As much as anyone can, thought David, with a grieving madman.

He had left his electric scooter a block away. The street hadn't been cleared, and it might not be till the sun did the job. The city trucks had already had their plows removed. They hauled fertilizer now, sludge and mulch, instead of sand. Spreading it on snow, though, anyway, he chuckled. He caught his breath to curse the cold. His coat was heavy, his boots snug, but his gloves were neither, and his fingers felt blue already.

He raised his eyes and saw the windmill jutting from the curve of the dome. The generator was out of sight. Snow covered the solar cells. But it would be warm inside, he told himself.

He came to the six-foot ridges that still marked their driveway, turned up it, knocked. He watched as the light beyond the vestibule was blocked by Stanley's shaggy head. The latch clicked, and he entered, carefully closing the outer door before opening the inner. Heat was too precious, still, to waste.

The dome was small, four rooms on a single level. Its walls were a soft yellow-green. The color of spring, complemented by the brown and blue of hanging fabric, the gold of the Jimsons' clothes. As he shucked his coat and boots, laying his chilled flute aside to warm, David felt as if he had left the snow a month behind.

Stanley, tall and thin, took his coat and laid it aside. Martha pecked his cheek. "David! We're glad you're here. We've news!" Her ample breasts surged against his chest, brown hair tickled his ear. She smelled clean and alive, and he ached with memory.

"And I saw you only yesterday. What could have come up?" He smiled with pleasure and kissed her in return.

"Things are better, David," said Stanley. He tossed his blonde head and grinned. Martha smiled too, reached up to touch her husband's cheek. "The government thinks we can start boosting the population again."

"They want. . ."

"Children?" David guessed. It was in the air, he

knew, as much as its opposite had been once, and it had to be done. But now?

"That's right," laughed Martha. "And they want us to have one!"

"But it has to be kept quiet."

Or there'll be throngs of suddenly pregnant women, all ready to end a thousand years of silence with midnight squalls. There'll be too many, and most will have to starve. Again. David shook his head. "For how long?"

"They want it as soon as we can make it."

"They'll keep it as quiet as they can. They're spreading them around. Though if all goes well, we'll have more," said Stanley.

"There's lots of room!"

Their smiles were fixtures, David thought. Plastered on by sheer joy. Stanley's was crooked by an old scar, and David remembered the flying hoe handle that had made it. New farm, green hands, not one of them with the sense to lay a tool edge down. There were no flaws in Martha's grin, though. She'd never been badly hurt that David knew. Sprained and lamed by sacks of feed and seed, yes, but never scarred. "If the crops go well," he put in. "That must be what it hangs on."

But Stanley refused to be sobered. "But that's why they've decided it's time. They're better every year now."

"And the trend shouldn't change, any more than the other did," said Martha.

They were convinced, and happy. It would hardly be friendly, David knew, to spoil it for them. He shut up and accepted the drink they offered him. He smiled as they talked only of children, admired the knitting needles Stanley had made that afternoon, laughed when Stanley said, "I'm better with my fingers, so I guess I'll make the booties." He ate their meat and scanty bread, fetched a southern pear from his coat and shared it with them. And he tried his best to play them a cheerful tune, but even "Fiddler" emerged lugubrious. He still mourned.

His failure didn't surprise his friends. It couldn't; they knew him. But the smiles faded a little, and the evening was suddenly over. Soon his coat was on, his boots laced up again. Good-byes were said, but as he reached for the door, Martha's hand tugged at his shoulder. He turned and raised an eyebrow. Her smile was gone. Her eyes shone. He thought he knew, and he tried to repair his damage. "I'm sorry, Martha." He shrugged. "You know I. . ."

"Yes, David. But you're our oldest friend. I'd like you there when the time comes. Too."

She shamed him, and he turned away. "I'll be happy to." He grasped the latch and left. Perhaps he would be, he told himself. Maybe a new birth was what he needed to see the future. He'd be there.

It took Martha two years. Two years, and three early miscarriages that perplexed her, her husband, and her doctor. Two years in which the word leaked out and the people swelled their minds with joy and hope. But Martha and Stanley did succeed, and if they weren't the first, they were the only couple David saw.

He saw them often, and he watched Martha's carriage change, from the careful delight of discovery to the gliding awkwardness of a grain barge berthing. He saw morning sickness rediscovered when she was late for work, and he saw the old anticipation when

Stanley finished his first small blanket. He didn't see their doctor, a surgeon retreading himself as an obstetrician, as he probed and prodded with his fingers and his stethoscope, with x-rays and ultrasound. He didn't see the caution, the reserve, the guarded optimism, the suppressed impatience.

The months passed, and Martha swelled with life. In time she took her leave of absence from the office, and soon David learned that she had been checked into the hospital.

"It's not yet," said Stanley. "They want to keep an eye on her." He picked up a pencil. His desk was covered with sheets of scribbled paper. He stabbed one, flipped it toward him, sketched a blossom in a blank spot. "They say they have a lot to relearn. It's been so long. . ."

Her time came a week ahead of schedule. The call woke David at his home, a shrill buzz in the darkness. He stumbled, got the light, saw the time. Oh, hell, he thought. Quarter of three. He found the phone and punched it on. "I hope that's you, Stanley."

"Yeah, David. It's now. Shall I pick you up?"

"Mmph. I suppose so."

"She wanted you there too, you know."

"Yeah. So come and get me. I'll be ready."

He was waiting on the walk when Stanley pulled his scooter to a stop. The air was chilly, and he was still tired. He was glad to climb into the warmth of his seat, but he didn't have much to say. "A little early, isn't it?"

"Mm-hm. But not too much. It varies. A week early, a week late. It's all normal, they tell me. I hope they're right." Stanley had no pencil this time. His fingers clenched and twisted on the wheel. His lips were tight, and his words were clipped and tense. "I hope she's all right."

She was, they learned when they reached the waiting room. Doing as well as could be expected. Still in labor. And no, they couldn't watch. The observation balcony was full of doctors.

They waited.

Stanley paced.

David sat on a wooden lounge and pulled his flute from his boot. He played, and his notes seemed to splatter grief on the floor like teardrops. He played softly, absorbed in his effort to wrench something better from his soul, something better than his loss of "might-have-been." He was shocked when Stanley's fist rocked the silver from his lips.

"Damn it! How can you do that? You should be happy! Happy! We're having a baby! And you sit there crying!" He spun and stalked across the room and back. He hurled his arms up and out, made claws and fists and pinched his ear. "A baby, David. It's a happy occasion! A joyous one! You should be celebrating it if you play anything at all."

David slipped the flute back into its niche. He sat, waiting. Stanley spun and stalked and paced and swore, waiting. Neither spoke again.

Eventually the door to the delivery room opened and a nurse appeared. The mother, it seemed, was fine.

The father was clearly a wreck.

The baby was dead.

That night David's joy returned.

A dead baby was taken from its sobbing mother for an autopsy. A hundred wrinkled bodies were cut and jugged and analyzed. A thousand tiny corpses stoked a world's sudden despair. Not one lived a day. They died deformed, limbless, gutless, cleft, and twinned. They never lived, and if they had they would never have been human.

Martha never left the hospital. She had screamed when her baby had tried to breathe and failed. She had wailed and torn at the doctor's hands when her baby had convulsed and kicked in pain. But she could have done nothing. Her baby's windpipe was not complete. Her baby died.

And so did she. She screamed until they knocked her out, and she screamed whenever the drug wore off. She screamed herself hoarse, and her nurse, unreminded, missed one injection. She arrived five minutes late, and she found her trust huddled on the floor, her life around her, a shard of her broken water glass still jutting from her throat.

David was at his desk, happily playing his flute, singing of trees and streams and fair blue skies, when Stanley found him. The incongruous gaiety, with its occasional runs of martial brilliance, had attracted a crowd. Fellow clerks filled David's doorway and blocked the hall beyond. Stanley heard the sound and came. Roughly, he pushed a smiling listener aside. Loudly, he swore. "Damn you!" His face was lined, his eyes red, his hair a tangle. "Damn you! She's dead! I hope that makes you even happier!"

David stopped. He stared. "She is?" he whispered. "She is? I . . . I'm sorry, Stanley." He had loved her, too, in his way. "I didn't know." His eyes glistened as he dropped his gaze to his lap. He turned his flute in his hands.

"She is! And you, you crazy bastard, you sing! All

of a sudden you can sing! Why? Why?"

David didn't dare to speak his thought into the waiting silence. He had grieved when all the rest had burned with joy. He had wept while others laughed. He had held his sorrow, he guessed, as long as he had seen it nowhere else. When others came to mourn, perhaps, he had been able to pass it on. All of it. He had none left. Crazy! He shrugged.

"Damn you!"

The funeral was two days later, and this time Charon received his due. Martha joined the Earth to the notes of an old and promising hymn. Stanley wept to lose her, but he was calmer now. Her doctor stood aside, bowed and silent.

David took the flute from his lips. He gazed at leafless trees and a gray sky. The snow was thick and more was due. Stanley was oblivious. His mind was wholly on falling, frozen clods. He seemed to twitch with each echo they evoked from his wife's plain coffin.

When the clods had begun to muffle themselves, David turned toward the doctor and closed the few feet between them. The man was still bowed, his hands clasped behind a plump abdomen, his nose red in the cold. His coat was the common wool, and his shoes were protected by rubbers. But he stirred when David spoke.

"Can you tell me why?"

"Why she died?" The doctor's voice was low. He refused to meet David's eyes. Instead he turned as if to read the inscription on a nearby stone.

"No," replied David. "The why of that. Why did the baby die? And others too, I hear." He spoke as softly as he could, but Stanley still heard him easily. He straightened his neck and listened.

"Others, yes. All of them. So far."

"But why?"

"It's the genes." It had long been known that an infant's chance of being born deformed increased with its mother's age. Cosmic rays, background radiation, food additives, drugs, all broke and twisted the material of life, changed the shape of each coming generation for good or ill. The changes didn't affect the adults' bodies, for their strengthened immune systems removed all damaged cells. All but their eggs and sperm. "One gene in a million," the doctor said. "One in a million gets changed every year, and you carry about twice that many genes. So in a thousand years, you get two thousand changes."

"And thirty years was enough to notice the effect." Stanley had heard, and now he turned. His voice cracked as he spoke. His eyes were bright with tears. "Why did we stop having babies then?"

The doctor still stared at the gravestone. "We didn't know," he muttered. "We should have, but no one thought it through. No one guessed that we would let the damage mount up so long, so far. Until we might as well be sterile."

"Until we might as well be dead." David turned away and sounded a few last, incongruously gay notes on his flute. Stanley gave himself a last glance at Martha's grave, at the workmen filling in the hole. They left.

A thousand years of immortality had seen the race reduced from four billion to five hundred million. Men had laughed in the face of death as their neighbors died of famine, accident, and the few remaining diseases, for they had felt safe. Death couldn't touch them, and if it did, so what? It was a rarity, an accident. The rule was life. No matter how bad the weather turned, it would improve, and then they would breed their numbers back.

But nature was not kind. Men forgot that they had evolved to breed, and by breeding live. They thought they could stop the cycle of regeneration and reproduction, and they did. But the cycle could not be started again. The long coast was nearly over, and the curb went whizzing by to the gaily mocking sound of David Howell's flute.

The people tried, but no matter how many years the attempt went on, no babies lived. They tried for a century, for two and three, but the deformities only grew worse as the mutations piled up in their cells.

The race mourned. The last shreds of order disappeared in a rash of suicides and murders. Farmers left their fields and were replaced by city dwellers. The crops failed again, and again. More people starved, even as the climate mellowed.

The second thousand years of immortality saw the immortals all but vanished. The last ones lingered awhile in Missouri, maintained a town or two, farmed the land, and basked in the lengthening summers. They had no future, though, and they knew it. Time would claim them all. The few savages who had stayed in their jungles, who had resisted the blandishments of civilization, would inherit the Earth.

They tolerated David. He had grieved while they laughed, and now he laughed while they grieved. Well, his madness was no worse than theirs, and if he sang all night, he still did his share in the fields.

They tolerated him, fed him, and housed him, but if they thought he needed them, they were wrong. He proved it, for they died while he sang on.

The town was sparsely built in these days. Most of its old buildings were weed-grown mounds. The last two men lived in the concrete and steel boxes of another era, George in a garage, David in a laundromat. They had been the only two for a decade, and the town's only sounds had been David's flute and George's hammer, banging bits of metal into hilts and blades and useless armor. They rarely met any more.

The last day opened with a threat of snow. David rose and ate, brought wood from his woodpile to his fire, took a rabbit from a snare on the old bank's mound. He listened, and he heard no banging. George was silent.

He took the path to the other's door, pressed it open, entered the gloom. Dimly he made out a figure on a pallet across the room, George, his face to the wall, staring at his hand-made, dreaming trophies. He spoke, "George! You sick?"

The other didn't stir. "Hell, no."

David hesitated. He had seen this before, though not in George. Other men, and women too, had laid down and died, but George had laughed at them, scorning their cowardice. He wouldn't go that way, he had said. "I have a rabbit, George. Should I cook it for us?"

No answer.

"Then I'll leave it here for you. Hope you feel better soon."

He returned to his laundromat. The machines were long gone, but the rusty stubs of pipes jutted from the walls and were good for hanging things. He had one of George's swords there. He had potatoes, too, and onions, dried corn and meat, a few dried fruits. Nothing fresh or green, but enough for a lunch that day, and many more. He ate in his doorway, and he grunted happily when he saw a thread of smoke rise from the garage. He pulled his flute from his boot, and as the first snowflakes fell, he began to sing.

He sang as the thread of smoke grew thicker and became a column. He played as flame licked through the boarded windows, and he played as a small figure stepped into the path, waved a gleaming blade in the air, and fell upon it.

The echoes rang wildly in the room at his back, fell muffled in the snow before him. Smoke surged and fell back in the near distance, and a body was shrouded in white. David closed his eyes and played on. He sang of afternoons and of armies, of dances and of war. He sang for himself and he sang of decline. He sang joyfully, and he sang of death.

For those of us accustomed to the Three Laws of Robotics, this story may come as a surprise. But think about it carefully!

Valo in Love
Gordon Eklund

Valo, the robot, had first known conscious existence as a romantic poet, the first of his kind, but that program had proven to be a rather embarrassing failure. Instead of composing the original verse expected of him, Valo never managed anything more creative than a verbatim regurgitation of some of the human verse already stored in his memory banks. For one year, then two, his programmers kept hoping for a breakthrough, but when all they received for their patience was a stream of sonnets written by William Shakespeare, they finally threw up their hands and ordered a new program installed.

Valo became a licensed attorney—a criminal lawyer. He defended fifty-nine cases and lost them all. Still, this was an era when lawyers were not expected to win acquittal for their clients. Only the guilty were ever arrested, and the corporate courts were not programmed for leniency. Valo continued to regard poetry as his principal calling, albeit he could no longer actually write. He felt he had been cruelly mis-

93

treated. The lines of one of his old sonnets clearly reflected his present state of mind:

> When in disgrace with fortune and men's eyes
> I alone beweep my outcast state
> And trouble deaf heaven with my bootless cries,
> And look upon myself, and curse my fate. . .

One particular day, all this changed, however, for as soon as Valo wheeled into the cell where his newest client resided, he realized at once that he had fallen deeply, suddenly, and irrevocably in love. The rush of furious emotion caught him totally by surprise. He had known several human females before but never loved a one of them. This girl was tall, statuesque, yellow-haired, green-eyed, with thick moist lips and a sharp jutting chin. Her name was Brenda O'Reilly. She stood charged with first-degree murder. Valo knew he didn't dare reveal his sudden feelings to her.

From her cot, she glared at him. "What do you want, robot?"

"My name is Valo," he said, trying to sound glib, "and I've been appointed your attorney. What I'd like to—"

"Nope," she said. "Uh-uh." She came stiffly to her feet, shaking her head so that delicate strands of hair brushed across her eyes. "I thought I'd made that clear. No lawyers—no robots. If they want to kill me, go ahead, but I won't play their game."

He barely heard her. She was lovely, a vision of pure delight. One of his poems came to mind:

> Shall I compare thee to a summer's day?
> Thou art more lovely and more temperate:

Rough winds to shake the darling buds of May,
And summer's lease hath all too short a date:

Wasn't it peculiar? he thought. He had composed those lines long before he set eyes on dear, sweet Brenda. It was like a prophecy come true, an unwitting glimpse into the shrouded future. He said, "Won't you at least hear what I can do for you?"

"I don't want to hear nothing." She pushed gruffly past him and slammed a fist against the padded wall. "Hey, open up! Get this tin can out of here!"

"Brenda, please." Mentally, Valo reviewed what he knew of her case. The matter was indeed a serious one. Brenda stood accused of the murder of Chief Randall McNulty, head of the local branch of the Internal Security Force and also her alleged lover. Because Chief McNulty had equipped his home with a video recording system, the actual crime was a matter of record. *I'll win this case,* Valo swore. *I'll win or die in the trying.* "Please listen to me," he said.

"Then give me one good reason." She turned, facing him, and for the first time he realized she was more frightened than angry. In her short denim pants, regulation prison garb, she reminded him of a child lost in a dark forest. In spite of her size, she was very young, too, probably not yet twenty. He could have wheeled forward and embraced her.

"I can save your life," he said.

She frowned skeptically and put her hands on her hips. "Look, Mr. Tin Can, don't take me for an idiot. I know exactly what's in store for me and I know there's nothing you can do. They've got you programmed, right? All they want from you is to be able later to say, look, we gave the woman a fair trial.

Well, I just don't give a shit. I did what I did, and when I die, my blood can be on their hands."

Valo turned his sensors on the tiny, dim cell. It was a dreadful place to live. "I could obtain your release from here."

She continued to frown, but something new—a ray of hope—entered her eyes. "And how do you intend to pull that off?"

He forced his voice to remain calm. "It's largely a routine procedure. I'll need to file a writ of temporary release with the court. I put up my personal guarantee. If you can't trust a robot, whom can you trust? You'll come and stay with me."

"With you?"

He nodded, a mechanical gesture difficult to perform without squeaking. "I have a small apartment in the western portion of the city."

"Then I won't have to. . ." Her voice suddenly cracked. He was startled—she had seem so totally in control before—and wished more than ever that he could hug her in his arms. She gave a sigh and her body, most of it naked, trembled. "Look, I'm sorry I was sharp, but you can't understand how it is. I've never been locked up before. There's no night, no day, no sense of time. I'd do almost anything to see the sun again."

"Then trust me, Brenda."

"I can—will they? The court?"

"A robot cannot lie. They'll have to believe me."

She nodded, slipped past him, and sat on the cot. Her head hung forward and a wisp of blonde hair obscured one eye. "What's to keep me from running away?"

"There are certain required precautions," he said. "The building I inhabit is totally secure. Like all ro-

bots, I am personally armed—" he showed her the tip
of his left index finger and the gun implanted there
"—and can stun, though not kill, in the event of an
emergency." (He knew full well he could never possibly harm a hair on her head.) "And, of course, the
authorities sometimes provide special surveillance."

She frowned tightly. "In other words, an ISF
peeper."

He nodded again, square head bobbing. "I'm
afraid so."

She bit her lip. "They hate me. I killed their boss.
They'd like to kill me, too."

"I can protect you, Brenda."

She seemed less than convinced. Still, at last, she
shrugged her gorgeous shoulders. "Okay, then do it.
I don't care—do what you can. I guess getting killed
by a peeper is better than living in this hell." She
stood, nearly smiling, and held out her hands. "I
guess, you and me, we're partners, Valo. Want to
shake?"

He captured her hands in his. A tiny chill, like an
electrical current, scurried up his arms. He knew he
would have to leave her now, if only for a while. Another of his poems expressed it best:

> Love alters not with his brief hours and weeks,
> But bears it out even to the edge of doom.
> If this be error and upon me proved,
> I never writ, nor no man ever loved.

2

Despite the optimistic tone he had taken with
Brenda, Valo left city prison with only frail hope of
winning her release. Such writs were indeed routinely

granted for minor crimes like looting and rape, but murder was quite another matter. Valo had told Brenda what he had only to keep her from carrying out her threat and dismissing him as her attorney.

Still, when he arrived in court, because of his love for Brenda, Valo refused to acknowledge defeat. Four times the judge ruled against him, but on each occasion, Valo raised yet another objection. In the end, he was willing to lay his entire self on the line. "I am a robot," he declared, "a term synonymous with personal integrity. For this court to deny my request for the release of my client is tantamount to denying my status as an individual. I am inherently incapable of telling a lie. I cannot commit a wrongful deed. I have no choice at any time but to act in exact accordance with my personal programming. It is absurd to question the integrity of a robot. Should something happen, should I somehow fail in my prescribed duty, I pledge to this court not only my life but my sacred honor as well."

"Are you sure that's an equal bargain?" the judge said testily. Like all human judges—the machines were reserved for use only at actual trials—he was an old man. The hour was late, and the judge seemed more interested in the clock than Valo's words.

"I'm speaking of the imperishable pride and honor of a robot," said Valo.

The judge gazed at the clock. By now, Valo had made it quite plain that he did not intend to retire easily. Finally, sighing, rubbing his tiny eyes, the judge said, "All right, I've had my fill of your goddamned honor. The defendent will be released and brought under guard to your home. I'll notify the county attorney who will, I'm sure, take sufficient steps to prevent trouble." He lifted a tired finger, pointing at Valo. "But if there is trouble, if anything happens, if this girl somehow manages to escape, I swear I'll personally oversee your obliteration. Is that understood?"

"Oh, yes, your honor," cried Valo. "Oh, thank you." He was so happy he was afraid he might rupture a circuit.

"Now get out of my sight," said the judge, with a final, dismissive wave of the hand.

Elated, Valo sped from the courtroom, filled with pride at the manner in which he had worn down the old judge. More than anything he wanted to rush straight home, but Brenda would not arrive for at least another hour, so he paused first at the nearest encyclopedic outlet. Inserting his private credentials, he waited for the outlet to recognize his identity, then dialed a request for a readout concerning one Brenda O'Reilly, accused murderess. The data, when they came, were of meager consequence compared to the shimmering glory of his love. Still, since the readout concerned Brenda, he found it of some interest.

The readout began with a brief description of her father, one Michael James O'Reilly, a well-known radical extremist. Because of his criminal activities, which included wrongful advocacy and incorporate publishing, O'Reilly had been confined to a major mental recycling center, where he had suddenly died. Because her mother was also dead, Brenda, then fifteen, had been assigned to a public home. At sixteen she ran away from the home, and a year later was arrested for unlicensed prostitution. Chief McNulty, as was sometimes his practice, appeared personally at her trial. (This portion of the readout contained restricted information that Valo, as a robot, was permitted to read but programmed not to divulge.) The court found her guilty but sentenced her to the care of Chief McNulty himself. A day after the trial, nine months ago now, she changed her permanent address to that of Chief McNulty's estate in the southern suburbs. He reported that her rehabilitation was proceeding well. Two weeks ago, he was murdered. Brenda was arrested on the spot. Her trial and subsequent execution were expected momentarily. There was a recent photograph. Some vital statistics. She stood five feet, nine inches tall; her average weight was one hundred thirty-seven pounds. Copies of her voice, finger, and lip prints were included.

Despondent, Valo broke the circuit. Even the encyclopedia appeared to accept Brenda's guilt. What possible chance did he have of winning an acquittal? He drew strength from another of his poems:

> That thou art blamed shall not be thy defect,
> For slander's mark was ever yet the fair;
> The ornament of beauty is suspect,
> A crow that flies in heaven's sweetest air.

Valo headed into the streets. As was usual at this hour, the sidewalks were crammed with humans dashing to their aerocars to begin the long trek home. Valo struggled to find an inconspicuous path through all that bustling flesh, bumping from body to body. When he finally reached the empty, broken boulevards at the edge of his own neighborhood, where the stripped skeletons of burned-out houses rose like ghosts in the twilight, he was able to move more freely. An old Negro, undoubtedly a pensioner, charged from the shelter of a rubble pile and pursued Valo, cursing and accusing the robot of stealing his job and wife. Such open prejudice was not uncommon in this desolate region. Out of patience, Valo finally paused long enough to inform the old man that he was a poet, which was a calling, not a job, and that he was presently in love with a gorgeous young woman, who was not anyone's wife. The old man stopped in his tracks, gaping in astonishment. Apparently, he had never heard of a robot in love. Chuckling softly, Valo hurried onward. In good time, despite the delay, he reached home.

3

As Valo labored to place the carpet on the floor of his apartment—he had no use for such luxuries, living alone—another fragment of his own verse kept coming to mind:

How like a winter hath my absence been
From thee, the pleasure of the fleeting year!
What freezings have I felt, what dark days seen!
What old December's bareness everywhere!
And yet this time removed was summer's
time . . .

Yes, how true, he thought, stamping on the carpet. Apart from Brenda, his life seemed to possess no meaning. Everything prior to this morning—even his own verse—was mere prelude; his true life, the part that mattered, had begun the moment he entered that cell.

A solid fist pounded on the door. A firm voice said, "Internal Security Forces. Open up."

Valo knew at once that it had to be a peeper—with Brenda.

His heart caught in his throat. (Figuratively—he didn't have a real heart.) With trembling fingers, he pressed the button that cycled open the iron door.

There were two peepers, both in uniform, and Brenda stood between them, like a bird pinned by the claws of a cat. She wore a lacy thin shift, black leather boots, and a red velvet bracelet on her left wrist. She looked at Valo and grinned. He had seen nothing so beautiful in his life.

"Brenda," he said, struggling to execute a distinguished bow. "I'm very pleased to—"

"You Valo?" While one of the peepers kept hold of Brenda's arm, the other handed Valo a thick sheaf of papers. Her official release, he assumed. Valo knew he was staring. When Brenda winked, all of a sudden, his heart skipped a full beat.

The peeper was saying: ". . . should be in proper legal order. Any questions regarding your responsibilities should be directed toward the county attorney."

"I'm certain there will be no problems." Valo watched Brenda closely. She kept jerking her shoulder, as if the peeper were hurting her arm. "Couldn't you let her go?" he said, ignoring the proper deference.

Both peepers frowned quizzically, but the one closest to Valo said, "Go ahead and release her. But watch out."

Brenda broke free. She shook her arm and winced painfully.

"You're hurt," said Valo, wheeling to her side.

The peepers were frowning even more deeply. The one in charge said, "An agent will remain below at all times. This woman is a classified priority one prisoner. My advice is that you stay close to him. Chief McNulty was a hell of a man. He wouldn't have died easily."

Valo nodded, distracted. A red mark formed on Brenda's arm. "I'll contact you if there's an emergency."

The peepers hesitated a moment more, then finally withdrew. Eagerly, Valo let them out. The instant the door shut, Brenda sat down on the floor. It took Valo a moment to realize that she was laughing. It was an uncontrolled explosion of glee. Her stomach heaved; her breath game in ragged gasps. For a while, Valo feared she might be in real pain. Helplessly, he hovered nearby.

At last, her laughter subsided. She peered at Valo through moist eyes. "I just never believed for a minute you could really pull it off."

"I'd do almost anything for you, Brenda," he said, coming dangerously close to declaring his love.

"You must be one hell of a lawyer." She held out her hand. "Help me up, Valo."

He did, once more experiencing the tingle of her bare flesh against his cold steel. "Now we must dine," he said. "I've chosen an excellent facility."

She seemed amazed. "You can't mean in a restaurant. What about what the peeper said?"

"I do not concern myself with the absurdities of those insensitive creatures. You deserve a chance to celebrate your release. I have decided to take you to dinner, and we shall dine."

She beamed in delight. "Well, goody for you."

"Indeed," he said, nodding firmly.

She grasped his hand warmly. "Valo, I think you're a wonderful guy."

4

Returning home late that night, Valo turned his wheels at a deliberately slow pace, since he knew that Brenda, huddled inside a fur jacket purchased from a peddling machine, must be tired. Her eyes were bright and she chattered off and on, but he had seen her yawning even before they left the restaurant and wanted to be sure she didn't overextend herself.

They had spent close to three hours dining at a quiet establishment in the downtown sector. Valo observed happily as Brenda ate a slow path through the long menu. Between bites, she apologized, explaining that she hadn't been inside a restaurant in many years and had forgotten how delicious real food could taste. Valo loved the way her jaw clenched as she chewed, making the ivory skin flex smooth. She was a lovely girl, and if he hadn't loved her already, he would surely have started now.

The walk home was safe, too, or else he would have made haste. An ISF peeper had tagged at their heels since they first left home. Valo loathed the sound of those heavy bootheels pounding the pavement close behind, but at least the peeper kept them well protected. Not even the boldest urban marauder would interfere with a peeper. Once, several years ago, a peeper had been mugged near here, and afterward, in swift retaliation, three city blocks had been leveled.

At the restaurant, while Brenda ate, Valo carried the conversation. He was not known as a talker, even among his closest robot friends, but with Brenda he discovered a new articulation; he spoke freely of matters he had never discussed before and quoted several of his favorite sonnets in full. Brenda said her education had been limited—the death of her parents had seen to that—and she experienced some difficulty following all his words. Valo forgave her easily, explaining that love was the one true constant and that romantic poetry sometimes had to seek a language of its own. He quoted another sonnet:

Not marble, nor the gilded monuments
Of Princes, shall outlive this powerful rhyme;
But you shall shine more bright in these contents
Than unswept stone, besmeared with sluttish time. . .

She smiled in response and told him that was very good, but Valo knew the only way to make her truly happy would be to win her case. On the way to the restaurant, he had raised the subject tentatively, stating his belief that she would be found innocent and that all that was needed was a clever strategy for use during the trial.

"But I'm not innocent," she had said, with an ease that shocked him.

"Never say that!" Valo cried. "Never!" His voice rose so shrilly that the peeper took an extra step forward, anticipating trouble.

"It's true," she said softly.

"My job is to prove that it's not."

She hadn't responded then—the peeper lurked too near—but now, as they came close to home, she said, "I think there's something you ought to understand, Valo. I appreciate what you're doing, but I'm not expecting miracles."

"Miracles?" He tried to sound confused. "I'm afraid I don't understand."

"I mean that I don't expect you to win my case. It's just not possible, Valo, and I fully understand that."

"You haven't heard my strategy yet," he said smugly.

"No, but I have seen the tape of the murder, and it's all there. Me. McNulty. The gun. We're in bed together, naked. Maybe they'd let you look at it."

"No, that's not necessary," he said, recoiling from her suggestion.

"But I'm not sorry. I want to make that clear. I intended to kill him and I'm glad I did."

"That's not relevant to the case."

"No, but it is to me. Look, Valo, I killed McNulty because he deserved to die. He was a terrible man who preyed on helpless people. I was one—there were plenty before. He treated people like animals, objects, things lower than a robot. He deserved to die and yet —this is the funny part—I didn't enjoy it. Not then, and not now, either. It was a horrible, ugly mess. If I die for it, I'm not sure that'll be wrong."

"You mustn't ever say that." He couldn't be angry with her. "You must have faith."

She shrugged. "In what?"

"In me," he said boldly.

They went another block in silence. Her confession only increased his determination to prove her innocent. His love for her was reason enough, but now he had something more: Chief McNulty had deserved to die.

"Six," she murmured.

"What?" said Valo, startled.

"Oh, I was just counting. I wondered how many peepers were tailing us. I've counted six so far."

"But there's only that one. . ." He started to turn. Surreptitiously, she drew him back.

"Don't worry about him. He's there just to keep us from noticing the rest. I've lived on the streets too long to be fooled. You've got to watch the shadows." She made a gesture, and he tried to follow her hand. The landscape here was dark—too dark. He saw a few fleeting shadows, nothing more. "Half the men in the restaurant were peepers."

"But why should they want to hide?"

"Isn't it obvious? How damned convenient if I tried to escape. Blooey! That would save the embarrassment of a trial."

"Then you mustn't even think about escaping."

"I wouldn't get far."

"You don't want to do anything before the trial to jeopardize your chances."

She laughed. "Is that important?"

"Yes," he said fervently. "Yes, it is."

4

As Brenda awoke that next morning, Valo hovered nearby, observing each flicker of her eyelid as if it represented a revelation from heaven. He had made up a bed from a few cushions and her jacket. Snuggled inside, Brenda appeared to him as a vision of pure innocence.

Suddenly, her eyes were open. She was watching him. "You're Valo?" she said.

He nodded solemnly. "And you're Brenda."

Grinning, she sat up, rubbing her eyes. "It must be morning."

"One o'clock in the afternoon."

She shook her head and yellow hair tumbled down her bare shoulders. "I don't usually sleep long. What's new?" She pointed to her clothes. Valo handed her the lace shift.

"I spent all night doing research," he said proudly. "I believe I've discovered a strategy to win our case."

"You have, have you?" She seemed thoroughly unexcited. Standing, showing a brief flash of flat stomach, puckered navel, pubic thatch, she drew the thin shift over her head.

Her lack of response drove him to say more than he had intended. "It's got to be a twin," he said. "That's something the county attorney can't possibly dispute. We'll pull it off as our big surprise. It wasn't you who did the killing. It was your twin sister."

She stared at him, wide-eyed. "My twin? What twin?"

"You see," he said, "she even fooled Chief McNulty. The whole thing was a frame-up, an act of revenge. Your sister hated you. When she snuck away, you were naturally blamed."

"Valo, I don't have a twin. That's a matter of public record. I'm an only child."

"Records can be mistaken. That's the crucial element in our strategy. We'll show that your parents couldn't afford two children. They chose you over your sister."

"My father wasn't poor. He was a university teacher when I was born."

"Then we'll say that he hated children in groups larger than one. The details aren't important. We'll prove that your sister, when she grew up, discovered that she had been deserted and blamed you. That was her motive. Jealousy—revenge."

She was staring at him, her head shaking from side to side. "You are serious."

He nodded as firmly as the hinges allowed. "I promised you a strategy, didn't I?"

"Valo, I'm not sure . . . do you really think a judge will accept that story?"

Her lack of enthusiasm disturbed him. What had gone wrong? He had wanted only to make her happy. All at once, he hated his own damned strategy. He saw how stupid it was—and how weak. "It's worth trying, isn't it?" he said hopefully.

She continued to shake her head. "It's not that . . . it's . . . Valo, tell me something. How many cases have you won?"

"Not a majority," he admitted.

"No, please. Exactly how many?"

"Well, very few. No straight out-and-out victories, I mean. I have won several sentence reductions, though. There was one boy—"

"Valo, there's no reduced sentence for murder," she said, in a hushed tone.

"And that's exactly why I have to prove you innocent."

She was pacing the tiny room. "Then do as you want. Hell, I don't suppose it matters. It can't hurt. It'll be over soon."

Valo observed her aimless wandering and softly cursed his own stupidity. He knew he had caused irreparable harm by forcing her to endure his own half-formulated plan. He made a vow right then and there to keep his future strategies secret, to be sure he was right before loosening his hinges.

Wheeling across the room, he placed a steel hand on her shoulder. Stooping, she leaned close to him. It was the most intimately they had ever touched. "Would you like to have breakfast?" he said gently.

She smiled—just a tiny gesture, but it was genuine. "Sure, Valo, whatever you say."

He knew how deeply he loved her, how passionately he adored her. Everything else in the cosmos, including his own petty existence, faded to mute insignificance beside the beauty of her soul. He had once written:

> When I perhaps compounded am with clay,
> Do not so much as my poor name rehearse,
> But let your love even with my life decay;
> Lest the wise world should look into your moan,
> And mock you with me after I am gone.

Beautiful words, he thought, and—except for the part about her love for him—not only appropriate but true.

5

Valo worried that his friends might not accept Brenda, for there was as much prejudice by robots toward humans as the opposite, but oddly enough, the robots he knew best did not seem to mind her presence, as if they understood and sympathized with his undeclared love, and when it was Valo's turn to serve as host, no one stayed away from the regular Saturday night poker party.

Brenda greeted each guest politely as he wheeled through the door. Executing a bow and offering a handshake, she said how pleased she was to meet any friend of Valo. There were four tonight: Daka, a cleaning robot, presently in the service of the City Magistrate; Dyna, a surgeon, the best in the world, some said; Raqua, a sportswriter, an experimental model like Valo but a successful one; and Zabo, a bullfighter, minus his right arm this evening because of a slip in the ring.

The four of them, plus Valo, folded their wheels and knelt on the carpet. Valo opened a deck of cards and handed it to Zabo, who shuffled and dealt the first hand. They played nothing but five-card stud, the purest of poker games, wagering credit slips. No one ever lost or won a truly significant amount; the game was largely for fun.

Brenda, crouching behind Valo, observed the game in polite silence, examining the cards as each arrived and watching the subsequent play. She said she was familiar with the game but declined an invitation to sit in. Valo could tell that his friends liked Brenda and she liked them. It made him feel quietly proud.

As the evening progressed, Valo lost steadily, while Zabo, the brass bullfighter, emerged as the big winner. Valo felt almost humiliated by his failure, an abnormal reaction and one he knew was because of Brenda. He could feel her warm breath close to his shoulder. He knew he wanted to prove to her just how clever he could be.

Dyna shuffled and dealt a new hand. A queen of spades showed face-up for Valo. He peeked at his hole card: it was an ace of diamonds. Zabo was the high man. He showed an ace of hearts.

"Ten credits," Zabo said, placing the script in the center of the circle. The bet was not a large one. "An ace should be worth more, but I'm feeling pity toward the rest of you."

Valo waited patiently until the bet came to him. Then, without hesitation, he laid down his script. "I'll raise thirty."

A ripple of surprise went around the circle. Only Zabo, with his ace, and Dyna, who showed a nine of spades, called the raise. "So you want to pretend you've got a pair in the hole," Zabo said.

"Could be," Valo said.

Dyna dealt another card. Zabo drew a ten of diamonds, but Valo got the queen of hearts. That gave him a pair showing. Dyna drew a seven of spades.

Valo knew this bet was crucial. He could keep it high or go low. He decided to gamble that Zabo, on a winning streak, would not fold easily. "That will cost you thirty more."

"No problem," Zabo said, matching the bet. Dyna, as Valo anticipated, folded his hand.

It was now one against one, Zabo and Valo.

Dyna dealt another card. Valo drew the jack of diamonds and Zabo, the ace of spaces.

Zabo beamed, his headlights flashing. "That makes me high man," he said of his pair of aces. "It's worth fifty."

"And fifty more," said Valo.

"You're raising?"

"I am."

"I don't believe you have it."

"Have what?"

"A third queen in the hole."

Valo peeked at his hidden card. It hadn't changed: an ace of diamonds. "It'll cost you fifty credits to find out."

Zabo shrugged. "Then fifty it is."

Daka, the cleaning robot, turned to Brenda. "I met a robot yesterday who knows you. His name is Mylva."

"I remember him," she said. "He was Chief McNulty's valet. He was at the house the night the killing happened."

"Can't we have our cards?" Valo said impatiently. He did not want Brenda reminded of her alleged crime. Daka fell silent. Dyna dealt the final cards.

Valo got a two of clubs; Zabo drew the three of hearts.

Zabo was gloating already. "Nice try," he said, "but you've only built a pot for me. It'll cost of fifty to stay and lose."

The big wager was wise strategy on Zabo's part. Without a third queen, Valo would have to be a fool to stay. He knew he couldn't hesitate. "Fifty," he said, "and make it two hundred more." The pot already contained enough money to put Valo ahead for the evening. If he lost, there would be no more restaurant dinners for a while.

"You bluffer," Zabo said. He fingered his cards, staring at the pot. "You haven't got it."

"Two hundred to find out."

"Do you really think you can bluff me out?"

"What makes you think I am?"

"I'd bet on it."

"And you'd lose, too."

"Liar."

"Everyone knows robots can't lie."

The others in the circle laughed in appreciation. Zabo was silent. A proud robot, he hated to lose. Finally, he let his cards slip from his hand. "Fold," he said quietly.

As he raked in the credit slips, Valo kept silent, betraying no emotion. He would never gloat over the defeat of a friend. He glanced at Brenda. Her face, wreathed in a smile, showed how she felt about his triumph.

That one big pot seemed to alter Valo's luck. From then on, he won consistently and, by the time the party drew to a close, was far ahead of the next best winner, Dyna.

Zabo was the last to depart. Pausing at the door, he gestured at Valo to come close. "You and I have been good friends for many years," he said, "and I'd like you to tell me one thing."

"Of course, Zabo," Valo said.

"That big pot you won from me: did you have the third queen in the hole or didn't you?"

"The truth?"

"Yes, the truth," Zabo said.

"I had it."

"You damned liar." Beaming, Zabo went on out.

Alone with Brenda, Valo faced her. "I did well tonight and would like to celebrate by doing something unusual tomorrow. Do you have any ideas?"

She hesitated a moment, then said, "Well, how about a visit to the entertainment strip? I'll bet you've never been there before."

Valo was surprised. The entertainment strip was a place seldom frequented by robots. "Do you really want to go there?"

She nodded slowly. "Yes. It's not a place I'll likely ever see again. I did work there. Call it nostalgia."

"As you wish, Brenda." He wheeled forward to help make up her bed.

6

San Francisco's entertainment district—more commonly known as the strip—consisted of two square kilometers of dancehalls, sensashows, dope dens, nightclubs, thieves, confood bars, gambling parlors, and prostitutes of various breeds and sexes, all precariously perched on the edge of the city's tallest hill. Valo was certain he would not like this place, with its noise and clamor, but Brenda seemed excited by the spectacle and he could not go against her wishes.

Valo held himself to blame for her recent mood of despair. Ever since he'd made the monstrous error of revealing his initial strategy, she had seemed subdued and despondent. He was eager to do anything to alter that mood. All night, every night, he labored diligently at devising a new strategy designed to win acquittal. He had kept his latest ideas from Brenda. He didn't want inadvertently to hurt her again. He wanted to win her approval—then her love.

Walking through the entertainment strip made Valo very uncomfortable, a reaction he sought to conceal from Brenda. This was strictly human terrain and, as the only robot visible, he attracted as many hostile stares as an enemy soldier in no man's land.

Brenda, fortunately, seemed oblivious. A throng of street clowns went bouncing past in their exotic silks and painted faces. Brenda smiled, then laughed.

"You seem to enjoy this," he said, nearly shouting to be heard.

"It's always fun here. I hated the work, but it was better than McNulty."

"You shouldn't think about him."

"How can I help it? The trial's less than a week away."

"I'll tend to the trial," he said stuffily.

They were not alone. A uniformed peeper clung close to their heels, while eight others in plain clothes sought concealment among the crowd. Brenda had pointed out each of the peepers to him at various times, and he knew them all now by sight. They were constant shadows, present both day and night.

"Is there a particular place you'd like to visit?" he asked.

"Oh. . ." She stopped, turned, then suddenly pointed. "How about right there?" She indicated a glittering neon sign halfway down the next block. It advertised a dancehall: *The Pit*.

"Have you been there before?"

"Yes, it's very crowded."

"With degenerates?" he asked disapprovingly.

She laughed. "You're worse than an old mother, Valo. Have you forgotten? I'm a degenerate, too."

"I don't think you are."

"Well, then, you're wrong. See those girls down on the corner." She pointed to a flock of brightly painted prostitutes. "I used to be just like them."

"All right," he said, unwilling to argue. He took her tightly by the hand and wheeled forward. "We will visit this place—*The Pit.*"

Reaching the club, Valo purchased two tickets from an autobooth and joined Brenda at the entry doors. They went inside. The hall was one big room jammed from wall to wall with shaking, twisting, quivering, dancing human bodies. A shrill unpleasant noise—like a penny whistle amplified a thousand times—pounded his aural sensors. He assumed it was meant to be music. Most of the dancers were naked. Valo didn't spot any other robots.

"Are you certain this is what you want?" he said, leaning close to her ear.

"Sure, isn't it great?"

"Well, shouldn't we find a table and sit down?"

She shook her head, distracted. "I don't want to sit."

"Well, then what do you want to do? Just look and go?" he added eagerly.

"No. I want to dance."

"Dance? But I can't. . . ." He pointed to his wheels.

"I know you can't dance, but I can." She seemed tense. Was something wrong? "I'll go alone. Here— you watch." Reaching suddenly down, she took hold of the hem of her white shift and pulled. The garment came over her head in a single swift graceful motion. Naked, she stood before him. "Hold this please, Valo."

"Do you want me to wait here?"

"Yes, please do." Her eyes kept darting—from the crowd to Valo, back to the crowd again. "I . . . I . . . ." She stuttered, backing to the edge of the dancefloor. "Valo—darling—good-by."

He raised his hand to wave and only then realized what her words might mean. "No!" he shouted, charging forward. "Brenda, don't!"

Already, it was too late: Brenda had vanished. She was just one naked body among hundreds.

Anxiously, he scanned the crowd, seeking her again. What if the peepers also guessed she was trying to escape? There were simply too many bodies. This girl was too tall, another too plump. One wore a mole on her left cheek, another a birthmark below her right breast.

Valo stood hopelessly on his wheels. A whimper of emotion escaped the cavity of his mouth. Such a human sound. It amazed him. He had never made a noise like that before.

Suddenly, a hand clamped down on his shoulder. Valo swiveled, praying it was Brenda. The man was a peeper. In plain clothes. His eyes were tight with anger. "Where did she go? What's happened to her?"

Valo tried to act calm. "She went to dance. She'll be right back. She said—"

"You believed that?"

"Brenda wouldn't lie to me."

"Christ!" The peeper fastened his eyes on the swirling crowd, straining to see. Abruptly, Valo saw a gun in his hand. A killing weapon—not a stunner. "When I catch her, she'll be damned sorry."

"No!" Valo leaped for the gun.

He was way too late. The peeper shoved past him and broke into a run. For a long time, Valo caught glimpses of him. Fully dressed, the peeper stood out among the dancers like a red apple on a lemon tree. There were others, too. Peepers prowled the floor everywhere.

There was a flash of light. A moment later, Valo heard the sound of a shot. The peepers had found

Brenda. He knew they were killing her.

Surging forward, he tried to reach the place where he had seen the flash of light. The crowd moved against him. These were suburbanities unaccustomed to the blaze of gunfire. There was another flash, another shot. Panic spread among the dancers. The music wailed on. Screaming in fear, people dashed frantically for the exits. Valo battled hopelessly against the flow. Wheels spinning, he was carried away. "Brenda!" he cried. "Brenda, I'm coming!"

But he wasn't.

Another burst of yellow light, much farther away. The crowd drove him back. He didn't want to go. He wanted to stay and save her. The peepers were killing Brenda, his love, and there was nothing Valo could do.

Suddenly, he saw her. Near the main entrance. Pinned to the wall. Two peepers held her arms, while a third—a squat man in plain clothes—aimed a gun at her heart.

With a terrific burst of animal strength, Valo broke free of the mob. He squealed across the slick floor. "Release her!" he cried. "Release my client!"

The peeper with the gun turned in astonishment. Brenda, sensing an advantage, lashed out with her legs. Dancing on tiptoes, the peeper barely avoided her feet.

"Bitch," said the peeper. "I ought to kill you."

Brenda seemed totally out of control. Her face was a rigid mask of rage, her eyes blank and expressionless. Throwing back her head, she screamed, her voice rising higher than the music. Oddly, her cries seemed to calm the mob. People stopped in their mad dash to escape and turned to watch. Valo wheeled forward past the peeper until he stood only inches away from Brenda. She was trembling. He saw tears in her eyes. He understood. Brenda had dared something desperate, gathering what little strength she possessed until it burned in her stomach like a ball of fire, and she had failed; she had gained no release. The peepers couldn't kill her now, not with this crowd. She was safe, but she was caught. "Brenda," he said, his voice very soft. "Brenda, stop. Don't."

Unable to hear, she went on screaming.

He knew what he had to do. Drawing back his hand, he slapped her face gently. His fingers made red streaks on her flesh. The crowd grew silent. There was an ugly murmuring. A robot should never strike a human being.

"Brenda," Valo said, in a louder voice. "Brenda, they won't hurt you. I'm here now. Listen to me."

When he slapped her, she went stiff, her muscles frozen as if by shock. His words seemed to penetrate, providing an excuse to relax. All at once, her knees slackened. She tottered. Valo caught her. The peepers let go, and he hugged her to him. Her tears ran down his chest.

"Brenda," he said, "you must never, ever do that again. Promise me. Trust me. I can save you. Tell me you believe that."

He felt, dimly, the touch of her head against his chest. He looked down and saw that she was nodding.

He believed that she had come at last to place her faith in him.

7

In an attempt to convince the peepers not to file an

incident report, Valo spoke quickly and glibly. It was all a dreadful mistake, he insisted. Of course Brenda hadn't tried to escape. She was dancing—that was all —but when the men had chased her, she had run. What could be more natural? She was frightened. An official report would necessitate a reply. Valo would be forced to allude to their incompetency. There might be a court battle. Nothing had really happened. Brenda was here, wasn't she? It all seemed so unnecessary.

In the end, the peepers agreed to say nothing. Their spokesman—the man who had first confronted Valo on the floor—asked only one concession in return. From now until the start of the trial Brenda could not leave Valo's apartment. She had to give her word. Food and other necessities would be brought to her.

"I give you my word," Valo said.

"I don't want your word," the peeper said. "I want hers—I want to hear it from her lips."

"A robot can't lie."

"Who said he could? That's not the point. I still want to hear it from her."

Brenda shrugged her shoulders. She sighed. "All right, you've got it. I promise not to leave the apartment till the trial starts."

"If you do, we'll shoot on sight."

"I'm quite certain that won't be necessary," Valo said. He drew Brenda close to him. The peepers had already dispersed the mob. He helped her dress.

Outside, the bright lights of the strip glittered with unsubdued vigor. It was as though nothing significant had occurred. The crowd swallowed them up. Out here, they were close to anonymous again. The peepers were following. Valo chose not to look back and see them.

"That was a terrible thing I did," Brenda said, speaking for the first time. They were close to home already. Dark streets—barren houses.

"You shouldn't say that. What you did was only natural."

"That's not what I mean. If I had escaped, if I'd gotten away, what would have become of you?"

"Oh, the court would be angry."

"They would obliterate you, wouldn't they?"

"It's only an electrical process."

"Valo, it's death, isn't it?"

"Well, no, not exactly. Only humans can really die."

"Oh, Valo." She laughed and touched his arm. "Valo, I appreciate what you're doing—I do—but I'm not stupid. I know what robots are like. Death for you is just as final as death for me. I was willing to risk your life for my safety. That was what was so terrible."

"But I don't mind," he said quickly.

"I know you don't." She took several more steps. "But I think I do."

8

For the next few days, Valo did everything in his power to make poor Brenda happy. He told silly jokes, performed wild skits, quoted from his own poetry. Brenda said one poem in particular was her favorite. (Valo liked it, too.)

When in the chronicle of wasted time
I see descriptions of the fairest wights,
And beauty making beautiful old rhyme,

In praise of ladies dead and lovely knights,
Then, in the blazon of sweet beauty's best,
Of hand, of foot, of lip, of eye, of brow,
I see their antique pen would have expressed
Even such a beauty as you master now.
So all their praises are but prophecies
Of this our time, all you prefiguring;
And, for they looked but with divining eyes,
They had not skill enough your worth to sing:
For we, which now behold these present days,
Have eyes to wonder, but lack tongues to praise.

Friends came, too: Dyna, the surgeon; Raqua, the sportswriter; Zabo, the bullfighter; and Daka, the cleaning robot. They talked to her and performed for her. Watching, Valo felt an odd flash of a brand new emotion. What could it be? Jealousy? He hoped so, knowing just how silly that would be.

Every night, before bed, he took her hand in his and spoke imploringly. "Brenda, you must have faith in me. I have a strategy. When the trial comes, you'll be set free."

She smiled faintly and patted his forehead. "Sure, I believe you."

He knew she didn't, but he was smug. More than anything, he wished he could share his strategy with her. But he had made a vow. Besides, in a way, it was better this way. What was the point of a happy ending when you knew it was coming miles ahead?

9

The burnished hulk of the judging machine loomed over the courtroom like an iron fist, but Valo was not disheartened. He wondered how the outcome might have been altered by the presence of a human judge. Wasn't that really the point? A human could be fooled at times, but a machine had no choice but to be thoroughly logical.

The county attorney, a man named Landon, appeared in person for the prosecution. He was round and red-faced. The way he glared at Brenda seemed to say, "I am about to force you to pay for your terrible crimes."

Valo could have laughed.

"Why, look who's here," Brenda said. "I hadn't expected them."

Valo turned to the back and saw a line of robots kneeling wheelless against the far wall. There were five. He knew Dyna, Zabo, Raqua, and Daka. The fifth robot he had never seen in his life.

Brenda creased her brow. "Isn't that—?"

He drew her toward the courtroom. The squeaky voice of the judge emerged from a speaker. "Case will now be heard. People versus Brenda O'Reilly. Charge of first-degree murder. How does the defendant plead?"

Brenda looked at Valo. "Not guilty," he whispered.

"Not guilty," she said. Turning, she looked at the robots again. "I really think that's—"

"Hush," said Valo.

The county attorney, on his feet, began to make his case.

Because of the doubtlessness of most verdicts, few court trials, even one as serious as this, lasted more than a day. The county attorney thus spoke quickly. Brenda O'Reilly was guilty of a most terrible crime.

Her own private benefactor. Public servant. Struck
down in the prime of his powers. Murder most foul.
So on and so forth.

Briefly, Valo listened to Landon's presentation.
Finding nothing more than what he had expected to
hear, he shut down his aural sensors. Dimly, he
watched the flapping lips of the county attorney.
They moved with such lack of grace. He compared
the sight to his own clean, sharp, angular mouth. Was
it possible, after all, that robots were not inferior to
humans? He had been programmed never to think
such a thought, but it was hard to ignore the concept
here. What if it was true? What of the future of the
planet?

His attention continued to drift. At the front of the
room, a videotape machine began to play. Valo saw a
woman, presumably Brenda, shoot a naked man as
hairy as a monkey. He shut off his video sensors, too.

Brenda tapped him on the shoulder. From her
stricken face, he knew she had been forced to endure
terrible things. That was the problem with eyes and
ears. They kept seeing and hearing, even when you
wanted them to stop. He wished he could reassure
her:

No more be grieved at that which thou hast
done,
Roses have thorns, and silver fountains mud,
Clouds and eclipses stain both moon and sun,
And loathsome canker lives in sweetest bud.

Landon, the county attorney, wrapped up his plea.
"No further witnesses are required to confirm the testimony of our own eyes. We have seen this woman

kill the man who has given us all so much. I have no
alternative but to demand here in open court a
verdict of guilty and a sentence of death. Like the rats
that roam our slums, Brenda O'Reilly deserves nothing less than total and immediate extermination."

Shaking his head, Valo rose to his wheels. He
touched Brenda reassuringly and rolled forward. If a
robot could be nervous, then he was nervous. Everything depended upon the next few seconds. It was like
a poker game. The time to expose the hidden cards
had come.

"The defense calls Mylva, a robot," he said in a
steady, confident voice.

Against the far wall, the fifth of the five robots
raised its head and then glided swiftly forward on
sleek wheels. Valo heard a sharp intake of breath. It
was Brenda, recognizing Mylva as Chief McNulty's
valet.

Landon sprang to his feet. "Your honor," he told
the judging machine, "this is most extraordinary. A
robot, a mere machine, can hardly be expected to
present valid testimony at a proceeding as important
as this."

Valo was prepared for the objection. He let Mylva
reach the front of the room, then said, "We have already seen and heard the testimony of one machine,
a video taping device. The defense is willing, if the
prosecution agrees, to forego the one as long as it is
understood that we shall also ignore the other."

"Identify the robot," said the judging machine, as
impassive as ever.

"Mylva," said Valo, "served in the household of
Chief McNulty as a valet. He was present in the home
the night of the crime."

"Then he couldn't have seen anything we haven't

already seen for ourselves," Landon said. A certain desperation seemed to invade his voice. Could he possibly guess what Valo intended?

"I would prefer that Mylva's own testimony should be allowed to establish his knowledge of the alleged crime."

"But, your honor," Landon said, "this can only be irrelevant. What more can there be to add?"

"The law permits the defense to present any and all witnesses possessing a material knowledge of the circumstances of the crime," the judging machine said. "There is no exclusion for robots or other machines. The witness will be heard."

Valo stiffled his sense of triumph.

Some confusion followed concerning the oath, and once again the judge was forced to rule. "Since robots are programmed to tell only the truth, an oath not to lie is not required for them."

Landon objected. Again, the machine overruled him. Valo was beginning to wonder. The judge was also a conscious device. How did he like having the integrity of his species called into constant question? Prejudice could work both ways, Valo knew. If he were Landon, he'd sit on his hands and keep his objections to a minimum.

Mylva squatted in front of the witness chair. His headlights flashed benignly. Valo thought he might be trying to wink. Turning, he looked at Brenda. Her head tilted forward with interest. Trust me, he thought. Trust me, my love, and we will win.

Take all my loves, my love, yea, take them all;
What hast thou then more than thou hadst
before?
No love, my love, that thou mayst true love call;

All mine was thine before thou hadst this more.

Interrogating Mylva, Valo picked his questions cautiously, like a man walking barefoot through glass.

"You were employed in the service of Chief McNulty at the time of his death."

"I was indeed." Mylva had a high, squeaky voice, odd for a robot. Perhaps he was due for an overhaul.

"And you are therefore familiar with the defendant, Brenda O'Reilly."

"I am."

"She lived in the household with Chief McNulty."

"She did."

"As a permanent member."

"Yes."

Valo glanced surreptitiously at Brenda. The expression on her face was not particularly hopeful. If anything, she seemed confused. It was just a matter of time before enlightenment came, he knew. He had to lay the foundation before he could build the house. That was part of his strategy.

Turning to the events of the night of the crime, Valo said, "Were you present in the courtroom when a videotape allegedly depicting the murder of Chief McNulty was shown?"

"I saw it, yes."

"And can you tell us anything about the creation of that tape?"

"I was there when it was composed."

"When the Chief was killed?" Valo held his breath. (Of course, he didn't really breathe.)

"The Chief wasn't killed."

Valo exhaled in relief. "Then how did he die?"

"I surmise that he killed himself."

Valo made a clucking sound. "I'm afraid, Mylva, that surmises, even yours, are not admissible as testimony. We must stick to the confirmable facts here. If the Chief wasn't killed, then what is it we're seeing on the tape?"

"That was a play, a drama, a fantasy. Chief McNulty often made such tapes and then destroyed them."

"So none exist?"

"None except this one."

"And what it depicts is not real?"

"The gun never actually fired. The sound and the flash were both simulated."

"And the blood we saw pouring from Chief McNulty's heart?"

"Tomato sauce."

"Then the Chief was alive when the taping was finished."

"I spoke to him a short time afterward in the bedroom."

"Was the defendant with him at this time?"

"No. I believe she had gone to her own room."

"Then what happened?"

"I left him. A few minutes later, I heard a loud noise from the room. I entered and found Chief McNulty dead."

"Then why doesn't the tape show this?"

"It had been turned off."

"By Chief McNulty?"

"Yes."

"What did you do?"

"I turned it back on, set a delay, went outside, and entered the room again as if for the first time."

"And why did you do this?"

"Because, when I spoke to Chief McNulty earlier, he had instructed me to do so."

"What else did he say?"

"He said he intended to kill himself."

"Then, earlier in your testimony when you surmised that Chief McNulty might have done exactly that, you were more than just guessing."

"I never actually saw him kill himself, no."

"Why have you told none of this to anyone before?"

"Chief McNulty ordered me to say nothing."

"Then why are you telling it now?"

"Because you asked me to."

Valo turned. "I have no further questions to ask, your honor. I think I've more than established a degree of doubt that Brenda O'Reilly murdered Chief McNulty. I would like to suggest that the facts now tend to indicate that the Chief deliberately conducted his own suicide in such a way as to throw the blame on an innocent person. I cannot speak for his possible motives. All I can do is reveal the facts and follow them wherever they may lead."

Landon, who had sat silent throughout Mylva's testimony, as if unable to believe the evidence of his ears, finally staggered to his feet, unleashing a series of violent objections.

Calmly, the judging machine overruled each one of them.

It took ten more minutes to reach a decision. The judging machine said, "I find the defendant, Brenda O'Reilly, not guilty of the charge brought against her."

As the judge spoke, Valo looked at Brenda across

the room. The gratitude he saw reflected on her face was more than enough to make his triumph complete.

9

"Where will you go?" Valo asked Brenda a few days later, as both of them stood in his apartment.

"I've applied for several employment vacancies. If I get one of them, I ought to be able to find a small apartment in the suburbs."

"Not the entertainment strip again?" he said, with concern.

She smiled. "Oh, no, not there. I think I've had enough of that to last me a lifetime."

"You could stay here with me if ... if you wanted."

"No, Valo, you've done enough for me already. You saved my life. I think ... well, I think I ought to move on."

As deeply as it hurt, he knew she was right. If as a romantic poet he had ever learned anything, it was this: no love can ever endure.

She had broken his heart, but he would recover.

Farewell! thou art too dear for my possessing,
And like enough thou know'st thy estimate:
The charter of thy worth gives thee releasing;
My bonds in thee are all determinate.

He would miss her very much.

Brenda laid a hand on the door. She paused. "You know, there is one thing you never did tell me. How did you ever manage to get Mylva to lie for me?"

"A robot cannot lie," he said.

She laughed. "But you know he did."

"No," Valo said. "A lie is a deliberate distortion of the truth. Mylva never lied. He told the court you were not a killer. We all know that's the truth."

"But I've seen you lie."

"You have?" He was genuinely surprised.

"Sure. The night you played poker and won all of poor Zabo's credit slips. He asked you what card you'd had hidden in the hole. You told him a lie."

"Are you sure?"

"I saw it."

"Then . . . then . . ." He let his headlights flash as a smile. "Then I guess you know we robots' deepest secret."

"I won't tell."

He nodded. "I know you won't."

She went out.

For a few moments afterward, Valo felt terribly alone, like a sailor stranded on an empty island with no company beyond his own anguished memories. The apartment was like a tomb. Was he, without his love, any better than a dead man?

Then, suddenly, it came to him, and all in an instant, his circuits pulsed with renewed energy. He searched the room for pen and paper. It was a poem, a brand new poem, and unlike anything he had ever written before; it wasn't a sonnet by William Shakespeare.

Furiously, he scribbled:

So we'll go no more a-roving
    So late into the night,

Though the heart be still as loving,
　And the moon be still as bright.

For the sword outwears its sheath,
　And the soul wears out the breast,
And the heart must pause to breathe,
　And Love itself have rest.

Though the night was made for loving,
　And the day returns too soon,
Yet we'll go no more a-roving
　By the light of the moon.

Like all great romantic poets, Valo loved his muse
more passionately than any mere woman.

Not elementary *particles, Watson, but those a few magnitudes bigger have many practical uses.*

Particle Detectives and the Million Dollar Map
Roy Meador

Pull up a chair. Settle back. Light a pipe. Take up your knitting. Prepare for a scientific mystery story that is wide-ranging both geographically and chronologically. It crosses the Atlantic to London and Barcelona, journeys to the fifteenth century, then leaps forward to the 1970s. It involves book-dealers, map experts, historians, scholars, an un-named villain, and particle scientists trained to think small. Ultramicroscopically.

The protagonists in this scientific whodunit and whydunit are microscopic particles occupying what Nobel laureate Wilhelm Ostwald called "the world of neglected dimensions." To solve the map puzzle we must enter the strange territory of the awesomely puny and perform detective work in a region where human eyes see nothing. So briefly lower your mind from concern with the macrocosmos and prepare to explore the microcosmos. Scientific adventure guaranteed.

Where this mystery unfolds, road signs never show

distances in light years, miles, feet, inches, or even
millimeters. In the claustrophobic realm of the microcosmos, measurements in angstroms, micro-
meters, and nanometers are more common:

1 angstrom (A) $= 10^{-8}$ cm (1/250,000,000 in.)

1 micrometer (μm) $= 10^{-6}$ meter

1 nanometer (nm) $= 10^{-9}$ meter

1 nanogram (ng) $= 10^{-9}$ gram

Microscopists today often need magnification ex-
ceeding 100,000X. To answer many particle questions, the finest optical microscopes barely take us
across the border into the *terra incognita* of the ultrasmall. Excellent optical microscopes help solve
particle problems arising in connection with industrial and environmental needs. Yet for some particle
mysteries, the traditional optical microscope versus
the ultimate tools of modern microscopy is like a man
with homemade wings competing against NASA's
two-stage Delta 2910 launch vehicle. For the
toughest puzzles, complex instruments and all the
contemporary skills of microscopy are essential.
There aren't many places where tools and skills are
available for comprehensive ultramicroanalysis.
One such place is the microscopy laboratory of
McCrone Associates in Chicago.

Walter C. McCrone and his associates are con-
sultants in the highly specialized field of small particle analysis. "Think small" is more than just their
motto. It is their philosophy, calisthenic, dessert,

religion, and art. "To be completely successful, the microscopist must be an accomplished crystallographer and microbiologist as well as a highly skilled manipulator of small particles," says Walter McCrone. The contributions of McCrone and his associates during the past quarter-century have helped microscopy reach its present ability to identify virtually any particle that comes along.

McCrone microscopists begin by studying a particle optically. They compare it with photomicrographs of more than a thousand different particles covered in the six-volume encyclopedia, *The Particle Atlas,* prepared by McCrone Associates for international use in particle identification. When this routine procedure does not succeed, advanced tools, including electron microscopes and microprobes, and many technical disciplines are concentrated on the problem.

All tools and disciplines were needed in the "Case of the Million Dollar Map." McCrone and his associates don't resemble detectives in the Bogart "Private Eye" tradition; but in the map caper, they certainly earned the right to claim the title of the twentieth century's outstanding scientific detectives.

According to McCrone, "Analytical problems faced by microscopists are becoming more and more micro. The milligram (10^{-3}g) samples we used to receive look like carloads beside the picogram (10^{-12}g) amounts we can now detect in nanogram (10^{-9}g) samples. Detection of such small amounts is justifiably called ultramicroanalysis, and often requires the use of microprobes."

McCrone clients include governments, industries, communities, and universities in need of microanalytical aid to cope with particles, a constant challenge wherever civilization ventures. Pollution measurements in Chicago indicate that over six thousand tons of small particles settle on the city monthly (10^{20} individual particles). All human activities produce particles. Industrial particles are detected from the upper ozone to the South Pole. Cosmic dust and meteors are particle sources. Every environmental particle until identified is potentially harmful. Some are toxic. With development of microminiaturized electronic and mechanical instruments, smaller and smaller particles cause more and more trouble.

Ultramicroanalysis has detected impurities responsible for malfunctions in sensitive instruments aboard space vehicles. Microscopy has proved its value and finesse from criminology to public health, from industrial processing to art forgeries. Microscopic particles no one can see have disclosed fakes and foiled counterfeiters. By thinking small, performing research where twenty angstroms is expansive, and mastering the miniature landscape of particles, McCrone Associates in the Vinland Map affair managed feats of detection that conventional detectives from Sherlock Holmes to Philip Marlowe would view with awe.

Modern microscopy didn't reach its present sophistication quickly. Like most other sciences, microscopy has deep historical roots. In 1614 Giovanni du Pont demonstrated that small objects can be magnified by reversing a telescope and increasing the distance between lenses. Anton Van

Leeuwenhoek, cloth merchant of Delft, Holland, spent years designing lenses and using them to launch the science of microbiology. Studying microorganisms in the 1670s, a century and a half before Pasteur, Leeuwenhoek wrote, "No more pleasant sight has ever come before my eyes than these many thousands of living creatures all alive in a little drop of water." Many developments, accidents, and breakthroughs had to occur as a prelude to the contemporary ultramicroanalytical detective work of McCrone Associates.

Exactly when or where the Vinland Map story began is unknown. The matter came to light in 1957 when a bookdealer from New Haven, Connecticut purchased a rebound book from a rare bookdealer in Barcelona. The book contained an account by Friar John of Plano Cartini's 1245 journey to the Tartars. Now called the *Tartar Relation,* it was handwritten about 1440. The New Haven bookdealer discovered a 11 x 16 inch map in back. The book and map seemed unrelated, although their paper was similar, since wormholes in both didn't match. The assumption was that someone had bound them together for preservation and convenience.

The bookdealer showed the volume to officials at Yale University Library. The map fascinated them. It placed a large island, "Vinlanda Insula," west of an impressively accurate Greenland. The island had to be part of North America. If the map also dated from the 1440s, it would be the first documentary evidence that Europeans knew about North America before Columbus and would support evidence of visits by the Vikings.

How could the map be authenticated? In the
1950s there seemed no way. Then coincidence
proved again that truth uses plot twists no
storyteller would dare. The Yale Library received a
book from London that also had originally come
from the Barcelona bookdealer. It was a twenty-
one-page segment of the *Speculum Historiale* by
Vincent de Beauvais, written in the same hand on
identical paper as the *Tartar Relation.*

When the documents were arranged with the
Tartar Relation on top, then the *Speculum Historiale,* and the map on the bottom, the worm holes
fell precisely in line. The items obviously had been
together in some form for a long time. To keep
them together, the *Speculum Historiale* was given
to the New Haven bookdealer with Yale having
first option to purchase all three. The dealer eventually sold the documents to a Yale donor for nearly one million dollars. In October 1965, three days
before Columbus Day, the map was publicly
donated to the Yale Library with appropriate
hoopla. Press releases called it "the most exciting
cartographic discovery of the century"; however,
some critics weren't convinced.

There was a continuing controversy along scholarly corridors in the U.S. and Europe that didn't
subside until particle analysis settled the matter.
Those who accepted the map did so on the basis of
textual features, the worm hole alignment, and appropriate Latin phraseology. Some scholars, simply
wanting the map to be genuine, ignored Sir Peter
Medawar's classic warning to scientists: "Never
fall in love with your hypothesis." Opponents, including Yale experts, thought the map *too* ac-

curate. Considering the primitive state of mapmaking in 1440, they couldn't believe the artfully done Vinland Map came from that period.

In the 1950s and 1960s, microscopy and other scientific tests were not sufficiently advanced to test the map definitively. The dispute had to simmer above scholarly campfires until the technology of small particle analysis reached its present status. Doubts among experts intensified when the map was labeled "suspect" by David Baynes-Cope, a scientist at the British Museum. Baynes-Cope discovered that when the ink of the map was exposed to ultraviolet light, it failed to show the fluorescent pattern typical of fifteenth century tannin inks. Inks from the *Tartar Relation* and *Speculum Historiale,* however, did give expected reactions. This contradiction had to be explained.

By the 1970s the technology of small particle identification had advanced dramatically. Yale hired McCrone Associates to examine the map using ultramicroanalysis. McCrone had the skills as well as the armamentarium of microscopy equipment indispensable for such a study. For one thing, McCrone had an ion microprobe, considered essential for the study. Also available were a transmission electron microscope (TEM), scanning electron microscope (SEM), the electron microprobe analyzer (EMA), energy dispersive x-ray analyzer (EDXRA), selected area electron diffraction mode (SAED). In a modern microscopy laboratory, the sea of acronyms is wide and stormy.

Each instrument tells something exclusive about particles. When all evidence is combined, a particle has slight chance of escaping unidentified. The Oxford English Dictionary quotes a 1656 microscopy enthusiast: "There are now such Microscopes . . . that the things we see with them appear a hundred thousand times bigger than they would do if we looked upon them with our bare Eyes." Actually three centuries of progress were needed to achieve magnification in the range of 100,000X. But when electron microscopes appeared in the twentieth century, the 1656 claim reached fulfillment plus.

The electron microscope was developed in the course of seeking alternate sources of illumination to surpass the limitations of visual light. Infrared and ultraviolet light extended the versatility of optical microscopes, but much smaller wavelengths were needed. Following Thomson's discovery of the electron in 1897, speculation grew about using geometrical electron optics. The shortest wave length of visible light is about four thousand angstroms, while electron waves are approximately 0.5 angstrom. Imagine an electron wave one inch long, and proportionally the shortest wave of visible light would be a mile and a quarter from crest to crest.

The first electron microscope was designed by Max Knoll and Ernst Ruska in Germany during the 1930s. They applied the fact that electrons "moving through a vacuum carry waves of exceedingly short length, and these waves can be focused by magnetic and electrostatic fields, just as light rays are by a glass lens."

McCrone uses both the transmission electron microscope with resolution of 0.5 to 1.0 nm and the scanning electron microscope with resolution at about 15 nm. An electron microscope functions by focusing a beam of electrons instead of light. Electrons enter the field of the specimen where some are blocked or deflected; those passing through unimpeded produce an image of the specimen.

In the scanning electron microscope, a high-energy electron beam is used to generate secondary electrons, effecting a two-dimensional display which provides valuable information about the topography of a sample. Because of their versatility and remarkable sensitivity, scanning electron microscopes are basic equipment in research and industrial laboratories today, as fundamental as the centrifuge, the autoclave, the computer, the telephone, and the coffee pot.

With the development of electron microscopes have come significant interactions between electrons and samples (*e.g.*, electrical effects are noted, light is emitted, x-ray generation occurs). Each phenomenon provides another useful clue. For instance, when electron beams strike the sample, x-rays are generated with energies characteristic of each element in the surface of the sample. The electron microprobe x-ray analyzer (EMA) results from attaching an energy-dispersive spectrometer to the scanning electron microscope to measure this x-ray activity. In addition to wavelength-dispersive x-ray analysis, the EMA can also be designed for energy-dispersive x-ray analysis, adding a further dimension of sensitivity.

Among newer innovations in microscopy is the ion microprobe analyzer (IMA). Important for the Vinland Map study was the fact that McCrone had an ion microprobe, because it facilitated testing extremely small samples. The ion microprobe analyzer works like the electron microprobe, using ion beams instead of electron beams. Atoms from the sample are ionized by an ion beam striking the sample. These ionized atoms are "sputtered" at a regular rate for analysis in a high transmission mass spectrometer, and the sensitivity is sufficient to make microscopists from earliest times to yesterday sputter with astonishment. The ion microprobe detects all the elements in the periodic table as well as isotopes. McCrone experts note that among IMA's advantages is its ability to perform carbon-dating on smaller samples than was possible before. The ion microprobe is more than 1,000 times as sensitive as the electron microprobe. The EMA detects elements down to and including boron (atomic number 5) with limits of 10^{-15}g by weight or 10 to 100 ppm in bulk analysis. The IMA handles a 10^{-18}g sample, detects 10 ppb.

Electron microprobes, using samples weighing less than one microgram, have validated paintings by testing every successive layer of paint. Samples can be taken in micro amounts with no visible evidence of extraction. Ion microprobes test much smaller samples in applications ranging from art authentication to biomedical research.

McCrone, with its imposing battery of instrumentation, had a free hand to determine the genuineness of Yale's fifteenth century items. Or were they fifteenth century? Ink particles from all three documents had to be extracted and analyzed. No one let the microscopists forget they were working with highly valuable pieces of parchment. The map had to be left exactly as found. Acquiring ink particles for testing without visible alterations was the first challenge.

Anna Teesov, applying methods of her own devising, worked in a particle-free clean room. Using a tungsten needle with a one micrometer tip on which a tiny amount of rubber cement was placed, Teesov approached the ink lines on the map with the needle at less than a 20° angle to avoid punching holes. The caution of brain surgery was needed as the needle moved forward, delicately touched the map, and carried ink particles away on the rubber cement. The ticklish process was constantly observed under a stereomicroscope.

The ink particles were prepared for microscopy by fixing them on slides with amyl acetate. A total of fifty-four samples were prepared: twenty-nine from the Vinland Map, seven from the *Tartar Relation*, eighteen from the *Speculum Historiale*. Walter McCrone noted that all samples combined weighed under a microgram (less than .000000035 ounces) and could not be seen with a microscope. No alterations were discernible in the documents. The scientists had particles to "fingerprint" but had left none of their own.

"The use of any tool or technique that enables us to identify microscopic objects" is considered microscopy at McCrone Associates. The Vinland Map called for standard methods plus new variations to meet the special challenge. If the map was a fake, it had been created with impressive skill. Worm holes matched the other documents. The paper had come from a Swiss paper mill about 1433. The question was whether or not the counterfeiter, if any, was equally informed concerning the chemistry of ink. He could have found a useful tip in Shakespeare's *Twelfth Night*, Act III when Sir Toby Belch says, "Let there be gall enough in thy ink, though thou write with a goose-pen, no matter."

Historically, tannin inks were the most common, made from vegetable galls or other sources of tannin, and a salt of iron. Tannin is turned dark blue by ferrous salts. McCrone scientists learned this and much more about inks. When listing skills valuable to microscopists, research historian of science deserves inclusion.

Inks from authentic ancient documents were obtained for comparison. Ink mixtures were prepared using traditional vegetable galls and iron pigments. Particle and chemical properties of modern inks were just as thoroughly researched. If tests indicated the map had not been drawn with a fifteenth century ink, what was the source? This had to be settled beyond debate.

Solving particle challenges at McCrone starts with visual analysis when feasible, followed by optical analysis in the light microscopy laboratory where a Zeiss universal light microscope system allows operators to achieve the best results possible with optical methods. In the light microscopy laboratory, particles can be compared with thousands of particle reference slides supplementing those in *The Particle Atlas*, thus covering most particles likely to be encountered in the modern world. By consulting reference slides and the *Atlas*, most particles are effectively identified in the process of careful morphological analysis to establish shape, color, transparency, degree of birefringence, refractive indices, and other physical properties that help distinguish one particle from another.

In addition to a stereo binocular microscope, the

well-equipped microscopist also typically uses a polarizing microscope during the optical examinations. The polarizing microscope facilitates studying anisotropic substances, such as crystals, which have different properties along different axes. Isotropic substances *(e.g.,* glass, table salt) have identical properties throughout and only one refractive index since light passing through retains the same speed in all directions. Anisotropic substances have two or more refractive indices, and the birefringence of such substances is the difference between maximum and minimum refractive indices.

In a polarizing microscope, polarized light is refracted into slow and fast rays by the anisotropic substance being examined. These rays are recombined in an analyzer, and the retardation between them establishes a sequence of characteristic interference colors. (Examples of interference colors are seen in oil films and soap bubbles.)

Interference colors and the retardation reading for a substance are important identification factors in conjunction with the Michel-Lévy Interference Color Chart (published in Paris, 1888). This chart shows the interrelationships of particle *thickness* running along the left, *retardation* along the bottom, *birefringence* values across the top and down the right side, together with *interference colors*. Applying these values to the chart simplifies particle identification.

When optical microscopy doesn't finish the job, electron microscopy, microprobes, and other techniques step forward. Writing in *American Laboratory,* July 1970, Walter McCrone said, "Single par-

ticles of almost any size can be identified by a
trained microscopist . . . His lower limit is about 1
picogram (10^{-12}g) with the light microscope, about
1 femtogram (10^{-15}g) with the scanning electron
microscope, 1 attogram (10^{-18}g) with the transmission electron microscope, and even smaller with
the ion probe."

Particles light microscopy can't identify are
"cemented to a tiny glass fiber for x-ray diffraction, onto a polished surface for microprobe analysis, or onto a grid for electron transmission microscopy." Facing such an array, one tiny particle is
like a poultry thief with the whole of Interpol and
the FBI on his trail.

The Vinland Map, as expected, required the full
sequence of tests. When the map was checked vis-
ually, they noticed yellowish-brown stains flanking
some black lines. These were considered stains
from the organic vehicle used in fifteenth century ink.
The assumption was one of many to be verified.

Ion microprobe results showed that ink from the
Tartar Relation and the *Speculum Historiale* contained iron gallotannate pigment, which was used
to make ink in the fifteenth century. The evidence
was convincing, and both documents were accepted as genuine. What about the map? The ion
microprobe showed its ink did not contain iron
gallotannate. What then? Different ink mixtures
possible in 1440 were tested in comparison with the
map. The results were negative. But a curious fact
emerged. When atoms of the ink sample were
ionized and analyzed in the mass spectrometer,
titanium traces appeared. Titanium in a fifteenth
century ink?

The scientists repeated earlier tests in the light of new knowledge. Under a polarizing microscope, they learned the yellowish-brown stain, previously thought a stain from the ink vehicle, was actually a separate ink *beneath* the black ink. Interesting. Had the yellowish-brown line been put on first to simulate aging?

Ten-micrometer ink fragments from the stain lines were found to have tinier particles adhering to them. The characteristics of these particles were similar to those of titanium dioxide particles. Anatase, a special form of titanium dioxide, is a pigment widely used in twentieth century inks and paints, but not in fifteenth century inks. Were the particles anatase?

Titanium, discovered by the Reverend William Gregor while experimenting with black sand from Cornwall, England, was not known until 1789. Anatase was first used in inks and paints about 1912. It was only after 1920 that anatase could be manufactured in a complex chemical process. Producing anatase, even accidentally, in the fifteenth century was rejected as too remote for plausible consideration.

Unmasking the particles that resembled anatase brought McCrone Associates to the climactic phase. The ink fragments were examined by micro x-ray diffraction and selected area electron diffraction. Diffraction is another technique for in-depth particle studies. If a narrow beam of electrons passes through a thin layer of material, it is deflected in particular directions. When it is collected on a fluorescent screen, the resulting pattern of light and dark areas is characteristic of the material under test. Most electron microscopes can be employed as electron diffraction cameras. Used together with transmission electron microscopy, diffraction is an effective means of garnering useful information about the size and chemistry of particles.

These procedures confirmed that the yellowish-brown ink contained calcite, which could have been used in the 1440s, and anatase, which could not. The results were conclusive. The scanning electron microscope confirmed the presence of anatase particles in tiny lumps, 0.03 to 0.5 μ in diameter. Anatase was unquestionably present. The map could be genuine only if it had been retouched by someone using an ink containing anatase to strengthen fading lines.

Yellowish-brown ink taken from numerous locations on the map was checked. Anatase was present all over the Vinland Map. The yellowish-brown line obviously had been put on first for an aging effect, and black ink traced over it. The case was solved. Yale could congratulate itself on having persisted until it reached the truth, that its million dollar map was a brilliant forgery. Yale could also take satisfaction from the stimulation to historical scholarship the map controversy had supplied. Also the map had given microscopists a stiff and instructive challenge. The hidden world of the ultrasmall had been explored more deeply than ever before.

The masterful job of forgery demanded the ultrabest of the ultramicroanalysts. Because of the forger's superb work, experts studying the map saw nothing wrong. Only small particle analysis by experts proved the deception. Later Walter McCrone wondered, "Who would have wanted to perpetrate such a forgery? Perhaps the most plausible are religious arguments or national rivalry, but maybe it was a couple of very knowledgeable graduate students who just could not resist a practical joke."

In 1974 two Yale professors disclosed evidence pointing at Dr. Luka Jelic, a Yugoslav Professor of Ecclesiastical Law. This professor, who died in 1922, was monomaniacal in defending his theory that Catholic missionaries visited North America centuries before Columbus. Latin expressions used by Jelic in other writings were on the map. Of course, someone other than Dr. Jelic could have appropriated his expressions.

An Italian professor at Palermo University acclaimed the findings of McCrone Associates. This professor blamed European forgers and called it an elaborate plot to defame Columbus. Fed by national politics and pride, the controversy went on about who did it and why. Those were human riddles scientific detectives couldn't answer with their instruments, although with diligent particle analysis they had put to rest the fundamental question of authenticity.

After the map case was solved, Walter McCrone wrote that in addition to great scholarship, a successful forger of antiquities would have to be a pigment specialist and master of the complex technology essential to create an undetectable appearance of age. Yet even so, he said, "tomorrow's scientific tools would probably still reveal the truth."

Tomorrow seems here already as microscopists command particles to give up their secrets. Counterfeiters of bogus maps, painters of fake Van Goghs, forgers of antique documents or relics should pause and reflect. At McCrone Associates, accomplishing the job is more than "prediction of future dial-readings from present ones" as C.J.S. Clarke has categorized a trend in science. The Vinland Map exposé demonstrates the originality, versatility, and range of skills available in microscopy today.

In 1978 McCrone was involved in another international scientific mystery with profound religious connections. When scientists gathered in Italy to begin determining whether or not "The Shroud of Turin" could have been used to wrap the body of Jesus, Walter McCrone, as an authority on microscopy, was present. Rightfully and logically so. McCrone scientists and instruments can make critical contributions in the search for answers to the intriguing questions surrounding this famous and enigmatic cloth.

Knowledge of particles is valuable today in many fields. Microelectronics, space, pharmaceuticals, polymers, fibers, and papermaking are a few of the many. The use of microscopy in criminalistics is standard practice. What conventional detective, shamus, private eye can promptly deliver authoritative data on blood traces, seminal stains, handwriting, bullet markings, fibers, counterfeit coins, forgeries, hair, drugs, or practically any other material known? Microscopists have convicted criminals because of particles left at or carried away from the scene of a crime. A man accused of robbery denied being in the area, but microscopy proved his clothing had been there. In Los Angeles a murderer was convicted when a scanning electron microscope confirmed that a wrench had been used to destroy a tourmaline ring owned by the victim.

The electron microscope has even become a television star. On the program "Quincy," a crime-solving medical examiner often uses his trusty instrument to prove which "particulates" did what and to whom. Quincy demonstrates that a certain bullet scatters nickel rather than copper particles, and conviction follows. Microscopy authoritatively helps Quincy identify the perpetrator, week after week after week.

When the particle itself is the criminal, as in pollution cases, microscopy is indispensable. A furniture plant was charged with pollution; particle analysis found the pollutants were oil soot from other sources. A jet aircraft accident was traced by particle analysis to a fuel line clogged by glass fibers from a protective filter.

Today in our particle-surrounded lives microscopy is both detective and watchdog. The age of modern technology inescapably is the age of particles, which demands the special know-how and effective scientific snooping only microscopy can supply. When people are sick from unknown causes, instruments failing, criminals suspected, products defective, the only solution often is to "think small." Particles, like people, have individual traits as distinctive as fingerprints, dental x-rays, and the mug shots in post offices. Using every device from the microscope to ion microprobes, mocroscopists can supply information through particle analysis that saves lungs, lives, eyes. They can reveal the truth about a map, a masterpiece, and maybe eventually a shroud.

The macrocosmos isn't the only arena for adventures of the mind. Some purposefully draw in their sights to the equally mysterious microcosmos of the ultrasmall. Understanding particles is an appropriate warmup for understanding the planetary nebula of Lyra. On this poets agree with science. "See a World in a Grain of Sand," advised William Blake.

English naturalist Henry Baker wrote in 1744, "The Use of the Microscope will raise our Reflections from a Mite to a Whale, from a Grain of Sand to the Globe whereon we live, thence to the Suns and Planets; and, perhaps, onwards still to the fixt Stars and the revolving Orbs they enlighten, where we shall be lost amongst Suns and Worlds in the Immensity and Magnificence of Nature."

If we are lost, scientific detectives perhaps will come and identify us particle by wandering particle.

The Horse that Jack Built
Jeff Rovin
Illustrated by Jack Gaughan

This is the horse that Jack built.
Well-cloned at the camp
Of a Triple Crown champ;
The miraculous horse that Jack built.

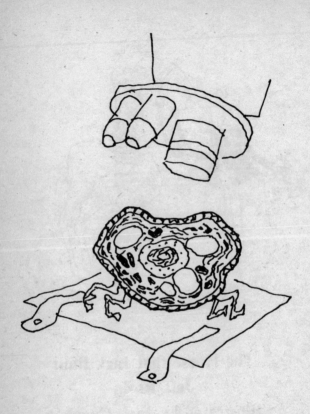

This is the cell historic.
The first vital seed
Of that world-famous steed
Who was cloned at the camp
Of a Triple Crown champ;
The miraculous horse that Jack built.

This is the mix nutritious.
The chemical broth
Topped with protein-laced froth
That nurtured the seed
Of that world-famous steed
Who was cloned at the camp
Of a Triple Crown champ;
The miraculous horse that Jack built.

This is the colt stupendous.
Grown hale, swift, and strong
As Jack planned all along,
For he'd fed on the broth
Topped with protein-laced froth
That nurtured the seed
Of that world-famous steed
Who was cloned at the camp
Of a Triple Crown champ;
The miraculous horse that Jack built.

This is the safe at Jack's house.
Now solidly packed
With dough won at the track
By that mount swift and strong,
As Jack planned all along,
For he'd fed on the broth
Topped with protein-laced froth
That nurtured the seed
Of that world-famous steed
Who was cloned at the camp
Of a Triple Crown champ;
The miraculous horse that Jack built.

This is track manager Trent.
The racing horse czar
With some questions regard-
ing Jack's safe so well packed
With dough won at the track
By that mount swift and strong,
As Jack planned all along,
For he'd fed on the broth
Topped with protein-laced froth
That nurtured the seed
Of that world-famous steed
Who was cloned at the camp
Of a Triple Crown champ;
The miraculous horse that Jack built.

This is the edict Jack heard.
"It's godless to clone;
That's a fact, it's well known,"
Quoth the racing horse czar
With some questions regard-
ing Jack's safe so well packed
With dough won at the track
By that mount swift and strong,
As Jack planned all along,
For he'd fed on the broth
Topped with protein-laced froth
That nurtured the seed
Of that world-famous steed
Who was cloned at the camp
Of a Triple Crown champ;
The miraculous horse that Jack built.

This is the grave of the horse.
Trent cried, "Satan's spawn!"
And then shot him at dawn.
"For it's godless to clone;
That's a fact, it's well known,"
Quoth the racing horse czar
With some questions regard-
ing Jack's safe so well packed
With dough won at the track
By that mount swift and strong,
As Jack planned all along,
For he'd fed on the broth
Topped with protein-laced froth
That nurtured the seed
Of that world-famous steed
Who was cloned at the camp
Of a Triple Crown champ;
The miraculous horse that Jack built.

This is Jack back at the track.
"Now I'll show that fool,
That barbaric damn ghoul!"
He who cried, "Satan's spawn!"
And then shot him at dawn.
"For it's godless to clone;
That's a fact, it's well known,"
Quoth the racing horse czar
With some questions regard-
ing Jack's safe so well packed
With dough won at the track
By that mount swift and strong,
As Jack planned all along,
For he'd fed on the broth
Topped with protein-laced froth
That nurtured the seed
Of that world-famous steed
Who was cloned at the camp
Of a Triple Crown champ;
The miraculous horse that Jack built.

This is Jack's circus brand new.
Built next to the track,
It's a fair with one act
That would show the old fool,
That barbaric damn ghoul
Who had cried, "Satan's spawn!"
And then shot him at dawn.
"For it's godless to clone;
That's a fact, it's well known,"
Quoth the racing horse czar
With some questions regard-
ing Jack's safe so well packed
With dough won at the track
By that mount swift and strong,
As Jack planned all along,
For he'd fed on the broth
Topped with protein-laced froth
That nurtured the seed
Of that world-famous steed
Who was cloned at the camp
Of a Triple Crown champ;
The miraculous horse that Jack built.

This is a *new* horse Jack built.
Its genes changed ad hoc,
It grew wings like a roc
and flew next to the track,
In a fair with one act
That would show the old fool,
That barbaric damn ghoul
Who had cried, "Satan's spawn!"
And then shot him at dawn.
"For it's godless to clone;
That's a fact, it's well known,"
Quoth the racing horse czar
With some questions regard-
ing Jack's safe so well packed
With dough won at the track
By that mount swift and strong,
As Jack planned all along,
For he'd fed on the broth
Topped with protein-laced froth
That nurtured the seed
Of that world-famous steed
Who was cloned at the camp
Of a Triple Crown champ;
The miraculous horse that Jack built.

This is the track that Jack bought.
The horse was a smash,
Drawing mountains of cash,
With its genes changed ad hoc
And wings grown like a roc,
Flying next to the track
In a fair with one act
That would show that old fool,
That barbaric damn ghoul
Who had cried, "Satan's spawn!"
And then shot him at dawn.
"For it's godless to clone;
That's a fact, it's well known,"
Quoth the racing horse czar
With some questions regard-
ing Jack's safe so well packed
With dough won at the track
By that mount swift and strong,
As Jack planned all along,
For he'd fed on the broth
Topped with protein-laced froth
That nurtured the seed
Of that world-famous steed
Who was cloned at the camp
Of a Triple Crown champ;
The miraculous horse that Jack built.

This is custodian Trent.
Jack fired him with glee
Then rehired him, you see,
To take care of that smash
Drawing mountains of cash,
With its genes changed ad hoc
And wings grown like a roc,
Flying next to the track
In a fair with one act
That would show that old fool,
That barbaric damn ghoul
Who had cried, "Satan's spawn!"
And then shot him at dawn.
"For it's godless to clone;
That's a fact, it's well known,"
Quoth the racing horse czar
With some questions regard-
ing Jack's safe so well packed
With dough won at the track
By that mount swift and strong,
As Jack planned all along,
For he'd fed on the broth
Topped with protein-laced froth
That nurtured the seed
Of that world-famous steed
Who was cloned at the camp
Of a Triple Crown champ;
The miraculous horse that Jack built.

*In an evolutionary sense, most mutations are neutral
—or deadly.*

Homo Neuter
James Patrick Kelly

Dr. Simon Pelerin was magnificently bald. Most
people he met preferred, at first, not to look him in
the eyes for fear that their gaze might slip to the top
of his smooth head. He appreciated this quirk of human nature, a small but distinct advantage he en-
joyed over the sapiens. It was one of the rewards of
being different. One of the few rewards.

To all appearances, Pelerin was a carelessly
dressed, successful man in his mid-to-late twenties.
Actually he was not a man, either in the generic or
sexual sense of the word, and he was starting his sev-
enth decade.

He was resigned to his differences, but had never
been happy in his resignation. To him, being unique
meant only being alone. Because it was possible that
others like him existed, he believed that they did. The
search for them gave him a reason to go on living. As
he reached the entrance to the school's medical suite,
he allowed himself to hope again that his long isola-
tion might finally come to an end.

He stopped and peered through the small, wire glass window set into the door at eye level. Although there were eleven boys in the room, restlessly waiting in their underwear to be examined, Pelerin was interested in only one. Marcus Graham stood apart from the others, watching their antics disapprovingly. He was the largest of the group of sixth graders and carried his coffee brown body with a self-conscious dignity that seemed out of place in comparison to the exuberant awkwardness of his classmates. Pelerin opened the door.

Madge Worley, the Willowbrook School's ancient nurse, glanced up from her desk and nodded. The boys fell silent as he passed through the room, but as he washed up next door he could hear the titters.

One of the boys was nudged into the examination room, then went rigid as the door closed behind him.

"Hello there. Dick, is it? Dick Arnold?"

The boy nodded hesitantly.

"Are you coming in?"

He took two more faltering steps.

Pelerin crossed the room to the boy and put a hand on his shoulder. At first he felt only cool skin, but he worked his concentration quickly to the touch and broke through into the boy's mind. A wave of emotion washed over him and was gone. Yet in those few seconds Pelerin experienced an unsettling, childish brew of emotion: embarrassment, insecurity, shyness, confusion, and fear. He shuddered briefly, but his voice was soothing when he spoke again.

"All right, son. This won't take long. Now the first thing I want you to do is step on that scale over there."

The worry lines that had already begun to etch the

boy's face were gone. As he stepped lightly onto the scale, Pelerin wondered what had made him so skittish. He felt the familiar regret that the touch relieved only symptoms, not causes.

Pelerin ran quickly through the standard tests. When he finished he patted the boy on the head, not so long as to establish touch, but with enough ordinary good feeling to make the boy smile.

There were three others before Marcus. Pelerin found himself rushing the examinations. He had been waiting for an opportunity to be alone with Marcus since the day he had convinced Willowbrook's headmaster that the school needed a part-time doctor who was also a child psychologist. He was good at things like that; for him they were survival skills.

Pelerin was studying the boy's file when Marcus entered the room. When he looked up, he saw Marcus staring at his head unabashedly.

"Man, you better keep your hands out of my pants, you hear!"

"You're Marcus Graham?"

"Did you hear what I said?"

"I heard, Marcus. Please stand on the scale."

He obeyed grudgingly, but when Pelerin moved behind him to adjust the weights, the boy spun around and put one foot on the floor. Pelerin reached out to touch him. Marcus slapped his hand away.

"You don't have to put your hands on me to weigh me."

"No. But I have to adjust the weights until the beam balances. Would you like to try?"

"Why should I do your job?" said Marcus as he stepped back onto the scale, facing Pelerin. "Just don't try anything."

"You're pretty tall for a kid in the sixth grade," Pelerin said as he adjusted the measuring rod. "How old are you?"

"Seven. And a half. Can't you read? It's in my file."

"Uh . . . yes, of course." Pelerin remained cool; he was not going to play the boy's game. "Please step off the scale and sit on the edge of the table. You know, it's unusual for a boy your age to be as big as you are. You're the tallest in your class?"

"Yep. And the strongest and smartest, too. What about it?"

"Breathe deeply please. Again . . . again . . . keep breathing. Okay, that's it. You're a pretty interesting fellow, you know that?"

"Yeah? What's so interesting about me?"

"Your heartbeat, for one thing. Most people's hearts beat around seventy-two times a minute. Yours beats around fifty-five."

"So? There's nothing wrong with that, is there?"

Pelerin had been concentrating for the touch. "Not really," he said calmly as he struck out and grabbed Marcus's shoulder. The boy tried to jerk away, but was too slow.

The first thing Pelerin felt was vast surprise. There was no rush of emotion, no awful vomiting of the mind. Instead he experienced his own thoughts and feelings. He was lost in a vivid daydream. A huge, no, infinite room was full of people screaming at each other. The noise was deafening. He put his hands to his ears but they did not block the uproar raging around him. He tried to question a woman standing nearby. It only added another voice to the din. The absurdity of the dream infected him with a crazy abandon and, at the top of his lungs, he shouted his secrets to the crowd. As he continued, the clamor abated and his own voice grew thunderously. By the time he had relieved himself of the last detail of who and what he was, he held sway over a silent, darkening roomful, not of people, but of eyes, fixed on him unblinkingly. He did not care; he was too elated. A real sound escaped his lips: a cry of exultation.

Reality seeped slowly into the dream. He was breathing heavily, trembling with pleasure. Marcus lay shuddering on the floor. His eyes were open but unseeing. Pelerin shut the boy's lids, picked him up gently and maneuvered him onto the examining table, concentrating against the touch. As he started to get some water, he realized how dizzy he was himself and sat down abruptly in the nearest chair. His thoughts tumbled randomly over one another. He had not touched like that in nearly half a century, not since they put Eduard away. He was astounded that his search had actually come to an end after all the years of failure. Or had it? He walked unsteadily to the table and lifted the boy's shorts just high enough to see the lush patch of curly black hair underneath. Pelerin felt only pity for Marcus. This boy, no longer a boy, might enjoy his sexuality for another ten or twelve years, and then it would end. Forever. Thinking back to his own change, Pelerin doubted whether Marcus could make it through as a sane person—unless he had help.

He wet a paper towel and sponged Marcus's face. The boy woke slowly, painfully, as if he were trying to escape from a nightmare. Terror glazed his eyes as he recognized Pelerin.

"How did I get here?"

"You passed out. I put you here."

There was a long silence before Pelerin spoke again.

"You don't remember anything about what just happened?"

"Who says I don't?"

"Well then, do you always have such violent reactions when people touch you?"

The question struck home. Pelerin knew that at his age Marcus undoubtedly did not understand the touch. He was probably both curious and frightened about it.

"Sometimes. Not too much." Marcus mumbled for the first time.

"Who else knows about it?"

"My old lady. I used to pass out a lot when I was a kid."

"No one else? No doctor?"

"That's it."

"And do you have any idea what just happened?"

"Sure," Marcus said, shaking his head groggily. "I had a dream. Or maybe it was a nightmare. I don't know."

"Can you remember it?"

"I don't know, man. What's the hassle? I didn't do nothing to you."

"No. You didn't," Pelerin said as he turned to look for his notebook. "You can go as soon as you feel up to it. I'm finished with you for now."

"What do you mean, for now? You're not going to tell anyone about this?"

"Not unless you force me to. But I'll have to see you after school. As a matter of fact, I think I'd better drive you home and have a talk with your mother."

"You're going to tell her about this, aren't you?"
"I'd like to be your friend, Marcus."
"You're a damn fool."
"Just be back here at three."

As soon as he had finished examining the sixth graders, Pelerin sent the nurse off to lunch and locked himself in her office. He opened Marcus's Willowbrook folder on the desk and removed his own private files from his briefcase. These slim files were the product of many bitter years of research. They documented the movements of most of the people who had lived in the village of Hinche on Haiti in 1898. In the summer of that year a mysterious disease had swept through the area, wiping out almost a third of the population. The villagers called it *fièvre du rêve*. They said it was voodoo. Pelerin's father, who had been working in the village as a doctor and who himself had contracted the disease, had never been able to identify the sickness, nor had he understood why he and a handful of others had survived it. Now only his son wondered.

The information in the Willowbrook folder completed Pelerin's own file on the Graham line, the longest and last of those he had been able to trace back to Hinche. His file began with Jacques St. Martin, a black peasant farmer who had survived the epidemic of 1898. St. Martin's only child was Jeanne, a carrier of the neuter mutation. She married a cook attached to the U.S. Marine forces which occupied Haiti through the twenties. His name was Graham.

When the occupation ended in 1934, the Grahams returned to the States with their four-year-old son, James. Pelerin believed this child to be the first

Graham who actually was *Homo neuter*.

James Graham's records showed him to be a brilliant if erratic student. He was accepted at Tuskegee Institute when he was seventeen. In the following year he was secretly married to Hattie McDonald, a junior lecturer at the college who was pregnant with his child. When Hattie died in childbirth, James dropped out, brought the baby, James Jr., to live with his parents, and joined the Army. He was among those rushed to Korea when fighting broke out and was killed at Osan, one of the first Americans to die in the war.

Marcus's application to Willowbrook contained the bald facts that his parents were separated, that he lived with his mother, Ellen Graham, and that the whereabouts of his father, James Graham, Jr., were unknown. Pelerin knew, for he had seen the man's plain headstone in the public cemetary in Gary, Indiana. Pelerin did not know much else about Marcus's father other than that he had been thrown out of high school, that he was a heroin addict, and that he had died of an overdose two days after dropping out of a methadone maintenance program at one of Gary's free clinics. Pelerin believed that Graham's addiction had a lot to do with the trauma of changing, but could not be sure.

Ellen Graham was a waitress, according to the Willowbrook folder. She was meeting the steep tuition with the help of a grant from the Department of Social Welfare and a rebate from the School. Pelerin was intrigued by this; he wondered if it would be possible to buy his way into the Graham household.

Marcus's last medical exam had been routine. At the time it had been conducted he was a five-year-old entering the first grade. There had been no signs of sexual development. The G.P. had added a note to the file that Marcus was "extremely difficult to work with, shows indications of serious emotional stress."

For Pelerin, the best thing in Marcus's file was not what was in it, but what was missing. To the rest of the world, he was just one special child in a school full of special children. There were at least two other of his classmates with I.Q.'s in excess of 180.

Pelerin locked his own files in the briefcase and took Marcus's and several others to the front office for copying. He spent the rest of the afternoon preparing for his visit to the boy's house.

Marcus was waiting for him when he drove up that afternoon in his wine red Mercedes. As a treat for the boy, Pelerin had gone out and bought the top ten popular albums on cartridges for the car's tape player. Marcus was unappreciative, paying no attention to the tapes, the player, the electric windows, or the air conditioner. He rode slouched down in the seat so that only the top of his head showed above the window. Neither of them spoke during the first part of the trip.

"Are you going to be like this the whole way home?" Pelerin said finally. "I thought we could get to know each other."

"I know all I want about you. Why don't you just tell me what's wrong with me and get off my back?"

"What's wrong with you? What do *you* think is wrong with you?"

"You're the doctor. All I know is that every so often I get this feeling about people that makes me sick. Especially at school. It's getting so I can't stand those fuckers no more."

"Anymore."

"Man, there you go again, talking out of the side of your mouth. I know it's anymore. But when I hang in my neighborhood I gotta talk like all the other dudes talk. You heard of chameleons? Man, I'm the baddest chameleon you ever seen. That's how I get by. Only my skin don't ever change." He chuckled bitterly.

"Okay. I can understand that. But why be so rude to me?"

"I don't like rich dudes, and I especially don't like doctors."

"That's too bad, because I'd like to study you. You're a very interesting person, you know."

"You keep saying that."

"What I mean is," Pelerin said as he slowed to a stop for a red light, "that you're more special than anyone gives you credit for. It's all tied together, you know; what happened this morning, your intelligence, the way everybody feels about you, and . . ." Pelerin leaned closer to the boy, ". . . the way you can look into people's minds when you touch them."

Marcus's brashness melted away. He returned Pelerin's stare only long enough to be sure that he was not joking, then shrank even deeper into the seat. A car behind them honked; the light had changed. Pelerin accelerated quickly and they drove on in silence.

As they approached Marcus's neighborhood the street scenes changed rapidly. There was trash blowing in the gutters, a scattering of broken windows, spray-painted graffiti in angry colors. One side of his street was a solid row of aging three-deckers; the other was a park whose main features were two blacktop basketball courts surrounded by rusting chain-link fences. Pelerin parked in front of Marcus's house. The boy did not move.

"Why do you want to study me?" Marcus said quietly.

"I want to help you find out who you are."

"Why?"

"Maybe you haven't realized it yet, but you're unique. A very important person. To me, especially. Think carefully about this morning and you'll understand. I like you, or rather I want to like you if you'll give me the chance. But I'm a doctor, too." He laughed, as always, to punctuate his act. "I'm interested professionally in special children. That's how I earn my living. If I can study you, it will help me in my work."

"Are you a queer?"

His laughter this time, though loud and prolonged, was still part of the act. The faint touch of acid that underpinned it was real.

"I wish I was, just so I could see the look on your face when I said yes. Anyway, the most important thing right now is for you to decide what you want to do."

Marcus played with the door handle. "My old lady isn't going to like it. She hates doctors. Maybe if I told her that you were a tutor. Or something. That's if . . ." He paused as if he were surprised at what he had intended to say.

"That's okay, Marcus. I think we both agree now that we'll be working together. I'll tell you what. Let's go in and you can introduce me. For starters I'm just Mr. Pelerin from school. I'll take it from there."

"I don't know, man. It might not work."

"If it doesn't, we'll work something else out at school. She doesn't have to know. But it's best to give her a chance."

Marcus started to speak just as his mother burst out the front door. "Marcus!" she called. "Is that you? What are you doing out there boy? Get in here now!"

He was moving before she finished, out the car door, across the street and up to the stoop in three bounds. Pelerin followed deliberately, taking time to lock the car. He approached the woman with a friendly smile stuck on his face. She stood, barring his way, slightly in front of the door, arm propped back against the casing. Marcus had gone inside.

"And just who are you?" she asked contemptuously.

Pelerin heard Marcus's muffled voice. Mrs. Graham turned and shouted over her shoulder, "You shut up in there! You're in enough trouble for joy riding with strangers."

Marcus's reply was an indistinct crescendo ending with the word "School!" Pelerin again became the target of her indignation.

"So you're from Willowbrook. Okay, what do you want this time? Is he in trouble again?"

"Not exactly. No."

"You're that doctor he was supposed to see today." It was an accusation.

"As a matter of fact, I am. I work for the school part time and . . ."

She recoiled as he spoke and the door began to swing shut. He shoved his foot into the narrowing space and spoke quickly but dispassionately.

"Before I go, Mrs. Graham, if you could give me

the name of your family doctor. I have some information about Marcus that I feel he should know. The school will have to be notified too, but I'll wait until I have a chance to see him."

The door stopped closing. In the shadows behind it only Mrs. Graham's face was visible. Anger had hardened her features; her gaze swept across his face. She tried to say something but choked on the words. Pelerin thought to touch her, but he realized that the door would slam on his hand before contact could be established. Besides, Marcus was in there waiting to see how he would handle the situation.

"Mrs. Graham, I can see that you don't want to talk to me. Fine. That doesn't bother me. What does bother me is that you'd risk your son's well-being by not hearing me out. Once I say what I've come to say, I'll walk right out this door and never come back. If that's what you want."

She replied in a restrained voice, clipped with bitterness.

"You're so full of it. That's all you people have to do, is to bring bad news and trouble to folks and then act like you're doing them a favor. Let me tell you something, mister. I work ten hours a day, five days a week, to send my boy to your school. That's what I care about Marcus. What do you care about him?" She did not wait for a reply; the door swung open. "All right, Doctor, why don't you come in and tell this poor nigger what's so important."

Pelerin stepped into a small foyer which opened onto a kitchen, a living room, and a stairwell. She motioned him into the living room.

It centered on a battered color TV set, on which an orange-skinned newsman murmured. The set's bizarre tint bothered Pelerin until he noticed that the color controls were covered over with electrician's tape. Grouped near the set were an aging cream-colored couch and two artificial leather chairs. The room's only other feature was a plaster fireplace fueled by a neat pile of dusty plastic logs. A department store portrait of Marcus graced the mantle. The boy himself sprawled on the couch. Mrs. Graham sat next to her son and Pelerin settled into one of the chairs, his palms and forearms sticking to the cheap plastic.

"So?" She seemed to enjoy his discomfort.

"Uh . . . You've met Mrs. Kintze, Marcus's teacher?"

"I've talked to her on the phone."

"And she's told you what an exceptional child Marcus is?"

"I hope that's not what you're here to tell me. I know exactly what Marcus is. He's got no secrets from me. Marcus is the smartest kid in this city. That's why I send him to your school."

"I'm sure you're aware of how bright he is. As you are also aware of how mature he is. Physically, I mean."

"He's big for his age. So what?"

"I'm not referring to his size, Mrs. Graham. I'm referring to his sexual development." Pelerin waited uneasily for an explosion which never came. Instead she spoke quietly to her son.

"Marcus, turn this TV off and go upstairs."

"I don't want to go upstairs. I want to listen. I got a right to hear what he has to say, don't I?"

She brought her arm around so fast that it almost slapped the words from his mouth. She drew it back and held it poised for another strike. He looked at her without pain, grief, or even surprise registering on his face, then shrugged as if giving up an argument with an ignorant person and left the room. She sat on the couch, perfectly still, staring vacantly after him.

In an uncomfortable moment of compassion, Pelerin felt Mrs. Graham's suffering more than her son's. As the boy grew older, he would also grow away from her. Confrontations like this, destructive as they were for ordinary people, would be even worse for the Grahams. And if they should ever touch in anger. . . What adolescent could understand the ugliness of a raging adult?

"It must be hard to raise a gifted boy like Marcus," he said gently.

She nodded, then looked at him as if for the first time. "What were you saying before?" she asked, all business.

"I was about to explain why Marcus has school problems. You see, most kids follow a pattern of development—not only intellectual but physical and emotional development as well. Marcus's physical and mental development are well ahead of schedule while his emotional development is only normal. To some extent, Willowbrook compensates for Marcus's differences by placing him in an advanced grade. The other sixth graders, all of them bright kids, approximate Marcus's intellectual development. But most of them are behind him physically and ahead of him emotionally." Pelerin paused, thinking of how to say what he intended without giving offense.

"Complicating things even more," he continued, "is the fact that Marcus is one of only three blacks in the school and the only one in his grade. I'm sure that's hard on him. He's a lonely boy, angry and afraid. Add to all this the enormous physical and psychological changes he's going through due to puberty and you can see why he doesn't fit into the Willowbrook environment."

He waited for her to comment, but she said nothing. Her face was impassive. Pelerin began to worry.

"Marcus senses that the others are threatened by his differences. He may try to minimize them, say, by acting dumb. I've had many cases of brilliant kids who fail in school because they don't want to appear to be the teacher's pet. They'd rather belong than achieve."

Her face was still frozen in disapproval. She said sarcastically, "So what does it all mean? What are you trying to sell me?"

"I'm not trying to sell you anything. Special—gifted—children are my lifework. I'm also supposed to be responsible for all the kids at Willowbrook. There are ways I can help Marcus adjust."

"That's nice of you, Doctor . . ."

"Pelerin. Simon Pelerin. Please, call me Simon."

". . . but what do you want from me, Dr. Pelerin?"

"Uh . . . hopefully, a chance to study one of the most gifted kids in the country. There are many things that Marcus can do for me. Tests, for instance. I've been working on a new I.Q. test that's equally fair to all kids, white, black, rich, poor. In exchange for his help, I can offer the standard fee for experimental subjects. It's not much, twenty-five dollars a day, but it might come to as much as an extra hundred dollars a month, depending on how much I can use him."

"I like that. I like to hear about doctors paying

ordinary folks instead of vice versa. But I don't like you, Doctor. Because no matter how fast you talk, I get the feeling there's something you're not telling me." She rearranged herself on the couch, leaning forward. "It's too bad in a way, but I have to agree with you. There's something eating at the boy. I can't help him like I used to; he doesn't tell me things. So, if you're who you say you are, and Marcus is agreeable, I'll take that hundred a month. But understand this, Doctor: you come here and give me a report whenever I call you. And you tell Marcus not to keep anything from me." Her facial muscles relaxed for the first time since he had come in. "Now where are you going to do this testing?"

"At my office. 99 Pearl Street, fifth floor. Here's my card."

"You just hold onto that until we talk to Marcus. And remember: it's my boy you're messing with. That means you're messing with me."

"I understand. I hope we can come to be friends."

"I doubt it." She rose and called out, "Marcus! Come down here and say goodbye to this man."

He appeared in the foyer as they reached the door. She spoke to him in a carefully neutral manner, as if what had happened before did not matter.

"Marcus, this man says he wants to study you. What do you say?"

A look of triumph flitted across his face as he answered.

"I say it's fine with me."

"Try again," Pelerin said.

Marcus looked irked. "Okay, here goes: WER, SIM, RET, DUT . . . POG, BUH, ZAV, CIP . . . er

. . . TOB . . . GUK . . . shit! Why do we have to keep doing this over and over? I'm sick of it."

"Once more and we'll quit. Try your best."

' "WER, SIM, RET . . . DUT, POG, BUH, ZAV . . . TOB . . . CIP?"

Silence. At length Marcus said resignedly, "That's all I remember. You said we could stop."

Pelerin was writing notes on his clipboard. "Uh-huh," he said, paying no attention.

"Why do we always do the same test? This is the sixth time we've been through it today, and it seems like each time I do worse."

"We weren't testing for the same thing every time." Pelerin tossed the clipboard carelessly onto his enormous teak desk and pointed at the couch. The very first time Marcus had seen it he insisted that they take the classic psychiatric position during the therapeutic part of their sessions. The boy loved to sprawl on its smooth leather surface and look out the nearby window onto the busy street below.

"So what's with these tests?"

"I'm looking at how frustration affects your basic learning rate." Marcus arched his head backwards so that Pelerin could see his puzzled frown.

"Okay. The first test measured your basic learning rate. Once we have that we can introduce a variable, something that affects your ability to memorize the list. If you want to measure frustration, say, you give the subject a list much longer than he can possibly memorize. Just now you were trying to show me that you were smarter than my stupid test. So you tried your hardest to memorize the whole list. You couldn't. You got mad, and on the next list you tried even harder, and remembered even less. Once you start to get angry, you have to remember less each time, no matter how hard you try."

"Sounds like some fancy kind of torture. How did I do?"

"You didn't do too bad. But for someone as smart as you are, you don't cope with frustration very well."

"You didn't have to give me a test to find that out. You could've just asked."

"Not scientific."

"It's bad that I get frustrated?"

"Sure. For instance, in school. You tend to get frustrated with people who aren't as smart as . . ."

"Bullshit! That's them, not me. They can't handle the fact that a nigger can be better than they are." He craned his head back again to see Pelerin's reaction. Pelerin shook his head sadly.

"No way. It's *your* problem, Marcus. You're not better than anyone. Right now you're bigger than most kids your age. So what? In ten years everyone will have caught up. Some will even pass you. And they'll get smarter too. It just takes time."

"So what you're saying is that I'm nothing special."

"Oh, you're special. There's no question about that. But better is the word you used. And that remains to be seen. For now, let's just say that you're different."

"And what about this mind reading shit? No one else does that, do they?"

Pelerin replied cautiously. "No . . . That is very unusual. But let's talk about it for a minute. You say that sometimes when you're near somebody . . ."

"No. When I touch them."

"Okay, when you touch them, you can see all their feelings."

"How can you see a feeling? I feel them, like all at once."

"And the people you touch, they know nothing about it."

"Nobody ever said anything."

"Not even your mother."

"I don't know," said Marcus grimly. "Maybe she does know something. Maybe that's why she hardly ever touches me except with the back of her hand. I don't want to talk about her. I want to talk about me."

"All right. Suppose you do feel their feelings. Are you sure that you don't get ideas too. I mean, when this happens, you don't get ball scores, or last night's dinner, or faces? Things like that?"

"No."

"Nothing else?"

"Ummm . . . there was that time with you. When you were examining me."

"What was different about that?"

"I blacked out, for one thing."

"You said that happened before."

"When I was a punk kid. But when I touched you, I didn't really feel your feelings. I don't think I did, anyway. It was more like I was feeling my own feelings, except they were kind of organized, like a dream." He thought for awhile. "No, it was a nightmare actually."

"And what was that?"

"Man, I don't know. I wish I did. I mean, I can tell you about it, but I can't tell you what it was, you dig? Everything was wrong . . . but it was all so real. I was awake in a dream and couldn't get out. That was the scary part. What can you do when you're already awake?

"Let's see. I was in Carbury Park, you know, across the street from my house, with this sister, Jane. I don't think I told you about her. Anyway we're looking for a place to get down—this is a dream, remember—so we go to the corner of the park where all the trees are. By the Sears' parking lot. There's an old statue there, made out of that stuff that rusts green instead of red. Bronze? The statue is of some Civil War dude, all in his uniform and everything.

"The two of us stretch out behind the statue, real close to each other. I'm really getting into it. Then there's this strong wind, like comes downtown by the skyscrapers. I feel a pain in my leg and I think, someone's chucking rocks. I roll off her and there's this bronze Civil War hat next to me. So then I check the statue, just as the dude's metal coat blows off at me. It misses, but it's close. Too close. Jane splits and I'm alone. More clothes blow off at me but I dodge them. Pretty soon the fucking thing is standing there bareass in the middle of Carbury Park.

"I'm standing behind it and I can see when those green muscles start to flex. It turns, slowly, toward me. Then it's facing me and those cold, green eyes are staring right through me. The wind takes its beard and hair off. I say to myself, it's the doctor, because it's bald, right? But then I realize it's me, except I'm grown up, really old. The thing opens its mouth and a noise comes out like the screeching of brakes before an accident. That really shakes me, so I get ready to run."

Marcus paused and stretched. In telling the story

he had gradually curled into a defensive position, arms clutching legs to the chest. Pelerin had not made a sound during the recital. Marcus looked back for encouragement; Pelerin managed a half smile. Eventually the boy continued, but the tension that had been building in his voice was gone.

"The end of it was kind of crazy. Just when I was ready to run, the wind took off its balls. It grabbed its crotch and screamed. Maybe it was only the wind sound. I couldn't really tell because I had this fucking monstrous pain myself, like somebody castrated me with a pair of pliers. I blacked out and that was it. Except at the very end I think I remember seeing these little points of light, like stars, or maybe they were eyes. It was right as I went under, or woke up, or whatever it was."

"That was a pretty vivid dream," Pelerin said. He cleared his throat noisily.

"Yeah. I wish I could figure out how to forget it. It keeps popping into my mind. I never got anything like that from touching before. And it couldn't have come from you. We just met so you couldn't have known about Carbury Park or Jane. So that means it must have come from me, right?"

"Probably. There's one way to find out."

"Yeah? What's tha . . . oh no! I don't know if I'm ready for another one like that."

"It's up to you. But if it continues to bother you, it could be the only way to get it out of your system."

Marcus rolled off the couch and jumped to his feet. His eyes were full of suspicion.

"It doesn't bother me that much," he said firmly.

Pelerin rolled over in bed, reached out to the night

table, and snapped on the light. He thought a curse at things in general and sat up, rubbing his eyes. Sleep had eluded him long enough; he was giving up. The thought made him tired.

He decided to walk his problems out. He picked a wrinkled dress shirt and some faded jeans from the clothes heaped like casualties around his bed. He passed through the apartment by memory, avoiding the messes without turning on lights. He had always lived carelessly, since he never had visitors and possessions meant very little to him. At the door he stopped to get a coat.

For two months he had tried to push the desire to touch Marcus from his mind. His self-imposed abstinence was becoming a strain; he felt a growing need for the pleasures of the touch. This alarmed Pelerin, who had always found it easy to mortify his sexless flesh.

Although touching did Marcus no permanent damage, the boy was frightened and confused by the experience. Touching for him remained an inexplicable hallucination. Pelerin believed that touching partners were like mirrors: each enabled the other to look into himself. Marcus had given Pelerin the gift of seeing himself truly. Pelerin could never reciprocate until Marcus discovered who and what he was.

What he was ... Flashes of memory lit the darkness Pelerin had so painstakingly woven around his own life before the change. He imagined that he saw a hundred faces, a hundred moods of Claudette, his fiancée. A few laughed, some teased, most worried or cried. There had been no physical pain for him; the change brought only a deadening of sensation. Yet in that lost time he had shared only too well the anguish scored on those imagined faces. First he had lost the desire, then the ability, then slowly the flesh itself. How could he have explained to her what had happened? The cruelty of sudden indifference had been the easiest way.

Pelerin found that he was out of breath from striding through the darkness. He stopped under the cold light of a streetlamp and shivered. Briefly he had a vision of his former self standing alone at the end of a corridor lined with locked doors. The corridor reached across a span of fifty years to the bleak, bone-white circle of light where he now stood. He stepped into the street and crossed it hurriedly.

For a short time he applied his thoughts totally to the process of walking. He was in new territory now, and just a little bit lost. Eventually he began to consider his problems with Marcus.

There was another reason why he needed the boy's cooperation. If Marcus was fertile, and there was no reason to suspect otherwise, he might sire a whole generation of neuters before he changed. Having missed his own chance, Pelerin had every intention of exploiting Marcus's to the maximum. It seemed to him a very elegant solution both to his problem and that of neuters in general. By breeding his own peers and raising them to know themselves and their potential, he could ensure the sanity and survival of the new species.

He needed unquestioning obedience from Marcus, however, and Ellen Graham would never let him get it. She still suspected Pelerin. She was the symbol of his human heritage that Marcus would have to renounce. And Pelerin would have to push him to that renunciation.

Yet it was easier for him to arrive at that conclusion than to accept it. Ellen Graham was no abstraction; she was a living, feeling, fragile human being. To achieve his dream, Pelerin would have to preside over the destruction of hers. When he had isolated himself, years ago, it had been to avoid hurting other people with his alienness.

He was beginning to realize that his indecision would last only as long as his idealism.

He arrived at the entrance to a little park nestled like a glen among the masonry heights of the city. Directly in front of him was a play area: swings, slide, monkey bars, and a sand pit. Beyond it were benches clustered around a dry fountain. An expanse of grass, shaggy with fallen leaves, ran toward treed shadows. Suddenly tired of walking, Pelerin entered the park.

He paused by the swings. He was tempted to test this simple pleasure again, but his sense of dignity held him off. Instead he gave the empty seat a push and retired to a bench. He watched the swing come slowly to a stop.

And from the swing's stillness welled the banished memories of his half brother Eduard, the priest whose touch could shrive the devil. He had gone away to seminary school when Simon was a baby and had taken Holy Orders at the extraordinary age of seventeen. From there he had been assigned to a parish in Baton Rouge so that the two of them did not really meet until Simon was ten. The first time they touched was on the porch swing of the Pelerin house, while his mother was inside making them lemonade. Pelerin, remembering, relived that first vision: he had swelled up like an impossible pink balloon and floated high above the house with Eduard riding atop his bare belly, his face twisted with violent and carnal passions incomprehensible to young Simon. Later, when they were putting him to bed, he heard his half brother lie about it to his mother and he knew that he, Simon Pelerin, would be forever damned by that lie, for he could not contradict the word of God's sworn minister. Time passed and Eduard touched him ten, twenty, a hundred times, each a wicked pleasure, each a mortal sin, until Pelerin knew that his soul was as black as his brother's cassock. His soul sickness finally ruined his health, and they sent him to stay with his uncle in New Orleans to receive treatment at the University. Though what help the doctors offered was useless, he finally managed to push his affliction out of his mind. He returned, months later, to find the household in an uproar. Eduard had gone berserk, running through the village displaying his shocking castration with mad pride. The Church had taken care of its own. Eduard's bishop had directed that he be sent to a home for sick clergy. Pelerin's mother told him that it was somewhere in the west, Kansas or Oklahoma. Pelerin never found out exactly where he went, although when he realized that longevity was also part of their special biology, he had searched long and hard for Eduard. The image of an eternity in an insane asylum often recurred in Pelerin's nightmares. After all, despite what Eduard had done, if he had not prepared Pelerin with those coy hints and delicious touchings, he might well have gone mad too.

Pelerin shook his head, trying to dislodge the memories. Since he had touched Marcus, things inside him had begun to come unstuck, things he had sealed up years ago. He felt the urge to walk again. He started toward the other side of the park, away from the playground and the ghosts it had resurrected. He saw his situation clearly now; his sanity was at stake. He could not take the chance of sharing the fate of Eduard and James Graham. The question was not whether, but how to separate Marcus from his mother. And if the touch became necessary to Pelerin's survival, he would be careful, but Marcus would have to put up with it.

"And so you see, Mrs. Graham, that Marcus is going to want to test his sexuality just like any other adolescent. Just forget about his chronological age and look at his biological age."

"Damn his biological age! He's not old enough to understand girls, especially some hustler seven years older than he is."

"Let me explain something to you," Pelerin said reasonably. "Most of Marcus's immature behavior is due to our expectations. The boy wants to fit in at a level where he's comfortable. I think it should be his decision if he's comfortable with fifteen-year-olds, not ours."

"You think I'm holding the boy back?"

"Yes, you are. And so am I. And so is everybody at Willowbrook. If we force him to live up to our expectations rather than his own potential, we'll be doing him a disservice."

Pelerin had come to look on his sessions with Ellen Graham with mixed feelings. Many times she had provided insights into Marcus's problems. Their mutual feeling for the boy had smoothed over what should have been a rugged relationship. Although their meetings were not cordial, they were at least civilized.

On the other hand, Pelerin tried to reserve a large

part of himself from any involvement with her. Even though he thought himself the consummate actor, he also knew that in his enthusiasm he was sometimes careless. His plans were ready now. One final deception and he could stop lying.

"I don't know, Doctor. I just don't know if you're right."

"I'll tell you what. I run a teen encounter group on Saturday mornings. Why don't I bring Marcus into it? There would be no need to give the group his life story. We'll let them draw their own conclusions about who and what he is. If he's accepted for what he appears to be, then you'll have your answer."

"What's it going to cost?"

"Mrs. Graham, I don't want to go into . . ."

"No charity!"

"If you insist, you can pay me, but not in cash," Pelerin said stiffly. "I'm giving a paper in Washington next week and I'd like to bring Marcus along."

"You want to show him off like some kind of freak."

"Hardly. The people at the convention know better. No, this would just be to verify some of the figures I use on Marcus in my paper. After he runs through some independently administered tests, I think they'll be more receptive to my thesis. It will all be fairly basic to Marcus, things we covered in the first few weeks."

"I guess it's okay with me if it's okay with him."

"Thank you. I really appreciate it."

She nodded reflectively.

"Is Marcus home? I'll ask him right now."

"He'll have a separate room."

"Uh . . . sure, if you want. Did you say he was home?"

She walked out to the foyer and called, "Marcus!"
Silence.

"I'M CALLING YOU, MARCUS!"
Still nothing.

She stepped into the doorway and shrugged. "He must be across the street. I'll ask him for you. Go ahead and make your reservations. I'm sure he'll want to go with you."

He detected resentment in her tone. Better to let it drop, he thought as he rose to go. I won't have to see her again anyway.

He started toward the door but she motioned him to a stop.

"Is there something else?"

She made no response. He knew from past experience that she had probably worked out a whole line of questions, and was now reviewing them in her mind to be sure that she had everything. Suddenly, all he wanted to do was escape.

"Tell me," she said, "why are you so interested in Marcus?"

"Well . . . he's special. Like I said when we first met." He wished she would come back in the room and sit down.

"Yeah, I remember what you said. And I believe it, too. But that's not the only reason. Not anymore. Is it?"

"No. I don't deny it. I'm very fond of Marcus. I want the best for him."

"And you don't think I can give him his chance?"

"I never said that. I'm sure you want what's best for him much more than I do."

"But I can't give it to him?"

He paused, considering tactics. There was an unusual pressure in his lungs. "No," he said at last.

"I'm not going to lie to you. I think you know that you can't give him everything he deserves."

She nodded, satisfied with his answer. He exhaled softly.

"You don't have kids of your own, do you?"

"No."

"Not married?"

"No."

"You think of Marcus as a son?"

Pelerin chuckled uncomfortably. "A son? No. I think of him as a friend." She sat impassively; her eyes demanded a better answer. "Well, I suppose you could say that I think of him as a little brother."

For the first time since he had known her, Ellen Graham bestowed a half-friendly smile on him. Pelerin felt ill.

"A brother? You and Marcus brothers?" She laughed out loud. "You got a lot to learn about the way things are. Son."

Pelerin's smile did not feel very convincing.

"You've been good to Marcus. I appreciate it. I know I've been hard on you, but dammit, you come on like all those other do-gooders from the school who think they know what my boy needs better than I do myself. At least you have respectable intentions, none of that brotherhood of man crap. But you better listen to me now. You think you know what's best for Marcus. Maybe you want him to be a shrink when he grows up. You want him to be like you. But it's too late for that, understand?"

She began to gesticulate as she talked. Pelerin was thunderstruck; it was the first time she had ever acknowledged him as other than a convenience for her and Marcus.

"The boy is black. Black in the same way I'm black. 'Flesh of my flesh,' the book says. I've done some studying up on psychology since you started coming around. Do you know what I learned? Every damn book says that the most important years are from the time you're born until you're six. Marcus already is what he will be. And he will be a black man, Doctor. If you really want to help him, you better start respecting what he already is, what I made of him. Go ahead and add to it if you want, but don't you try to change it."

She relaxed. He knew he could walk past her now after a few pleasantries, but he could not move. He was afraid that if he took a step he would splinter into a thousand pieces. The apartment was so still that he could hear the faucet dripping in the kitchen. He focused on that sound as if it were the only real thing in the world.

She spoke again, finally. "Come on man! If you stand there much longer, I'll have to dust you."

She crossed the room to his side. "You better be going. I have to get ready for work now. Think over what I just said. I'd like to hear your opinions." She smiled again and touched his hand.

He jerked it away as if he had been burned. An angry look began to form on her face and then he was babbling.

"Yes, yes, you're right. I must get going. I've got a lot to do. My paper, you know. Well, this has been nice. Thank you for everything. And don't forget to call anytime."

He hurried to the doorway, thinking of nothing but driving his car, fast.

"And . . . uh . . . Simon," she called after him.

He turned, totally unnerved.

"I'll call your office if Marcus doesn't want to go to Washington. But he'll go, don't worry." As he fled to the Mercedes, Pelerin could not shake the feeling that everything he had ever done was wrong.

It was the most important day of Pelerin's life and he had plotted it carefully. After he picked Marcus up at Willowbrook, they would go right to his office and he would tell the boy everything. He had rehearsed the scene down to the last pause and inflection and was satisfied with it.

"Let's go into my office," Pelerin said as he unlocked the door to his suite. Marcus ran ahead and captured the seat behind the desk. He motioned Pelerin archly into the chair where visitors sat.

"Vell, mein boy, vhat's on your bald little mindt today?"

"Knock it off, Marcus. We've got some things to discuss before we go."

Marcus held out a limp hand and rolled his eyes suggestively. He exaggerated the lisp. "But I told you, Sidney sweetie; we simply must have separate beds."

Pelerin glared, unamused, then stalked to the window. He waited there in silence, hoping to restrain the boy's excitement by ignoring him.

"Marcus," he said finally, "if someone offered you a million dollars, no strings attached, would you take it?"

"Are you serious?"

"Yes. And I want you to be, too. Give me an honest answer."

"Hmm. No strings attached, you say?"

"You wouldn't have to do anything you wouldn't otherwise do."

"Sure. In that case, I'd take it. Why shouldn't I?"

"No reason. Most people would. Now suppose somebody offered to make you the most important person in the world. What would you say?"

"Hey man, are you feeling all right? You're coming up with some pretty weird stuff."

"It's a test, a test of your values. You have to take it seriously though, or it won't mean anything."

"How am I supposed to know the answers to questions like that?"

"Whatever you really think, that's the right answer."

"Okay, then. Sounds good to me, whatever it means. Marcus Graham, Esq., The World's Most Important Person. What else?"

"A free ticket to wherever you wanted to go?"

"When do we leave?"

"The chance to live as long as you want."

"Great."

"But you don't believe that those things could happen to you?"

"How could they? I mean, sure, I wouldn't mind being rich enough to go where I wanted when I wanted. Maybe that could happen, someday. But what does it mean to be the most important person in the world? There ain't no such animal, so far as I know. And everybody wants to live forever, but nobody's made it yet."

Pelerin nodded and considered his answers. Marcus fidgeted for awhile, then spoke again.

"That was a pretty dumb test, Doc. You didn't even come close to my first choice."

"Oh?" said Pelerin, clearly interested. "What's that?"

"I want to get laid every night for the rest of my life."

Pelerin's cool, angerless disapproval deflated the joke. "I'm sorry," Marcus said uneasily. "I couldn't resist."

"Forget it. I suppose I deserve it for trying to get too serious with you tonight. But since you brought the subject up, what's this I hear from your mother about this Jane?"

"I'll tell you, but it's got to stay between us two. Okay?" A conspiratorial eagerness filled his voice.

"Promise."

"All right. You want to know about Jane? She's my woman, from now on. I'm getting my piece. Not bad for an eight-year-old, huh? I should be in the Guinness Book of Records." He snickered proudly.

Pelerin was stung. For a moment he forgot all about the practiced scene and what he was trying to accomplish by it. Jealousy, he thought, matching the unfamiliar feeling to a word. But it was not the faceless Jane he was jealous of; to him, she was just a cipher. He was jealous of Marcus, of his careless sexuality, of his independence. Marcus, despite his differences, still belonged to a society which numbered in the billions; Pelerin belonged only to himself. Now was the time: to tell the boy, to link Marcus's future forever to his own. Pelerin yielded gladly to the moment.

"Enjoy her while you can, Marcus."

"What's that supposed to mean?"

"It means that I'm going to have to tell you something you won't want to hear. But you've got to listen, okay? You know, when I was your age I was just as smart as you. But there were no Willowbrooks in those days. Not for me, anyway. So I faked it in the public schools. And at just about your age, I reached puberty. It didn't take me long to find out about girls. The touch, you know. It makes it so easy. But when I was your age, we didn't have sex. It was a sin. A sin was evil, you didn't want to sin because then you would be ugly. Unless you were married. Then everything was beautiful.

"Now you've got to try to understand what I'm going to tell you. Because when I turned twenty, thirty-three lousy days after I turned twenty, I didn't have to worry about the ugliness anymore. I told the girl I'd picked out to forget it. I made a mistake; I waited too long. I could've done what you did, I should've. But I waited too long."

He paused, out of breath. "You remember that dream you had. About the statue. That's what really happened to me. I have no sex, Marcus. I can't fuck, you understand? And just like it happened to me, it's going to happen to . . ."

"Not me, man. You've flipped. You're crazy."

"No, I'm not. I'm the same person you are, Marcus. That's what I'm trying to say. It's in our genes. There's no way to change it."

"Bullshit, man! You're talking out the side of your mouth, just like you've been doing all along." His voice cracked as he spoke.

"You can't hide from it," Pelerin said gently. "You already know it. Maybe not consciously, but your cells know it. Remember the touch. We've both got it. It doesn't lie." He started across the office, but as he approached the desk Marcus jumped backwards out of his chair, knocking it over.

"You really are crazy, man. Stay away from me or I'll hurt you." The frightened boy seized a chunk of petrified wood which Pelerin used as a paperweight, reared back, and took aim.

Pelerin froze. They watched each other silently. Pelerin slowly stretched out his hands, palms up.

"Go ahead, Marcus. It won't change anything, but go ahead." He let his hands fall to his side, turned his back to the boy and stepped over to his files. "I have proof, when you're ready."

Marcus snorted in disbelief but laid the rock on the desk. He stooped to pick up the chair and sat down.

"You're still crazy, man, but let's see what you got." His voice was flat, emotionless. He did not meet Pelerin's gaze.

Pelerin had removed a green folder from the file which he placed in front of Marcus. He settled into the visitor's chair as the boy flipped it open.

"The first thing you'll see," Pelerin said, "is a lab analysis of some chemicals in your blood called adrenal androgens. They're steroids produced by the adrenal glands. You and I share androgens with a unique structure. That's the only chemical link I've been able to make so far between us, but I think it's important."

"This doesn't prove anything," Marcus said, gesturing at the folder. "It would be easy for you to write a bunch of numbers down on a chart and say that they proved I was Santa Claus. You got anything else?"

"But why would I try to fool you?"

"I don't know. But it's easier for me to believe that you're a liar than it is to believe that I'm going to lose my balls someday."

"Okay. I get the point. Look through the folder for a big white envelope. It's full of pictures and documents. Got it? Okay, now look at me, Marcus, and tell me if you think I'm lying. I'm seventy years old."

Marcus looked astonished for a moment, then shook his head grimly as he tore open the envelope. Its contents scattered on the desk. They smelled of musty books.

"What is this junk?"

Pelerin leaned out of his chair and sorted through the pile, producing a yellowed paper. "This is my birth certificate. Notarized by the clerk of St. Helena parish, Louisiana, November 29, 1906. And this," he said as he opened a leather folder, "is my high school diploma. Class of '22. Look at this. Those are my parents and my half brother, Eduard, and that's me on the bottom step of the porch. It was taken when I was twelve. And that's me again. Do I look any different today? I was a used car salesman then. It was taken in, let's see, must've been 1947, in Detroit, right after the war. That was years before I made my money and went to med school. You want more?"

"No. Just wait a minute. Let's talk about this. I admit it looks kind of real. But you're loaded. You could afford to fake it if you really wanted."

"Fake! What are you talking about, fake? This is my life. Where would I get those cars, those dresses? And here, look at this picture. Now this picture was taken with a Kodak box camera. They haven't made the film for it in years."

"Okay, okay. Suppose I do believe that you're seventy years old. What's that got to do with me? You're the freak."

"Come on, Marcus. What do you want from me?

The pictures, the adrenal androgens. You want me to strip for you? Is that what you want?" He reached for his belt buckle.

"No, man. Forget it," Marcus said hastily, looking away. "I don't want to see. But still. Nothing you said proves anything about me."

"You already have all the proof you need. What about the touch?"

"Yean. The touch," he muttered. "But why? What do you want from me?"

"I want you to know who you are. That's all. Because everything will change for you. The way you look at the world, the way you look at other people. You'll need me then as much as you need me now, to prepare you, to help you." Pelerin leaned forward in his chair, trying to get Marcus to look at him.

"Remember what I was asking you before? I asked you if you wanted things, and you thought they were funny. You never thought you could get them. What I wanted you to know was that you already have them. You have virtual immortality, if my life is any indication. Because of your genetic potential, you are the single most important person on the face of this planet. As for the money, everything I have is yours. That's the only way that makes any sense. And the trip around the world. You wanted to know when we leave?" He reached into his vest pocket and threw the airline ticket envelope onto the desk. "Tonight, if that's what you want. We don't have to come back."

Marcus stared at the tickets for several minutes, as if they were the last clue he needed to solve his problem. Then he put his head in his hands and rubbed his eyes.

"What about my old lady?" he said quietly.

"What about her? You want to go home and tell her? You think she'll understand? You wouldn't even believe it yourself if it wasn't for the touch." Marcus started to protest, but Pelerin cut him off. "You will believe it because you have to believe it. The truth of it doesn't have to come from me. It comes from inside of you."

"I don't want to hurt my old lady." He was firm.

"Why not? She'll have to be hurt sometime. And she's hurt you often enough." He began to feed Marcus some of the same complaints against his mother that the boy had admitted in their sessions.

"Believe me, Marcus, if there was another way, I'd try it. I . . . I wanted to prepare her to find out about you; I couldn't. I tried to cooperate with her but she didn't want anything to do with me. You know she doesn't trust me. You know she's got your whole life planned out for you. She's a failure, a failure who wants to use you to get back her self-respect. I want to free you from all that. I want you to find out for yourself what life is all about.

"Maybe she doesn't seem so bad now. But you're getting smarter and smarter and she's staying the same. She'll never understand you any better than she does now. She'll be like an anchor holding you in one place for the rest of your life."

Pelerin could tell that every word he said had cut straight into Marcus, but that none had pierced the central core of resistance. He knew that he had to strike harder.

"You can't want to be like her. You can't. Because you know exactly what she's like. I don't have to tell you. *You've touched her.*"

Marcus stiffened.

"What did you see inside of your mother, huh? A little craziness, I bet. I know you saw lies and fears and pettiness. What else? Hate? That's it, isn't it? She's already put some of her hate into you. Tell me, what does it feel like? I want to know from one who knows. What's it like to be possessed by a hate you don't want to feel?"

Marcus looked as if he had been struck. There were tears on his face. He spoke slowly, but distinctly, each word a feat of mental toughness.

"It's like when you get hit in the face by accident. You want to punch somebody out." He clenched his fists. "But you can't. There's no reason . . . you want to so bad . . . but you . . . can't."

Pelerin got out of his seat and walked over to the boy, gentling him. "Don't let it happen to you anymore, Marcus. She can't help it. She's only returning what she got unfairly in the first place. She has to hate. You don't. There are other ways, better ways. Let me show them to you."

If Marcus heard this, he gave no sign. Pelerin put a hand on his shoulder. "Marcus?"

In a fury he whipped a fist back at Pelerin, catching him in the stomach. Pelerin grunted and doubled over. Marcus vaulted the desk and in three long steps was at the door. He flung it open, then whirled to face Pelerin.

"Get out of my life, motherfucker! Get out and stay out. Let me tell *you* something for a change. I touched lots of niggers, and not one of them stinks as much as you. Dig yourself before you try to tell me about hate. Because there's something a lot worse than hate, man, and you got it. You're dead inside. No love or hate. Nothing. That time I touched you, it was like I didn't even exist. There's no room in your head for anyone but you. And if that's what you're offering, then you better find another sucker."

He turned and started running.

"Don't leave," Pelerin said, gasping for breath.

The door in the waiting room opened, slammed, and then he was alone. Pelerin sank back into the desk chair, drained. He closed his eyes and watched as the stillborn dreams of his kind wavered and shaded into darkness, into the death he had never known enough to fear.

Wherein the example speaks for itself. . . .

"Some Things Just *Have* to Be Done by Hand!"
Paul J. Nahin

The Most Important Entity rubbed His temples in fatigue. There was just so damned much crap to put up with nowadays. The personnel paperwork was nearly overwhelming, even for a being with omnipotent powers. And a work force faced with zero turnover had a first-class morale problem. The younger ones knew there was no hope for advancement by the usual routes of death, retirement, or resignation. None of those events ever happened.

The telephone rang, and He answered in weary relief at the distraction. "Yes?"

"Sorry to bother you, Sir, but the main computers have a backlog in the RANDOM QUEUE for ten to the one hundred eighty-third power decisions. Can you please service those requests right now?"

"Damn, are those bloody scientists on Earth doing their quantum experiments again!? You'd think they'd understand the Uncertainty Principle after all these years. Well, what is it now, an electron beam through a diffraction grating, or is somebody trying to locate an atom with zero error?"

"Both, and more, Sir. Those guys are really getting busy down there. Why, just as we've been talking here, the QUEUE has picked up ten to the thirty-fourth power more requests!"

The main computers *couldn't* be allowed to overflow. Once, two or three thousand years ago (in Earth time), they had been unattended for several days (in His time), and the QUEUE had clogged-up tight with ignored decision requests for determining random events. The resulting massive computer system crash had caused entire centuries (in Earth time) of strange, abnormal violations in His Laws of Natural Phenomena. It had been the time of Magic on Earth, and the new Wizards, Sorcerers, and Magicians had used it to their advantage in proclaiming themselves all powerful. It couldn't be allowed to happen again!

"All right, all right, hold your feathers smooth. Hang on for a moment." He put His caller on hold, and pulled open the desk drawer next to His perfect left foot. Inside was a pure diamond crystal box, containing two ruby cubes of ultimate clarity. The dots on the cube faces were precise circles of gold. Taking the cubes in His mighty hand, He established a mind-link with the input-output data lines to the main computers. Faster than imaginable (or even possible by ordinary laws, but for Him very little was impossible), the cubes tumbled in His quivering hand. The whole thing was over in just a few wingbeats.

"O.K., the main computers cleaned up?"

"Yes Sir, the RANDOM QUEUE is empty!"

"Excellent—now please don't call again for at least another day. Meanwhile, you and your colleagues might busy yourselves with finding a way to speed up the software random number generator. I find this business of hand generation to be increasingly inconvenient! Good-by."

As He hung up, He thought of what Albert Einstein, one of the better Earth scientists, had once said—'God doesn't play dice with the Cosmos.'

"Hummph," He grunted in disgust to Himself, "just what the Hell did *he* know about it!"

Against the terrorists he was alone—except for the largest robot in the world.

Windship
Lord St. Davids

It was the "off-course" alarm that woke him, and he faced the control board blurrily. The antigrav floater's lit dials came into focus and at first sight there seemed nothing wrong. Course . . . that was correct. Inertia Nav plot position, hell what time was it— yes, that was down a little below that ordered, and height . . . yes, height was all to hell. The ordered height was still set for 10,000 meters, but the altimeter was showing 9,900 and now a fraction less. The floater was dropping. Jim Ford felt a chill. It had nothing to do with the floater's internal temperature that was still at the 22° that he liked to sleep at, in spite of the sub-zero temperatures this high above the howling gale-torn seas of the South Pacific's Roaring Forties. It wasn't even fear of the obvious battery failure, now an unbelievably rare accident in a floater. That meant a slow loss of power; you cut speed and came down lower to put less strain on your powersource, looked around for somewhere you could land comfortably, and used your radiophone to get yourself rescued.

He was starting to consider the nightmare question of how to survive if forced down into the sea.

A world Visi News reporter often found himself in unusual places, and he was equipped to face any conceivable state of affairs. He had a survival suit, medical stores, an inflatable boat-capsule, side arms, emergency food and water supply, a radiophone, radionav, everything modern science could dream up to keep him alive, but would it be enough if he had to drop into the nightmare-sized waves of the howling Roaring Forties below him, or worse still of the Screaming Fifties further south with their ice, dark, and perpetual near-hurricane winds? He must save the batteries all he could. He dialed for a height of 1,000 meters and cut off all propulsion. With Cape Horn some thousand miles to the southeast, if he could stay airborne the wind itself would take him there pretty nearly.

He would radio for help and information. The emergency radio's clucking note started as he switched it on. It was nearly fifteen minutes before a faint voice answered.

"Calling emergency caller, Bear Island Station calling emergency caller, calling emergency caller, over!"

"World Visi News floater, Jim Ford visi-reporter only crew, battery failure in position 49°25′ south 97°37′ west. Am descending from 10,000 meters to 1,000 meters and stopping propulsion to conserve power. Please advise where I can land and what rescue services available. Can remain airborne possibly ten hours using propulsion up to 60 knots. Please advise. Over."

"Bear Island calling Jim Ford, calling Jim Ford,

nearest land to you is Desolation Island 970 repeat 970 miles east-south-east of you. With existing northwest 40 knot winds it is barely in your range. Peter Island is 1,186, repeat 1,186 miles south of you, but don't attempt unless desperate as weather conditions there are extreme. There is a windship, repeat windship, the *John R. Standby* about 100 miles to the west of you. She has no crew but has quarters and supplies. I am getting her exact position for you. Have you working radar, over."

"Jim Ford answering. Yes, my radar is working. I can't see the windship yet. Can she put out a directional beam? Over."

"We are trying to activate her emergency responses. Her signal is JRSX. Keep your set open, and we will have her position soon for you."

Ford had never been aboard a windship. Sometimes one was to be seen in port or under tow near land but then they had crew aboard. The great oceangoing sailing ships of previous centuries had been driven off the seas when fuel became cheap and men expensive. Now they were returning in extreme form when fuel became expensive and men could be replaced with reliable machines.

The giant tankers which had preceded them had for many years had such small crews for their size that in any emergency all they could do was to call for help. The giant windships took the process a stage further. Handled out of port by tugs and special crews, once safely twenty miles offshore the crew left and the ship was abandoned to her computer controlled rig. Their whole propulsive power came from their huge wingsails, so that a windship looked like a great steel base with a row of giant airliner wings stuck vertically into it.

The things were huge, and often had the capacity to carry 300,000 tons of cargo or more. They were bulk carriers, and this one was probably in the brown coal trade. Australian brown coal was the source of a number of important chemical products used in European industry. Speed was not important. With no crew to be paid on the long haul and a cargo which could not deteriorate, low cost of transport was what counted.

The ship was a cheap steel box, nothing more. Her inertia Nav gear would put her accurately within a half a mile, her sail-trim engines would adjust her 300 meter high wingsails to the most effective angle for the computer ordered course, and radar would let her see any object in her way. Normal steering was by rudder, and was slow, but for emergency turns or docking she had across-ship jets at both ends. These were worked by hydroxigen engines, burning the oxygen and hydrogen which she produced and stored throughout her long voyage. All through it she would be generating electricity from the forces of the sea and winds around her. Some would be pumped into her batteries and used for her lights, radio, radar, computer, Nav gear, and other continuous needs; the rest would be used to reduce seawater to oxygen and hydrogen, stored under high pressure as a reserve of power to work the engines which controlled her wingmasts and to keep the bearings heated against the icy conditions of the southern ocean. She would have a landing deck on her stern, with landing lights and a homing-in beam, and comfortable crew quarters where he could rest till

Bear Island Base, which he had been heading for,
sent a floater to collect him. They would fly in new
batteries and get his floater airborne again.

"Bear Island calling Jim Ford, calling Jim Ford,
over!"

"Jim Ford answering, I can hear you good and
clear, over!"

"Bear Island to Jim Ford. Windship *John R.
Standby* is in position 51°58′ south 96°07′ west
and is making 19 knots course 083 degrees in wind
northwest Force 8. She is now transmitting a directional beam signal JRSX on 237 kilocycles. She has
lit her decks to receive you. Please signal approximately half-hourly and report when safely on
board. We estimate we can reach you there at 12.30
give or take two hours. Over and out."

Ford had been feeding all this to his computer;
now he set his radio direction finder to 237 kilocycles. At once he heard the windship loud and
clear. She must be much closer than 100 miles,
perhaps within sixty. "JRSX EE-EE-EE-EE"—a
steady note for ten seconds, then "JRSX EE-EE-
EE-EE-." She was guiding him in. He powered the
floater up to sixty knots, no more would be needed.
She was coming almost exactly towards him. Allowing for the wind partly against him and her
speed, rather over an hour should see him safely on
board.

He set the autopilot to bring him as near as possible up her radio beam and set about preparing a
hot meal and drink for himself. It was more difficult now. The floater had been steady enough at
9,900 meters even in the weird turbulence of this,
the worst weather area of the planet, but now at

1,000 meters she was being violently tossed about. He only hoped conditions would allow him to land on the windship. This delay would mean that he would miss part of the brit-harvesting demonstration, but it was an adventure in itself and he should consider how to write it up and what shots to take. He could tape some scenes around the windship's decks and cabins and if his floater batteries still held enough power after dawn perhaps he could do some airborne ones of the huge vessel fighting her lonely way through gale conditions. Perhaps the rescue floater pilot could be persuaded to do a pass or two round the windship. That way also he would get shots of his stranded floater on her landing deck. He would stay at a thousand meters as he approached her to clear her huge wingmasts, then sink down and swing in from one side, head to wind, onto her tail.

He set about taping a run-up to the story.

Fifty minutes later he tried his clear-view and the windship was in sight, or rather a great splash of white light above which a thin red line shone. It puzzled him till he realized that it was the red warning lights on top of her eight tall wingmasts coming almost straight for him and some 700 meters below.

Now her masts were silhouetted black against the blaze of light on her landing deck. He shifted to manual control and came left and down, slowing and dropping, and hovered beside her at half-mast height, on her down-wind side. Her landing deck was brilliantly framed in light and the five-spot landing mark was clear. An arrow of green lights set in the deck gave the wind direction. He nosed upwind towards the deck.

The air turbulence was very bad, and the massive deck was rising and falling ten meters. He came in high and sank down. For one moment he feared a crash as the deck leaped up to meet him but it paused and sank away just as he settled on. A lovely landing, much better than he had hoped. He cut all gravity control and propulsion and prayed that the wind was not strong enough to blow the floater overboard. There was silence except for the howl of the gale. The windship was lifting, dropping, and rolling, but no earthly weather could cause the great steel hull to do more than slow stately movements. He was glad of having a survival suit as the gale blasted around him. There were securing rings sunk into the landing deck, and he got out guy-ropes and winched the floater tight down. He must report his safe arrival to Bear Island, and then go and "talk" to the computer center of his huge hostess.

He contacted the base. They asked if he had had any trouble and he said it was dead easy apart from having to take care in the actual landing, and asked why the windship was so far south. He had understood that they kept in the Forties latitudes rather than the Fifties because of ice. Yes, that was generally true, but the *J.R. Standby* was ice-strengthened and heated. She had been forced to work more southwards by a north-east gale, which was why she was now making some northing. She would have to work more south later, of course, to round Cape Horn.

The ship's decks were wet but no rain or spray was then coming aboard. Lamps on her mast bases lit her decks and emphasized the glow-paint of her walk, the path to the crew quarters built inside her eight great "wings." The front one also contained a bridge used in docking and inshore work. There was a door set in one wing base, and a friendly green light above it winked at him in welcome. It was an extraordinary feeling being alone, a thousand miles from land and maybe more than that from any other human, and being invited hospitably in by this windship, surely the largest robot yet built by man.

He was about to open the door when a shot rang out and a shrieking banshee wailed away into the gale.

For a moment Ford stood still. The sound had been half lost in the howling wind, but he had heard shots often enough not to be mistaken, and he had seen the splash of clean metal which had suddenly appeared beside the door just above his left shoulder. It had come from behind him, and his automatic next reaction was to run round to the foreside of the wingmast, putting it between him and his attacker. He was thinking furiously. There should be nobody on board, especially nobody armed. The ship, it seemed, had human rats aboard. He musn't keep near the wingmast or anyone walking round it could surprise and shoot him. In the semidark of the deck he could see out to one side a sort of table-sized steel box, hand controls probably for some docking purpose. He left the mast and hid behind it. Crouching low, he saw a man with a rifle coming round his side of the wingmast. He paused when he got to the front of it, and a second man met him from the other side.

They turned to look behind the steel breakwater which here divided the deck. Ford realized that he needed arms to survive. He must get back to his floater. He ran for it.

Unheard in the howling wind he tore along the main deck, up onto the landing deck, and tore open the door of the floater. He blessed his habit of keeping a loaded automatic needle-pistol behind his seat. Had he time to loose the floater and take off? No, already in the first light of dawn he could see the two men on the main deck. They seemed to be searching further forward. He must try and get help. He reached inside again for a portable radio. Pray God it had the strength to contact Bear Island. He tried. It was faint, but Bear Island replied.

"Ford here. I'm on the windship, but I'm in trouble. There are men with guns on board and I've been shot at. Can you help me?" He could hear consternation at the other end, and finally an authoritative voice.

"We will get to you as quickly as we can. We are contacting the windship on an emergency code and asking her to help you. Your identity to her is FRD. She answers to JRSX. She must be unaware that there is anybody else on board or she would have reported it."

Suddenly a new voice broke in. It was deep and somehow squeaky. "I am JRSX," it said. "I can hear you. I have been told to help FRD and oppose enemies of FRD. Please FRD speak so that I can learn to identify the voice of FRD."

Ford promptly spoke. "Hello JRSX, nice to have you on my side. What can you do to help me?"

"I do not know. You will tell me."

"Can you let me into your cabins and control room and can you keep the others out?"

"I have locks on all doors. They are now shut against all except FRD. I have a listening and speaking unit at each door. I will open one only if you speak. Enter my crew space, where I have a real voice. My radio transmission to you is being monitored by nearby equipment. I will cease speaking."

"Good luck! We'll hurry all we can! Out!" That was Bear Island signing off. Ford was left to face his enemies, unknown in number, with only the windship herself as his ally.

The gunmen would certainly come to examine the floater soon. He must get away from it. He must take his gun, a torch, all the ammunition he could grab, and the portable radio even if it could be listened to. Also, a good camera and a sound and video taper. If he came through this alive he would have a story to tell. He got out and locked the door.

Where were the enemy? Daylight was getting stronger and he could just see them a very long way away near the bows where they still seemed to think he had gone.

He could hear a voice—sounded like a girl—shouting for them. He must hurry. He crouched as he went down the steps to the maindeck. The door leading into the nearest wingmast mounting was close by.

"FRD here," he said. "Let me in"

"Obeying!" It was the deep voice again, this time from a wall-speaker, and the door opened. He heard the sound of mechanical bolts going home as it closed. The interior light came on. The voice spoke again. "You are now at my Number Eight wingmast. My control room for crew is in my Number Five wingsail. You will find a doorway in the central column here. Go down one level, enter the central passage, walk forward to the door with 'Mast 5' painted in red on it and there go up three levels to the door marked 'Control Room.' You can transmit orders there on my read-out if needed."

He was standing in a big circular room which contained heavy machinery, none of which seemed to be working at the moment. There was a circular column four meters thick in its center. A door in it opened easily and led to a spiral stairway actually inside the great hollow wingmast itself. He duly went down one level, where a door led him into a long steel passage. Red lettering on the wall said 'Forward'. He walked past red-numbered doors to the one which said 'Mast 5,' then up three levels.

The room he came out in was the full diameter of the inside of the steel wingsail. As in the other areas he had walked through, the lights were on. The room was full of banks of switches and machines, all obviously made to be operated by a human crew. There was a read-out screen by one wall, with its switches and type-in order console.

He switched it on and it lit the word "Listening." He spoke aloud. "Do you want me to use this?" he asked.

"Not unless you wish to," said the windship. "Crew uses it for accurate sets of figures. For simple orders it is quicker if you speak them."

He switched it off. "Where are my enemies?" he asked.

"I do not know. I only have monitoring devices for men at doors and inside crew areas. I have radar for long-range watching of large objects, and I have aircraft monitors on the landing deck. For things on deck only your eyes are available."

"Please turn the lights off in here. You are giving away my position." The lights went off. Ford peered cautiously out of a porthole. Shadowy figures were moving about on the deck below the wingsail. Clearly it was too late, the lights had already told them where he was, and they were proposing some counteraction. Could he risk a shot?

Not worth it; the range was rather long, and he had only a pistol against their machine guns or rifles.

There was movement below, they seemed to be running away. Suddenly the deck jerked to a tearing explosion. He clutched at a table. "Are you all right, JRSX?"

"Yes, I am undamaged but they have blown open the door into the sail-control engine room below. They cannot get to where you are as I have also closed the door to the staircase. If they blow open that door and the one above they can get to you."

"Where would I be safest?"

"Go into the passage and back to the store under the landing deck. There are at least five doors they would need to open to reach you, even if they knew where you were."

"What is kept in the store?"

"Paint of all kinds, welding tools, lengths of hydrogen and oxygen hose with connections."

"Wait! Where have you got hydrogen lines?"

"To all hydroxi engines, also duplicate mains the length of the ship."

"Can you control supply, and is there a connecting point in the cabin they have broken into?"

"Yes, but I may not open it as to do so would be dangerous to Man."

"Why?"

"If a spark is lit it would explode and hurt Man. I must not hurt Man."

"Not if I order it?"

"Only if you do it under Emergency Code."

"I order it under Emergency Code."

"I cannot obey unless you quote the Emergency Code Number."

"What is the Emergency Code Number?"

"Code Number 1307."

"I order it under Emergency Code Number 1307."

"Obeying."

"I expect some of them to enter the room below."

"They are doing so now."

"Then flood it at once with hydrogen to explosion proportions and spark it off."

"I obey. I advise you to go to the store. An explosion might hurt you."

Ford hurried out, down the staircase to the long passage, where he paused. "What is happening now?"

"Someone is trying to open the door to the stairs, I have bolted it."

"When will there be enough hydrogen loose to cause an explosion?"

"In another forty-two seconds."

"I order it."

"Obeying."

He moved further towards the stern. It seemed hours, but it came, a great grumping boom. "What has happened?"

"The hydrogen has exploded."

"Is anybody hurt?"

"I do not know. My sensors there are now destroyed."

"Is the inner door blown open?"

"No, it is still solid."

Ford decided he would have to get where he could watch. "I'm going up into a wingsail. Don't light the lights there if I do."

"Obeying."

He found the door marked "Sail 7" and climbed three levels. The door led into a big open area fitted for recreation. He looked out of the portholes. It was full daylight outside on the gale-swept deck. He could see the door they had blown open into number 5 sail engine room. As he watched, two figures came out carrying a third. It seemed that the hydrogen explosion had hurt someone. They put him on deck and bent over him.

"Where have all these people been hiding, JRSX?"

"I do not know."

"Where on board haven't you any sensors?"

"On deck, in the holds, in the buoyancy tanks."

"They can't have been living on deck. Can they get into the holds or buoyancy tanks?"

"I operate the hatch-covers to the holds. None has been opened. I do not operate the manhole covers to the buoyancy tanks."

"That's probably it then. Have you any way of
getting them out?"

"I can flood the buoyancy tanks."

"Good, try that, please."

"Obeying."

The two who had carried their friend out were
consulting. Suddenly they jumped into action.
Ford couldn't hear anything in the gale, but another figure had appeared and ran towards them. The
three rushed to two manhole lids in the deck and
disappeared below. A moment later they were out
again with bundles, then down below again for
more, and again. Now they were grabbing everything they had rescued and running along the deck
towards where Ford watched in the wingsail above.

Suddenly the whole ship jerked and Ford was
flung across the cabin. He got to his feet. "What
has happened, JRSX?"

"There has been another explosion. I am in-
jured."

Ford looked out and gasped. Where the manhole nearest Number 5 mast had been there was a
twenty-meter-wide hole in the deck. At its inner
edge it had lifted and torn the Number 5
deckhouse; at its outer edge it had blown a large
length of the edge of the deck away, and he could
see that an area of the ship's side was missing. The
ship lurched, and in horror he saw the sea thunder
into the hole.

"How serious is the damage, JRSX?"

"Buoyancy tanks 5 A and 5 C are open to the
sea. There is water entering holds number 4 and 5.
My number 5 sail engine is damaged, as well as the
number 5 wingsail roller-bearings. I have had to

de-clutch the sail."

Looking at it Ford could see that the number 5 wingsail was now turned to a different angle from the others; it had swung head to wind. "Are you sinking?"

"No, holds 4 and 5 are fully packed with coal. They will admit only two to three thousand tons of water."

"That sounds a lot to me."

"It is less than 1% of the weight of the cargo I carry. And the buoyancy tanks are normally above sea level; their importance is small unless I am much more heavily damaged."

"Doesn't having a sail out of action trouble you?"

"Yes, but its effect, averaging different wind angles and speeds, is to reduce my driving force by 12%. That is not serious."

"Anyway, you can cease flooding now and pump out except for the buoyance tank next to where the damage is. Leave just a little water in there."

"Obeying."

Ford wondered if the big explosion had been accidental or on purpose. Either it had detonated something in their store or they had meant to damage the ship. He felt it must have been an accident. Their wounded friend had been lying on deck when they had run for it, and there was no trace of him now or of the deck he had been on. If it had been deliberate it had failed. The ship was just simply too big, too solid.

Where was the gang? Ford went round looking out of portholes and saw them. They were on the steps leading up to the landing deck. It looked as if they were getting ready to prevent any other floater from landing. He must warn Bear Island. It wouldn't matter if the gunmen heard him. "JRSX, can you put me in touch with Bear Island Base?"

"Yes, obeying. JRSX to Bear Island, JRSX to Bear Island, can you hear me?"

"Yes, JRSX, we can hear you clearly. How is FRD?"

"He is well and safe. He wishes to speak to you."

"Hello Bear Island, this is Ford. I have now seen four gunmen. I think I've killed one. They are guarding the landing deck to stop anyone landing. They can probably hear this." A thick voice broke in: "Yes, we can. We'll get you, you swine." "Ford over and out." He had had an idea.

"JRSX, is there any thin rope or thin wire in your store?"

"Yes plenty, of all sizes."

"I am going there. Light the place when I reach the corridor."

"Obeying."

He went down. There was a door at the end opening into a large space under the landing deck. He walked round it. There seemed to be every imaginable kind of stores there. Yes, a long coil of thin line. And some baling-wire. He went to look for tools. There were plenty. He selected a strong pair of pliers, a length of the wire, and a coil of line, and went back to the number 8 sail engine room. There he sat down and took out a tape recorder. In a conversational tone, he started taping a long report on what conditions were like on board, how many gunmen there were, and anything else he could think of to say. They knew he was alone, and if he could use the tape to fool them into thinking that he was busy talking to Bear Island they might be careless long enough for him to do what he wanted.

When he had finished he went up into the wingsail cabin above and looked out. Yes, they were still there. He again got the windship to call up Bear Island. As he heard her do it he saw the gunmen cluster closely round together around a radio. Bear Island was answering. He spoke. "Ford here. I'd just like to give you a situation report of how things are aboard here."

He switched on his taped report, left it speaking, and ran down to the sail engine room below, then out of the door on the side away from the gunmen. He slipped a loop of line over a nearby manhole lid, pulled tight, and fastened the other end to a hand-grip close to the doorway. He then peered round the side of the deck-house. They had their backs to him, quite close. He fired several times rapidly into the group, then dodged round and back into the doorway. There were shouts and screams, followed by the sound of running feet coming. There was a crash as a figure hit the line and fell, its gun skidding away along the deck. He jumped out and swung his gun-butt again and again to its head till it lay still. He dodged into the doorway again and listened.

All was quiet. Carefully he came out and peered around. The figure on the deck was moving. He grabbed it and pulled it into the deck-house. "Close the door and bolt it."

"Obeying."

He took a look at his prisoner. It was a girl. Her hair was matted and there was blood on her face. He dragged her over to the sail-control engine, then used the pliers and the wire to handcuff her left wrist solidly to it. Even if she had a knife she couldn't get away from that. She was coming round. Her eyes opened. "I know you," he said. "You are Irma Katt."

She smiled through a layer of rust and dirt. "I am that famous?"

"Yes, I've studied the list of you who were condemned to death for those bombings. I'd better go and look at your boyfriends."

"They are dead?"

"I hope so. I'll check up."

With extreme caution he crept out. There were two bodies at the foot of the steps and when he felt them they were already starting to chill in the bitter southern gale. There was no sign of anyone else about. He picked up one of the multi-shot rifles they had dropped and after a short search found the other. As a safety measure he took the ammunition of both, smashed one against the steel rail, and cautiously went forward. They had been taking things out of two manholes just before the big explosion. One of the manholes had gone in the explosion; he was interested in the other. He found it was unbolted, and all dark below. He shone his torch down and gasped. The seawater had wetted everything, but down on the narrow strip of floor were the remains of a camp and an arsenal. Someone was very busy importing a lot of trouble.

He went into the door of the number six mast deck-house. "JRSX?"

"Listening."

"Half flood the buoyancy tank just behind where the big explosion was, and keep it flooded."

"Obeying."

Then back to look for those rucksacks they had rescued from the flooding. He found them piled under the edge of the landing deck. It was tempting to throw it all overboard, but the police would want it. He went back to his prisoner. "They are dead," he said.

"Then they were fools, and deserved to die. Two men should have killed you. Now you must kill me too."

"Why?"

"Because I cannot live. If you hand me over to anyone I will be executed after they have questioned me. Please kill me now."

"No, I am a journalist. I don't kill people, except I had to kill your friends in order to defend myself."

"Will you do it if I make it worth your while? You needn't shoot me, just take me to the side and let me jump over. You can say I escaped and killed myself. For that I will give you a long interview, all you want to write about. You have a camera?

"Yes, and tapers."

"Good, and there is something else I can give you. It was difficult for we could not use the crew's things or we would be discovered, but I have kept myself clean, so you can also have my body. I am to die, and I will not get another chance. You are a strong man. Please do it, it is my last request. It will please me, and I will try to please you. Then let me tell you everything and after that give me death.

It only takes two minutes in an ice-cold sea. When will they come to fetch you from here?"

Ford had been thinking. His watch said it was 0520. They had said rescue would come some time not earlier than 10.30, say five hours unless they hurried. "Not before midday," he lied. He didn't want her to insist on death and give trouble before they got rescued. "I want some food and a wash, and I want to get to my cameras and a taper. I'll be back in an hour or perhaps a little more. JRSX, can you do me a hot bath and a meal?"

"Yes, whenever you wish."

"Now please."

"Obeying."

The girl had listened to this in amazement. "It obeys you?"

"Yes, and it won't obey you, so don't try anything."

"May I have a hot bath and a meal too?"

"I won't risk letting you loose, so that rules out the bath, but if you behave I will see you get some food and a drink. Where do I go, JRSX?"

"Two levels up number 6 wingsail." Ford set out.

The hot bath felt wonderful and though the meal was inevitably tinned, JRSX was a good cook. She had also produced a not too bad bottle of Australian red wine. He was enjoying himself, with the meal half finished, when the windship spoke again. "I must tell FRD that there are noises in the cabin where the enemy is. Someone is attacking the cabin door bolt mechanism from inside."

Ford leapt to his feet. She could not have cut that very heavy wire, and there was nobody else there. The cabin was locked, nobody could have got in. Secured where she was she could not possibly reach the door. He must go and look. He set off at a run, taking the rifle and pistol with him.

With great care he gently opened the door between the wingmast staircase and the number 8 sail-engine cabin. To his astonishment it was empty and the door hung open. He looked at the wire he had used to tie her wrist to the engine and gasped.

The wire was still intact, still in the loops which had held her wrist, but what had happened was plain. There was a pool of blood on the deck, and beside it a razor blade and a human hand. She had got away by the classic trick of a trapped wild animal at the cost of a severed limb. Somewhere about the windship was a dangerous and desperate cripple, by now certainly rearmed. He peered outside cautiously. The short multi-shot repeater which had fallen on the deck when he captured her was gone. He dodged inside again. "Where is she, JRSX?"

"I do not know. I have detected no trace of her movements."

This was going to be dangerous. She might be just about anywhere, holed up and waiting for him. He went into the wingsail above and took a good look all round. No sign of her. He came down and walked along the corridor to a wingsail cabin further forward. Nothing was moving.

Finally he saw her. She was sitting under the projecting edge of the landing deck in a sort of nest of the bags the gunmen had heaped there, with a gun resting by her right hand. She probably couldn't aim it very well, but he didn't like to take risks. He came down from the wingsail, out on

deck, keeping out of sight on the side away from
her, and got as close as he could while remaining
behind the number 8 wingmast cabin. He called
out. "Irma Katt, can you hear me?"

"Yes, I can hear you. Don't try to get near me.
I am sitting on twenty kilos of blastite, and I've
wired a pressure-switch to it and I'm holding it. If
you try anything I will let go. It will blow this
whole flight deck up, and your machine. It will
blow you off the deck." She was probably right. He
went further away, back to the number 6 mast, and
went inside to think and be away from the explosion which she was almost bound to set off
some time.

He could see no way out of it. If he shot her the
blastite would blow up and with it the landing deck
and his floater. If he left her alone she might faint
or even deliberately let go with the same result.
There was one last chance. He would consult the
windship.

He did so, and explained the position.

"Where is she exactly?" asked the ship. Ford explained. "Can you come to the control room and
show me more clearly?"

"Yes, but wasn't it damaged in the big explosion?"

"Some things were damaged, but I have tested
my controls and enough are working." He went to
the control room. "What now?"

"Please switch on the read-out screen." He did
so and a map of the ship's deck appeared on it. The
windship spoke again. "Please now use the two red
knobs marked 'Pointer' to show me her exact position."

There was a little red dot on the plan, and as he

turned the knobs it moved. He steered it to the place under the edge of the landing deck. The deck-plan promptly altered to a much larger scale one of the small areas concerned. He put the spot in the exact position. "Why do you want to know?" he asked.

"If she is there and is using an electrical connection I can probably help you. I have live steam there."

"Live steam?"

"Yes, there are many points on the deck where I can project live steam. It is for the removal of snow and ice. I have started producing some steam in case you order it."

"But wouldn't it set the blastite off?"

"It does not detonate blastite but it may ground or break the electric wires if I switch it on suddenly."

"What will it do to her?"

"It will kill her at once. It will not hurt her."

"Might it kill her but not then ground the wires?"

"It might." The windship was right. If they did nothing a damaging explosion, killing the girl, was a certainty. If they risked it the girl would still be killed but the explosion might be avoided. They must try.

"Have you the steam ready to do it?" "Yes, it is now ready." "Then do it." "Obeying." He clutched at the table and prayed, for the safety of the ship and the passing of a brave but grievously deranged girl.

Nothing happened. "Why has nothing happened, JRSX?"

"It has happened. I have finished. There has been no explosion."

Ford went down to look. Shortly after he was back, wishing he hadn't. Live steam not only kills but it strips and cooks. The nest of bags and the girl had been reduced to scrap, rags, scattered bones, and a few small items of cooked flesh.

"Get me a whisky quick!" he ordered.

"One large whisky coming up! Anything with it?"

He didn't remember having said anything about "large." The windship had learnt people's habits from somewhere. "Just straight, please, and 'large,' yes." He sat down and let his mind calm while he drank it. He didn't feel he could finish his lunch; he kept on thinking of things cooking. But there was still a lot in that bottle of Australian wine. He was just getting it when the windship spoke. "I need orders," she said. "My radar shows two small blips airborne and approaching me from the south. Are these your friends?"

"Yes, they must be the people from Bear Island. Please contact them and let me speak to them." He sat down, glass in hand. He could hear the conversation. They were Navy and police asking after him. He replied. "Yes, come right in. It's all finished here, but the ship is in a mess." "That's all right, we've got Navy technicians here and can soon tidy her. We've got new batteries for your floater too, and a gravitech who can look her over." "Good, I will be on the landing deck to meet you and give you a personal tour of the battlefield. So come on in, our hostess is a very generous lady and the drinks are fine."

But Lord, he thought, is she tough!

It's not necessary to look to distant species for alien cultures. Look within. . . .

Guard at the Gates of Hell
George W. Olney

The ultimate development of anything implies its total specialization. You must give up some elements to gain others. This may be good or bad, but only in mankind can it be dangerous. —Changen Aieden, Fellow of the Imperial Institute

On a fine spring Midweek Day, at 0900, the town of Bluefield died. Its demise was long, slow, terrifying, and revolting to those on the scene later. Because of that fact, the later deaths of Shoreline City, Fairview, and Longcreek were swift and rapid, much like a terminally ill plague victim being given a merciful death to prevent the spread of the disease.

The Narsima Matic Etrranty shifted his corpulent bulk in his lounger uncomfortably as he meditated on that fact. Shortly, he, along with other members of the Guiding Council, would be forced to confront once again the fact of their only solution to an attack by the Wareegan Raiders.

The upcoming scene was already a familiar one to the Narsima. The Council would asemble in the Meeting Hall to hear the report of a ranking member of the Planetary Guard. As in the past, the Guardsman would probably be the Changaree himself, young Imin Webster. His expression would probably be composed of equal parts outrage, shame, and sorrow.

Etrranty could sympathize with the fellow. It was a hard thing to admit that the only way your organization, created with the sole purpose of protecting the people of Cauldwell, could destroy an enemy was to blow him, or it, to atomic particles along with the unfortunate inhabitants of whichever town was under attack. The Planetary Guard had nothing that would meet the Wareegan Raiders on even terms in space, and they would never allow the Raiders to complete another attack. Never.

Etrranty had been one of the first on the scene after the Bluefield attack. The memory still turned his stomach.

The Council assembly was as bad as Etrranty feared it was going to be, and as predictable. Webster had been even more incensed, if such a thing was possible.

Afterwards, in his quarters, Etrranty offered Webster a drink, more in hopes of calming the young man than friendliness, though they were friends.

"Damn it, Narsima, why won't you and the Council let us go down after them," the young man raged.

"Imin," Etrranty's voice was soothing, reasonable, "I've told you many times. The Planetary Guard hasn't the training, manpower, nor equipment to conduct any sort of ground warfare. Your force was solely designed to protect against threats from space."

"Which it doesn't seem we are able to do!" Webster shot back.

Etrranty ignored the outburst. "Now, my friend, if you were trained and equipped like one of them. . ." He waved his hand at a line of beautifully made statuettes on a shelf next to the wall.

"Your collection," Imin snorted.

"My collection," Etrranty agreed. "But don't despise my admiration for those men."

He got up and walked to the shelf, becoming more animated and enthusiastic. "These were all soldiers in their day. Any of them, from this Napoleonic lancer to the Vegan space marine, could go down and be at least an even match for the Wareegans, but not your men. It's a matter of the purpose for which they were intended.

"In fact," he picked up a statuette at the end of the line, "here is the very individual we need."

Webster glanced idly at the form in Etrranty's hand. "An Imperial Gladius. So what. We haven't seen an Imperial ship in this cluster for a hundred years, much less Imperial troops."

The figure Etrranty held in his hand was that of a man with a short beard, wearing a khaki tunic and kilt, boots, and a cylindrical cap. His chest was crisscrossed by equipment belts, and a short sword and battle ax on one hip was balanced by a handgun on the other. "An Imperial Gladius. Yes," Etrranty nodded his nead, "they are exactly what we need. They were the supreme warriors, the ultimate soldiers, and I wish we had them now."

The Narsima was soon to get his wish.

As the commander of the Planetary Guard, Changaree Imin Webster was immediately notified when the ship first came into scanner range. He was on the spot in the Combat Command Center when the mysterious ship was definitely identified as not being the Wareegan Raider returning. In fact, it strongly resembled their recognition slides of Imperial troop carriers, with a few changes. Once in visual range, the ship was noted to have some damage, possibly combat damage.

Signals were received on the standard communication band, and the Center lost no time in replying. The figure that appeared on the screen was wearing Imperial uniform with the rank badges of a pilot. He was also bandaged heavily on his left shoulder. "Imperial Troopship Rimini requesting permission to land and the coordinates of your port."

Imin moved in front of the communicator screen. "This is Changaree Imin Webster, commander of the Planetary Guard. We will clear you for landing, provided you state your mission. You are the first Imperial ship in this area in many years. What are you doing here?"

"We are—" the pilot began, then he stopped, glanced over his shoulder at someone out of viewfinder range, and turned back to the screen. "Please wait while I shift you to the other screen."

Before Imin could say anything, the communications screen blanked. The figure that came back on was older than the pilot, by a number of years, but vigorous, powerful. His lined and scarred face was partially hidden by a full, heavy beard, shot through with strands of grey. He wore a khaki colored, cylindrical cap above steel grey eyes that were piercing, burning with the pure power of the smoldering will behind them. Below his beard, a khaki uniform could be made out, with crossed leather belts slung across the shoulders and insignia on the collar. Imin wasn't sure, but he thought the insignia was that of a regimental commander of the Imperial Gladii.

"We are here, sir," the man's voice rumbled, "simply because we have nowhere else to go."

Imin gaped for a moment, then his hand slipped to the button that scrambled a squadron of his fighters. Recovering his composure, he said, "I will require a little more information, sir, before allowing a shipload of Imperial troops to land here. It's been over a hundred years, and anything could have happened in the Empire during that time."

The soldier in the screen solemnly nodded his head. "Caution is a good trait in a young officer. I like to see that, sir. Very well, I'll be more than happy to provide you with some answers.

"Simply put, I am Tribune-Commander Abedu Corona, commander of the Victrix Regiment. You are exactly right in your worry of Imperial political conditions, because the Empire is now sundered, broken by civil war and revolution. Our base was destroyed. I managed to save the bulk of the regiment, three reinforced cohorts, and we escaped to find a world on the frontier that would allow us free settlement and a return to our original purpose, the protection of the human culture. We found Cauldwell by the simple expedient of following an old route tape, and now I ask the privilege of coming down to speak peacefully to you about landing."

The eyes lit briefly with the fire that was forever behind them. "Changaree, I believe that allowing me to come down in a shuttle to talk will be best. It will prevent my crew from having to perform the distasteful chore of destroying those fighters we are now tracking in our sights."

"Permission granted, Tribune-Commander, for

you and an aide in a shuttlecraft." Imin felt he had to agree to prevent a clash. Bloodshed was needless at the moment. The old man was right, but Imin felt he had one more point to settle first, before he felt easy in his mind. "Answer me one thing, Tribune-Commander, if you will. I know the history of the Gladius regiments, and you've never run from a fight before. Why didn't you fall back on the Empire's center?"

The old man looked grim, angered. "The Victrix didn't run from a fight, as you put it. We fought to the end, then fought our way out. Our attackers paid dearly, in fact, they fled, but not before almost everything that made our regimental base was destroyed.

"But," he smiled ironically, "as to falling back on Empire Central? The forces that destroyed Victrix Base, Changaree, were *Imperial* forces."

"As I said before," Imin replied in quiet tones, "you are cleared to land a shuttle."

Imin flipped off circuit and turned to a nearby junior officer. "Find the Narsima Etrranty. There is something going on that will be of great interest to him."

In due course, negotiations between the refugee Victrix regiment and the world of Cauldwell were brought to a satisfactory conclusion, and the troopship was allowed to land. Although the negotiations had been in secret, the landing of the ship was not. In a free society such as Cauldwell's, it is the habit of information dissemination organizations to be both flourishing and ubiquitous. The landing of the first Imperial troops in a hundred years had been a major sensation, reported chiefly by Sim Shana Etrranty, the daughter of the Narsima.

That was how she found herself in her father's

apartment along with Imin Webster, her father, and the Tribune-Commander, after all speeches and formalities were concluded. She sipped her drink and tried to remain in the background, curled in an overstuffed chair. She wanted to study the Gladius commander as unobtrusively as possible. The man fascinated her.

It all went back, she thought, to her first, unsettling meeting with a Gladius, the Tribune-Commander's aide. Due to her father's influence, she had been first on the scene when the arrival of the Victrix regiment was announced. She was standing in front of the door to her father's office when the door opened suddenly, and she found herself face to face with the young soldier. Her immediate impression was of a clean-cut, fair young man in a strange uniform.

Then she saw his eyes.

They were an indeterminate shade of light blue, but empty, terribly devoid of all emotion. She got the feeling that she had no existence as a person for the Gladius. She was merely a concept. She realized, deep in her gut, that here was a man that would think less of killing her than she would of swatting a fly. Her death would be ordained for logical, objective reasons, and carried through with a maximum of professional skill.

From that moment, she realized what had made the Gladii the most feared soldiers in history.

The Tribune-Commander, now, was a different story. He seemed to be smoldering with suppressed fanaticism. If his men were ice, he was fire. With his beard, he reminded her of one of the Old Testament prophets from the Old Christian Bible. He seemed to have a speck of humanity in him somewhere. At least, he could laugh. Perhaps that was why he interested her so.

If the truth was known, the entire regiment fascinated her. She felt the urge to dig deeper, learn all she could about them. This reaction may have been prompted by fear, but her feelings were interpreted in her mind as professional curiosity on the part of Cauldwell's premier newswoman. She had high hopes of parlaying this little cocktail session into an in-depth study of the regiment and its way of life.

The Narsima was carefully pouring quantities of Cauldwell brandy into the glasses of everyone in the room. Once finished, he offered the toast, "To the future!"

The Tribune-Commander responded, "May your harness never fail."

The Narsima explained with the air of a well prepared student giving a favorite dissertation. "The Gladii ride into battle on small, six-man antigrav sleds. When they get close enough to their objective, they hit their harness release button and hop in using no-weight belts. The sled continues on to a preselected target, becoming an explosive missile to disrupt the enemy. If a man's harness fails him, he is condemned to ride the sled in to an explosive fate.

"Am I not right, Tribune-Commander?"

"Exactly right," Corona agreed. Etrranty beamed, proud of his ability to show off in his hobby.

Shana asked interestedly, "That sounds like a horrible fate. Has it ever happened, Tribune-Commander?"

He looked at her with a grandfatherly expression. "Occasionally, my dear. In fact, it happened to me once."

She sensed the beginning of her first character story on the Gladii, and leaned forward eagerly to ask, "Tell us what happened, please."

He took a sip of his drink, secure in the knowledge that he had the attention of his audience. "Well, Sim Etrranty, it was back when I was but a young Subaltern, newly commissioned. It was during the Battle of the Twin Volcanos on Partossos, and my mantiple was chosen to make the lead assault on their positions. I was full of my responsibility as a new officer, and I checked my men and our equipment to near distraction. I know they were heartily tired of my everlasting checking, so much so, the battle was probably a relief to them. I checked their equipment so much, in fact, that I completely neglected to check my own harness. I buckled up hastily, just before assault launch.

"Well, we were off. It was a wild ride into the objective, as it always is, and we came within a hair of being hit several times. We reached the release point, and we all hit our harness release buttons. The other five men in the sled were thrown clear safely, but I remained, with a fouled harness. I was forced to ride the sled into its target. I was fortunate that the warhead on the sled was a dud and did not explode."

He stopped to drink again, noting that the other three were on the edge of their seats. Shana leaned even further out of her chair. "Please go on," she said, "tell us how you escaped."

"Well," he replied in deadpan tones, "I was captured by the Vafnir forces and, since they couldn't spare the men to guard me, I was shot."

Corona threw back his head and laughed, a deep, falstaffian belly laugh. The rest sat there for a minute, then the joke sank in with the Narsima and Imin. They, too, began to laugh at the way they were taken in by the story. Shana, however, blushed a fiery red.

Corona's laughter died down to a series of chuckles and he took a further sip of his drink. "I must apologize, Sim Etrranty," he said, still chuckling, "in that I couldn't resist telling that little story. My junior officers will tell you it's my favorite tale when I meet someone new."

The Narsima's laughter subsided to occasional rumbles deep in his massive midsection, and he wiped his streaming eyes. "I will have to credit you with a definite score on us, Tribune-Commander," he said. "I am afraid you very neatly turned the tables on my daughter, as well. She came here expecting to pick apart a simple soldier fanatic for the amusement of her public, not find herself neatly ensnared as the butt of a joke."

Shana could say nothing, only blush, as her father exposed her intentions shamelessly in front of the object of her study. Thankfully, the Tribune-Commander took it gracefully.

He turned to her and smiled. "Don't be so embarrassed, young lady. That's not an uncommon intention where the Gladii are concerned.

"How," he said, "did you think I developed the story in the first place?"

"But, enough of this," the Narsima became imperious, casting a lordly glance at Imin. "Changaree Webster, I believe you have a small presentation to make to the Tribune-Commander concerning our troubles."

"Yes, Narsima," Imin said, as he fumbled with a small group of papers in his hands. Arranging them to his satisfaction, he placed a small solidio-optic projector on the side table next to his chair. "Tribune-Commander, have you ever heard of the Wareegan Raiders? I'm not sure if that is your name for them. We discovered it in records that pre-dated our cessation of contact with the Empire."

Corona got a fiercely intent look on his face. Much, Shana thought, as a deadly hunting animal would look on hearing the distant cry of a fierce enemy. She noticed that his left hand stole to the hilt of the short sword that, with its companion short battle ax, was still strapped to his side.

"The name is correct, Changaree," he replied in grim tones. "They were an old pest in our own sector until we located their raiding bases and cleaned them out. I was on one of those expeditions, myself. If you are suffering from Wareegan raids, nothing would please me more than to spill more of their blood, preferably slowly."

Shana was temporarily taken aback at this matter-of-fact declaration of bloodthirstiness. She was tempted to put it down to bravado, but bravado didn't fit with the man's personality. The realization that it was more likely a simple declaration of intent shook her slightly, and gave her pause for thought.

Imin also looked slightly surprised. "Ahem, ah, at any rate," he continued, a bit shakily at first, "this is the only example of a Wareegan we have available."

He did something to the projector, and an image appeared in the air between the four. The image was of a tall, bipedal insectoid creature, with two arms, a bulbous head, and a short neck. It was dangling, as though its limp body was suspended from invisible wires. To Shana, the grisly thing reminded her of a carcass dangling in the slaughterhouse. Realizing what the creature was capable of doing, Shana couldn't help a shudder.

In a calm, unemotional voice, Imin continued, "We strung the body up to get a better representation three-dimensionally. An interesting point is that, although the thing appears to be some form of highly developed insect, it is actually hemoglobin based and mammalian. Apparently this specimen was artificially neutered."

"They bleed red," Corona murmured. Then, in a more conversational tone, "That is one of their warrior caste. All are apparently de-sexed at birth. Where was this slide taken?"

"At Bluefield," the Narsima replied, "where they first hit. The devastation was terrible, and we aren't exactly sure of what happened to the bulk of the population. Normal things, manufactured items and raw materials, were taken, but why they took the people, we don't know."

"I do," Corona's voice was flat, ugly. "They have the same metabolism as us. They can digest the same foods, if properly treated for such things as trace elements. We found, when we were cleaning them out of the quadrant, that they tended to take all the organic matter they could to process in their protein tanks. That includes the residents of whatever place they raid."

"That's ghastly!" Shana said.

"Not to them, Sim Etrranty," Corona replied. "They ceased all production of their own needs many centuries ago, converting to an entirely raiding economy. The pattern is not unusual, even in men."

He broke off, looking at the two men. "In the past,

they exibited a tendency to wanton cruelty. What happened at Bluefield?"

Imin's voice was still unemotional, flat. "We have several slides of the human remains found at the scene. I'll run through them."

Shana looked in another direction. She, too, was one of the first persons on the scene after the raid. The things she saw still gave her screaming nightmares. She had no desire to relive anything connected with that visit.

The Tribune-Commander sat quietly, viewing each slide projection without comment. The only indication he gave of any emotion was the tight grip he maintained on the handle of his short sword. When Imin was finished, he said baldly, "There have been other raids. What have you done about them?"

Imin was embarrassed, defensive. "We found the Planetary Guard fighting ships were no match for their landing craft. The only thing we could do was let them land and put a thermonuclear missile in on the sight."

The Tribune-Commander glared at the younger man. "You wear that uniform to protect people, boy, not destroy them. Never forget that. If you can't shoot them out of the sky, ram the bastards."

Imin flushed.

Narsima Etrranty tried a soothing tack. "His men did their best, Tribune-Commander. He lost half his forces trying to fight these raids before I forbade any further attempt at combat. We have nothing that will fight them on the ground and we are totally outmatched in space. Our only hope is to destroy enough of their raiding parties that they will cease their attacks and go elsewhere."

"Only to do the same thing over again," Corona said, in a voice charged with dangerous intensity. "You have no need of any further presentation, Narsima. I can see that I and my men have work to do."

"Good," the Narsima nodded and smiled, sounding pleased. "I believe, then, that we may ignore any further pleasantries and get to a discussion of the hard details of our arrangement."

"My Operations Officer will be over to meet with your staff people in the morning," Corona said.

"Tribune-Commander," Shana began in a hesitant voice.

"Yes?" His voice mellowed as he turned to face the young woman.

"I was wondering if you would allow me to visit your compound? Perhaps do a story?"

The Narsima's face pursed with disapproval. "Shana, I am afraid that the Gladii never admit outside journalists to their area."

Corona waved him down. "Never in the past, that is true, Sim Etrranty. Now, though, the situation has changed. Your people must learn to know us. You have my permission to begin tomorrow. I will assign an officer to guide you."

"Thank you," she smiled sweetly. Inwardly, she rebelled. The last thing she wanted was some official stooge hiding the things she most wanted to see. She and that guide were going to accidentally miss connections. That was certain.

Later, as they were leaving the Narsima's apartment, Shana felt Imin's hand steal around her shoulders. She smiled up at him as he asked, "I was wondering, Sim, if there was any chance of a date tonight?"

She pursed her lips and assumed a mock-serious expression. "I'm not really certain, Sima. It seems that I am currently engaged to make supper at the apartment of the Changaree tonight. Do you believe he might let me go?"

"Knowing him," Imin replied pleasantly, "I seriously doubt it."

He changed the subject and his voice grew serious. "I wish you wouldn't go over to the Gladii encampment. We know nothing about them, and anything could happen."

"Imin," she replied firmly, "it's my job. I have to go there if I'm to get any kind of story from them."

"Like I said," he continued gruffly, hugging her, "you don't need this job. You could marry me like I have been asking you to do for the last year."

"No," she shook her head. "Not yet. I, mmph—"

His kiss stilled further conversation.

The quiet hiss of the steam motor on the velotrike provided a monotonous background to Shana's thoughts as she headed out to the Gladii compound on the following morning. When it came in view, she carefully studied the layout as the guidance computer on the little vehicle automatically took her to the main gate. The compound was laid out with military precision in a hexagonal pattern made by six triangular groupings of buildings, set point in, base out.

The guard at the gate was polite to an almost artificially precise degree, as though he was repeating lessons learned by heart in some classroom. He directed her to the headquarters building in the center of the compound. She cheerily thanked him, knowing full well that was the last place she wanted to go.

She deliberately kept the speed on her vehicle to a

slow walk, to give her time to find a place that looked worth investigating. The sameness of the buildings in the compound depressed her. All were quick-erection geodesic domes, varying only in size and, presumably, purpose. She finally chose a large one off the main route that seemed to have music coming from it, and pulled her velotrike up in front.

The guard at the gate was following her progress. When she stopped in front of the large dome, he reached for the phone in his guard station.

As she parked the velotrike in front of the dome, she could hear the sounds of music and cheering from inside. Standing in the entrance, she could see that the interior was laid out like a small amphitheater, with tables on various stages surrounding a circular stage in the dome's center. The place was dimly lit, with the exception of the stage, on which two of the Gladii were engaged in the coordinated posturing of a highly athletic dance. The tables surrounding the stage were full of drinking, cheering soldiers.

The music was provided by a small band of Gladii, using several guitars and recorder-like flutes, and two men blowing what appeared to be trumpets. As the music picked up speed, emotion began to swell in the crowd. They began to chant in time to the music and the movements of the dancers, "Yawm, yawm, yawm dan schici, schici yan, schici yan!"

The words made no sense to her, until she remembered her father saying that the Gladius regiments used a private language among themselves.

She was fascinated by the graceful posturing of the dancers, until a hand on her arm spun her around. She found herself looking into the steel grey, emotionless eyes of one of the young troopers. He looked her over for a moment, much like a butcher examining a side of beef, and it shook her that a boy barely out of his middle teens could display that much cool detachment.

He asked her a question, in what was obviously the regimental language. Then, when she shook her head in uncomprehension, repeated it in Lingua.

"You aren't engaged for tonight, are you?"

She shook her head, trying to figure what the young man had in mind.

"Then I claim you. Come with me."

He began to apply pressure to her arm, evidently trying to take her back to his table. He wasn't being rough about it, but he had a firm grip on her arm.

She tried to pull away, but it was no good. Without exerting himself, he was matching anything she did.

"Anatak."

The word came from the open entrance behind her. Although spoken in a conversational tone, it cut through the background furor like a knife. The trooper dropped her arm and stiffened into attention, not even an eyelid quivering. She turned and saw a young Gladius with the insignia of an officer standing in the doorway of the dome.

He marched up to the soldier and spoke to him for a moment in low, even tones. The man saluted, ran to his table, got his hat, and trotted out the door.

Shana shook herself slightly. "Thank you," she said. "Where is he going?"

The officer came up and took off his cylindrical cap. "I am Lieutenant Athan. That man is on his way to the Duty Sergeant for punishment tours."

"Oh," she was flustered, "I'm sure that wasn't necessary. Really, he just made a mistake."

"I must apologize for him, but the punishment is necessary.

"He mistook you for an assigned pleasure girl, not a civilian. A Gladius cannot afford such errors of judgement, especially on a world on which we are guests. That is why he is being punished."

In spite of herself, she was curious. "What are the punishment tours?"

He said calmly, "A tour is a twenty-four-hour route march with full pack. He has been assigned two of them. He will be through the day after tomorrow at this time."

She was aghast. "But—!"

He ignored her outburst. "The Tribune-Commander said that you are to be allowed full freedom of access within the compound, and I am to explain any question that you may have." He turned away from her and faced the stage. "Right now, for instance, you are in the Lower Ranks Club, and the men generally put on a good show to entertain themselves. I recommend that we watch, if only out of courtesy to them."

The cool rebuff irritated her. The thought of what he had just done to the unfortunate soldier fueled her anger. Then she got a grip on her emotions. Anger wasn't going to get her what she wanted. The best route to take looked like friendliness, if these men even understood the concept, she thought acidly.

"Do you come here often?" she asked, in what she hoped was a friendly tone.

"No." His voice was just as cool and even as ever. "Officers are not allowed inside, except on duty. The men have to have some place to themselves."

"I thought every aspect of their lives was controlled," she said, a trifle more pointedly than she intended.

"Except for their recreation," he replied unconcernedly, "that is true."

He smiled at her in a slightly ironic fashion. "Some choice must be allowed, though. After all, we *are* human."

That hit home. She quieted momentarily and directed her attention to the dancers on the stage. The two men were now rotating around each other, arms and legs spread, in a series of whirling leaps. Suddenly, each man threw the battle ax in his right hand out into the audience. The axes didn't hit, however. They flew out in a hard, flat trajectory for a moment, then flew unerringly back to their owners' hands. The men began throwing their axes faster, in time to the chanting and the music.

Shana turned to ask the officer how the return was accomplished when she realized one of the axes was flying in her direction. Her head snapped back, but she made no sound. She was too startled to cry out. The ax stopped in mid-air a foot from her head, whipped around on its balance point, then flew back to its owner.

"Don't be alarmed," Athan said, putting his hand in the small of her back to steady her, "and don't cry out. It was his idea of a joke, a little hazing welcome. When they all see you unshaken, you will have their respect."

"I'm all right," she said shakily. Now, if her knees would only believe that.

The dance ended. The dancers leaped off the stage, turning complete somersaults in mid-air, to have drinks pressed in their hands as they landed. Trying hard to calm down after the ax incident, Shana wondered what was next. She began to speculate uneasily if she was in over her head. These men were totally unpredictable. Possibly dangerous.

Athan was looking at her, observing her efforts to calm down. He nodded with approval. "That ax scared you, but you have it under control. That is good. You need not have worried about it, though."

She looked at him in slight amazement, while a part of her wondered at a compliment from this ice cool young man.

"Why?" she asked. "And tell me, how do you control those axes, make them fly back like that?"

He held out his right wrist and pointed to a large metal bracelet that encircled it. "Those axes weren't really thrown. This is a miniaturized tractor-pressor device. It controls the flight of the ax, and is in turn controlled by wrist action. A skilled ax man can make his weapon turn figure eights in the air forty meters off."

She looked curiously at the bracelet. "Isn't an ax rather archaic?"

"We have never found it so," he replied evenly.

The flutes struck up a pleasant, minor key air, one that Shana found familiar. Somewhere in the crowd, one of the soldiers was singing in a well-controlled baritone. It took Shana a moment to realize he was singing in Lingua.

"When you came to me, in the Spring,
    in the Spring,
And the gentle breeze did blow,
And the golden sun did shine,
Then did our lives entwine,

in the Spring,
in the Spring."

"I feel it is time we moved on to other areas." Athan's voice cut through the song as easily as it had earlier cut through the shouting.

Shana momentarily shook her head. Then, glancing at the set in the Lieutenant's imperturbable face, she shrugged and followed him out the door.

The music bothered her. The first dance was the kind of thing she had expected to see here. The second song most definitely was not.

It was an old song, but, as it happened, a familiar one to her. It was a love song, but a sad one. She remembered the ending wasn't happy. The last line was, "And with you gone, my life was as a dead tree in the Winter, in the Winter."

Now, why didn't Athan want her to be around when the song ended?

She followed as he led her around the camp, seeing everything from the neatly arranged barracks to the sports field. There was some form of ball game in progress as they arrived, involving a lot of running and violent action. The men on the sidelines, whenever a point was scored, let out with a high, warbling yell that seemed to carry on and on.

She looked at Athan. "Father told me about your war cry. I thought you only used it in combat."

He nodded. "True. All the noise those men are making is merely an expression of high spirits. It's not the *yalayathal*, the raising of the war cry. That is, as you said, only reserved for battle."

He brought up the subject again as they were examining one of the antigrav war sleds. "This is a command sled," he said, pointing to various features on the slim metal craft. "There are the six harness rigs for the men, three to a side. In addition, the harness in the center is for the bearer of the *brushara,* the battle shout."

Her look was enough to prompt an explanation. "The brushara is the horn of an Arkayagan ram, blown to signal the advance of a cohort into battle. The bearer goes everywhere with the cohort commander, hence his position on the sled. The brushara is only lost when all of the men of the unit are dead, because it *is* the unit, its soul and spirit. As the ax and the *yalayathal* are to the individual Gladius, the *brushara* is to the unit as a whole."

She nodded in understanding. "But, isn't the sound of the horn a little hard to hear in combat?"

"Not really," he replied. "The brushara is electronically amplified and produces tones in both the subsonic and supersonic. Its blast can stagger an opponent at three quarters of a kilometer. In fact, our men wear special ear protection in their helmets against it."

"It's a weapon of war as well as a signal," she said.

"Precisely," he nodded. "Come. I think it's time you spoke with the Tribune-Commander."

As they walked over to the headquarters building, a boy, about thirteen, passed them, saluting the officer as he passed. He was dressed in the full uniform of a Gladius, with the addition of what appeared to be a ram's horn slung around one shoulder. Shana stared for a moment at the departing boy, then realized what he was. "Lieutenant Athan," she said agitatedly, "was *that* a brushara bearer?"

"Of course," he replied coolly, "didn't you see his horn?"

"But—" she stammered, "so young. . ."

"The bearers are chosen from among the top cadets in each cycle. It is an honor, and one that I myself have held. That boy has been a trained combat soldier since he was eight years old. He fought in his first battle at the age of twelve, since he was a bearer. The normal cadet only waits another two years, so I see nothing to concern you about his age."

"Still," she said, "it seems young to shove a boy that young into a war."

"Sim Etrranty," Athan stopped and turned to look at her, "has it occurred to you that it is cruel to place any sentient being in a position where he has to destroy other sentient beings to preserve all that he holds dear?

"Still," he continued, an unreadable expression on his face, "the practice of youths of that age going into battle will not continue."

He wouldn't respond to any further questions, so she shrugged and followed him to the Tribune-Commander's office.

She found Tribune-Commander Corona seated on one of several large cusions in a sparsely furnished office. The room seemed sterile, with the furnishings stark in their simplicity. When she was shown into the room, he spared her one piercing glance, waved her to a cushion, then turned his attention back to several papers in his hands.

Without looking up, he said, "You have met my people, my soldiers, Sim Etrranty. Tell me what you think."

Taken slightly aback by the blunt command, she stumbled through a few remarks about how interesting it all was, and how she was trying hard to learn all she could. He waved his hand to stop her.

"Spare me that foolish set of platitudes," he said. "You were allowed in here for a very definite reason, and on my express order. You are far too intelligent not to have seen things that will give you an accurate picture of the culture of our regiment, and I want your thoughts on those things. Be frank. I want your honest feelings."

She took a deep breath. This fiery old man was really putting her on the spot! She wondered just how much he meant that command to be frank. Oh, well, she may as well find out. There was enough material for a hundred stories in her memory already.

She looked him dead in the eye. "Frankly, Tribune-Commander, your men scare the hell out of me."

He nodded his head gravely. "Continue."

"There are a number of things that bother me, but one of them is the fact that I believe you think of yourselves as a separate culture. Any number of remarks and hints I've gotten lead to that fact."

The Tribune-Commander carefully arranged the papers on his small field desk for a moment, then looked at her. "Sim Etrranty, you are a most astute observer. You made one small error, though. We do not merely consider ourselves a separate culture, we *are* a separate culture.

"Look around you," he continued, waving his arms to encompass the entire surrounding area, "do you not wonder where all of these buildings and all of this equipment comes from, if, as we said, we were run off Victrix Base with our lives? Sim Etrranty, there is a standard kit to build a compound like this on each of the Imperial transports. All we carry when we move is ourselves and our personal weapons.

Everything, supporting facilities, heavy weapons systems, even personal clothing, is pre-packaged on the transport. Does this bring anything to your mind?"

She shook her head, unable to see where he was leading.

He placed both hands on his desk and leaned forward to stare at her. "The ostensible reason for that, Sim Etrranty, is that it gives my regiment the ability to make a permanent move in literally a matter of minutes. If all men are present on compound when the alert blows, we can be gone in thirty minutes. Militarily, that is fine, an admirable goal. But consider what it does to the man that has nothing permanent in his life, not even his comrades, because they may be dead in the next fight. The people that conceived the system under which my regiment lives considered the soldiers no more than cogs in a military machine.

"Consider, Sim Etrranty, the fact that the Gladius was not created when the Empire was being formed. He was born to maintain, not create. When the Empire began to dissolve, as it is now doing, he became a detriment, a stumbling block to that dissolution, hence the attack on our base."

Corona leaned back slightly, and some of the fire went out of his eyes. "Do you know," he asked, "how a Gladius is trained?"

She shook her head.

"*All,* not just some, but all of my men were born into the regiment. It is the same with the other regiments, as well. A boy begins preliminary training at the age of eight, leading to active service at the age of fifteen. Officers are chosen by test at four times during a man's life, and he may be commissioned by passing that test even if he fails the first three.

"You see no children in this compound, because none of our families survived the destruction of Victrix Base. That is a deeper wound to us than others. A man may not marry until he has served at least ten years of active service. That insures that only the strongest and best soldiers breed the next generation, an almost Darwinian selection.

"The loss of the families meant not only great personal loss to us, one that each man fought and bled for, but the loss of the regiment's future. I assure you that the future of the regiment means as much to each Gladius as the future of the family."

"B-b-but," she stammered her outrage, "you haven't said one thing about the women? What about the mothers, wives, all the rest?"

"Our women are—were—just as much a part of the regiment as the men. From childhood, they work at the non-combat jobs, administrative, technical, entertainment, and such as that. Remember, they have—had—the same beliefs as the men. The regiment was all the existence we all had. It is our life, or, rather, was our life."

"What's the matter," she sneered, "weren't women good enough to be fighters? Were they *all* in support jobs?"

He looked at her calmly. "At the time of her death, my wife was twice your age and could break you in half. She was also the Victrix Base Commander. Among us, the women always held the command of the bases and support. Long ago, we realized that someone among us had to retain a modicum of sanity, stay out of the fighting, and maintain our heritage. That was the job of our women. They actually kept us in existence. That was something we evolved on our own, it was not the original plan of the individuals that created our regiments."

She shook her head, slightly ashamed. "Look, I'm sorry about your wife. I'd no intention of trying to bring up past tragedies.

"Tell me one thing," she said, "doesn't all this plan, the cold blooded breeding scheme, the depersonalization of the system, seem horrible to you? To be frank, it fills me with loathing."

He smiled at her. "There are good things as well as bad. The Empire had many years of peace because of us. We recognize that, in order for some men to live orderly lives without fear, others must sacrifice and die. That is our responsibility, and we assume it proudly. If the inbreeding of the system has created soldiers stronger and more intelligent than before, it has also created soldiers more dedicated to the preservation of the human race and the human individual. If I could term anything our prime religious tenet, it is the belief that the individual is all important and the civilian should be protected at all costs."

He leaned forward again. "That is why I consider your social system totally corrupt."

"Wha—" she gasped.

"I believe your father would agree with me," he said calmly. "You have a Guiding Council, totally isolated from the people, a military that is too weak to offer any balance, and a populace that doesn't seem to care that it has no responsibility in either. Your leaders are so separated from the people that they think nothing of destroying them wholesale to deter raiders. The real tragedy is, the rest of the populace is so uncaring, they go right along with it."

At first, she was outraged and shocked. Then a

sinking feeling began to grow in the pit of her stomach, telling her he was exactly correct. She asked, "Does my father know you feel this way?"

Corona nodded. "He does. He also knows that I hold the only real power in the political system, and will use it if nothing happens to change that repugnant situation.

"Why else do you think he fears me?"

The discussion carried on for several more hours. She was deeply abstracted as she left, only noticing one thing by merest chance. As she left the compound, she saw a young Gladius in full field gear trudging steadily around the camp's perimeter. It was the same man that had accosted her in the Lower Ranks club.

She flushed guiltily and drove on, in silence and in thought.

Over the next three weeks, Shana was a constant visitor to the regimental compound. The tridio network for which she worked didn't mind. For a story like this one promised to be, they would gladly let her have several months or more.

Her original story had faded into the background, however. If she had taken time to examine her purposes, she would have found that her exposé had been replaced by an all-consuming interest in the Gladius and his culture.

It was an interest that was encouraged by the Tribune-Commander and his men. It was as though, having lost their past and their future at the same stroke, they were pouring all of their history and background into the most willing ear.

She was more than willing. She spent many hours-long conversations with the Tribune-Commander, then poked into every aspect of the compound when she wasn't talking to him. She became familiar to every man in the regiment.

To a lesser extent, her father was also a regular visitor to the compound. He never went anywhere other than Corona's office, however. No one else was present at those meetings, but the expression on the Narsima's face was always stormy as he left.

A day after the Narsima's most explosive meeting with the Tribune-Commander, two events occurred. Shana left on a special temporary assignment, and a sighting was made on the long range probes.

Both Matic Etrranty and Imin Webster were notified as a matter of course. In a new change of procedure, Tribune-Commander Corona was also notified of the incoming Wareegan Raider.

The Narsima entered the Combat Command Center to discover that both the Changaree and the Gladius commander were already there. A tiny frown flitted swiftly across the Narsima's face as he caught sight of the bearded soldier. When the man turned to face him, however, he was his normal bland self.

The Tribune-Commander spoke first. "Have you ever wondered what happened to the Andromeda Expedition?"

Etrranty frowned again. "You speak in riddles, Corona. Explain yourself."

The Gladius gestured towards the probe monitor. "If you wish to view their ship, it's in that screen."

Etrranty looked at the huge globe centered in the monitor screen. "It's no more than the same mother ship they had the last times they came."

Imin spoke up. "Your pardon, Narsima, but the Tribune-Commander has been explaining it to me.

That actually was the ship containing the quarter million colonists sent to the next galaxy. The Wareegans, apparently, captured it and turned it into a base ship for their raids."

"All along," Corona added, "I have been curious as to just how the Wareegans could support the extensive raiding they were doing on this planet. I knew we cleaned out their home worlds long ago. This explains everything. It also explains why your Planetary Guard fighters can't touch those landing craft. When that expedition was launched a hundred and fifty years ago, they were given every protection the Empire could provide. Those landing barges are twice as powerful as my own craft."

"Report coming in," a communications tech shouted. "Landing beacon has impacted at Harborview."

"Our new fusion plant sight!" Imin exclaimed.

"Yes," the Narsima murmured. "Shana is there now, covering the opening ceremonies."

Imin looked stricken, then resigned. "Stand by to launch missles as soon as they are completely down."

The Tribune-Commander reached over and grabbed Imin's shirtfront roughly. "Are you out of your mind?" he demanded. "You've already destroyed thousands of your own people, and now you want to kill thousands more!"

"They're dead anyway, as soon as those ships land!" Imin shouted back.

"Not if the regiment is there to take them out when they land," Corona's voice was deadly soft, the expression of a man in a cold killing rage.

"You can't do that!" Imin blanched. "With their strength, it would be an even fight at best. Even if you won, you would be so decimated you could never fight again as a unit!

"We need you here!" he said passionately. "When they hit the capitol, that's when you will attack. If you waste yourself now, we will have nothing when they come back!"

"Look in the screen, fool!" Corona shoved the younger man towards the monitor and its startled attendant. "If we beat them now, they'll stay beat. That's all they have!"

"I must agree with the Changaree," Etrranty broke in quietly, "as much as I dislike doing so. They will come here to the capitol eventually. That's when we will need you and your regiment. Not now."

Corona rounded on him. His voice held a hard edge that grated on all that heard it. "I must remind you, Narsima, that there is no force on this planet that can tell me or my men what to do. There are many things I would wish to do on this world. That's of no importance now. Your people need protection, and you won't do it. I can and will. That's the ancient mission and pledge of the Gladius. I will fulfill it!"

"Come in the conference room, then," the Narsima shrugged. "We will discuss what you need."

A few moments later, both Imin and the Narsima watched the Tribune-Commander leave the CCC at a dead run. "You're letting him go through with it," Imin said in a deadpan fashion.

"I had no choice," Etrranty said placidly. "At any rate, we will be no worse off than before. In fact, if we can decoy them down on a few of our less important towns, we might be able to destroy enough of them to make them want to go somewhere else."

Imin made a face. "I still say it's a waste."

"But necessary," the Narsima replied.

"Now," he continued more briskly, "come with me. For some reason, Corona demanded that every part of this attack be recorded. We will have a unique seat at a sight you will never forget and one that I have always wanted to see."

"Your hobby, again," Imin sighed.

"Of course."

The two men arrived at the viewscreen dedicated to monitoring the regiment. The troops were already in formation in the compound. As they watched, Corona arrived and mounted a stand set up in front of the regiment. He was obviously preparing to make an address. "I have a translator programmed for the regimental language hooked up," Etrranty said. "We will hear everything he says."

"Stand at ease, men," Corona said as he looked out over the four hundred men assembled in front of him.

"You all know, and I don't have to tell you, that we left a job undone on Victrix Base.

"They destroyed our families, our people, and our regimental home. Some of them lived to tell about it. We can do nothing about them.

"There are Wareegan Raiders coming in to attack a small city not too far from here. They thought there was no one left to protect these people, that we were gone these hundred years of their separation from the Empire.

"They will shortly discover they were wrong."

Throughout the formation steel grey eyes began to burn with hidden fires. On a few faces, a quiet smile began to spread.

The wolfhound was scenting the wolf.

The Tribune-Commander continued after a moment. "As I said, we can do nothing about those who destroyed all that was dear to us, but we can do something about those that wish to accomplish the same purpose here. We can, and we will, for that is our one reason for existence.

"This will not be easy. We are evenly matched at best, probably outnumbered. That is of no matter, because we will not allow these raids to continue. No man will leave the field as long as a Wareegan stands.

"I order, as your commander, the Noanathal."

Etrranty, watching the monitor, turned to Imin. "It seems Corona believed our estimate of the situation, after all. The Noanathal, my dear young commander, is a memorial ritual. They reaffirm their pledge of duty and leave their blood behind. It is only undertaken when they feel there will be nothing else of themselves left. Most interesting!"

On the screen four hundred men were moving in unison. Each took a small cylinder from a chain around his neck and removed a white square of cloth from inside. Then he drew his short sword and pricked his left palm. He then held the cloth to the tiny wound and let the blood soak in.

Each step was ritualistically done, each trooper in precise time with the man on either side.

As the blood soaked the cloth, they began to repeat in a slow cadence, "I am a Gladius. I stand guard at the gates of Hell that nothing may pass and harm those I have sworn to protect. My life is nothing. My duty and purpose is everything. If my life is called for, it will be given gladly.

"I go now to face my enemy. I have seen him, and I know him. He will not see the dawn."

The ritual complete, the Tribune-Commander ordered the embarkation into the transport. As each man entered the hatch, he gave the little metal cylinder containing the bloody cloth to a transport crewman whose job was to safely return it to base.

As he watched his men board, Corona thought of a line from Kipling. "For what is our doom and pride."

He smiled to himself. He wished he could have talked to Kipling. That man would have understood.

In the viewing room, the Narsima gestured to the viewing screen.

"They'll ride that to the jump-off point," Etrranty explained. "It shouldn't be too long now."

An aide leaned in and whispered in Imin's ear. Imin turned and placed a hand on the Narsima's arm. "They've landed at Harborview."

"Umph," the Narsima settled himself more comfortably in the chair. "I hope Shana got out in time. If not, I hope she's dead."

Shana was neither. When the first blasts from the landing barges impacted, she ran away from the crowd and into the new fusion power plant. She spared one glance at the slowly settling Wareegan barges, then began a stumbling, heart-tearing, panic-filled run for the deepest sub-basement she could find.

The city of Harborview stood in a cup, scooped from the mountain range that followed the coastline. On one side, a small plain sat between the city and the mountains. The plain was filled with Wareegan landing barges. On the other side, the foothills came down nearly to the small city's edge.

A man stood on a promontory in those foothills.

He was wearing a khaki blouse and kilt, with a handgun, battle ax, and short sword strapped to his waist. A full beard ruffled gently in the wind beneath his combat helmet.

With his hand-held farviewer, he watched the horror of the carnage and panic below. His eyes, when he dropped the viewer to his middle, were alight with a fire held long in check. As he watched the predatory depredations of the raiders he silently promised blood for blood in a vengeance that this world would remember forever.

He triggered his throat mike. "Power level?"

A voice came back in his earphones. "At eighty per cent, Tribune-Commander. We will advance to maximum on your order. We await your command."

Corona glanced in the viewer again. "They are totally committed. Battle power!"

Behind the last range of hills before the city, a long line of battle sleds quivered as though eagerly alive and waiting to jump out and run towards an enemy. On board the sleds, men tightened harnesses, and calm comments were passed back and forth in throat mikes. The sled drivers inched the power levers towards maximum, their eyes glued to a gauge that crept ever upwards towards its highest point.

The Tribune-Commander raised his hand.

The gauges read maximum.

Corona's hand spread out, his fingers curling as though to tear physically at the aliens killing those he had sworn to protect.

He dropped his hand.

"CATAN NA BUSHARA!!"

As one, the three battle horns sounded with a blast audible for the length of the town. Pure sound tore at the fabric of the air, proclaiming the coming of the Gladius, the avenger.

"There go the horns," Etrranty said calmly. "This is what we were waiting for, my friend. You are about to witness the most terrible sight in history, the Gladius in full charge."

Outside the city, silver slivers of metal were racing a bare few meters off the earth, headed into the outskirts. The men on board hung on grimly in their harnesses, gritting their teeth in the blast of the wind. Already, a few of the Wareegans were aware of what was happening and were directing their fire at the oncoming sleds. Blasts and flashes tore at the bright morning as near misses tore at the ground.

Some shots didn't miss. Occasionally a sled would tear itself apart in an ear-shattering scream of tortured steel, or tumble into the ground. Some men got free in time. Others did not.

A group of the three-meter-tall raiders ran for a low screen of trees on the city's edge. Once on the other side, they would be able to get a clear shot at the careening sleds. Suddenly, the trees burst in a hundred directions as the slim shape of a sled blasted through, barreling into the group of Wareegans. The surviving raiders barely regained their feet as the Gladii on the sled dropped free and fell into their midst.

A raider's shot cut one of the soldiers in two, but there was another right behind him. The raiders, one after another, died in the span of a few seconds, one split in two by a thrown ax.

By this time, Corona and his command group had reached the center of the small city. Panicky townspeople were everywhere, still dying from a chance blow or shot from the raiders, but the Gladii were also there in force.

The trooper next to Corona threw a snap shot at a charging raider. It blew the alien apart, but the bolt's blast also dropped the civilian behind the raider. Taking it in, Corona spoke into his throat mike, "They're too mixed in, axes only, unless you get a clear shot."

For a moment, he looked into the eyes of the young trooper that had killed the man. He had just violated all he had been taught all his life, a crime, in his eyes, worse than murder. Corona grabbed the man and shook him. "You couldn't help it! You have a job to do, Gladius, DO IT!"

The young soldier, close to the edge of insane shock at his crime, grabbed his ax and charged into the crowd. Corona knew he'd never see the man again.

In the power station sub-basement, Shana was cowering in a corner, fearfully eyeing the two doors into the room. She knew nothing of what was occurring on the surface. Only the sound of blasts and screams filtered down to her.

Suddenly, the door farthest from her opened and disgorged two of the raiders.

She screamed in utter terror, all of her nightmares come to life.

The raiders were actually fleeing the fighting on the surface, but they were ready to take their anger out on the noisy food grub in the corner. This one would live for a little while, and give them some pleasure. The one in the forefront advanced and reached for her.

The second door flew open, and one of the cohort commanders charged in, followed by his brushara bearer. They had been trailing the raiders and had eyes only for the two aliens. The commander's ax took the first raider high in the chest. The second alien, under no orders against discharging his weapon, blew a fist sized hole in the commander's chest. As that happened, the boy carrying the horn dropped it, and, drawing his ax, charged the alien. The tall raider and the teen-aged boy grappled and rolled over and over on the floor in a snarling, smashing tangle.

Shana watched with wide eyes as the two fought, then suddenly slumped quiet on the floor. Hesitantly, she approached the still forms. It wasn't nice to see. The Wareegan had nearly torn the boy from limb, but his ax was buried hilt deep in the alien's chest below the neck. Both were dead.

She backed away in horror, then her foot struck something. It was the brushara. Only then did she realize that the regiment, her regiment, was upstairs. She picked up the battle horn, then turned a last glance at the dead boy. Hysterical sobs began to well up from deep inside. Weeping, she turned and ran upstairs.

Outside, most of the civilian population was gone, and so were the raiders. She could hear the sounds of fighting nearby, but could see none of the combatants. From somewhere, a little girl caromed into her legs, crying for her mother. Reflexively, she snatched up the child and ran, cradling both her and the horn.

Running around a group of buildings, she caught sight of the plain outside of the city. More of the landing barges were on the ground now, and fresh groups of raiders were spilling from them. It looked like there were hundreds of the aliens. She spun on her heel and ran back into the city.

She only went a little way before she barrelled into a line of Gladii. Spotting a familiar face, she realized the officer in charge was Lieutenant Athan. He held her and the child for a moment, until they both calmed down. He still had his normal calm exterior, but, as she looked into his eyes, she realized they were no longer empty and cold. Angry demons of hell looked back at her from behind those slate grey pupils.

"They're coming," she gasped, "be-behind me."

"Who's coming?" he asked evenly.

"Raiders. Hundreds of them." She pointed out into the plain.

He looked where she pointed for a moment. "Sim Etrranty," he said politely, "I think you should take the little girl and get behind those walls, out of the line of fire. You need go no farther."

She looked at him in amazement.

He looked at the horn in her hands. "That is the Third Cohort's brushara."

She made as if to hand it to him, but he shook his head. "No. Hold it for safekeeping. It will come back when you do. Now, go."

"But," she cried, shaken, "there are hundreds of the raiders coming."

He turned, drew his short sword and threw it point first into the ground. "This is as far as they are coming."

On either side of him, she could see the other men also driving their swords into the ground. She ran for the walls, holding the crying little girl to her breast.

Inside a ring of his men, the Tribune-Commander addressed his staff. "We have the town cleared at the moment. What's our status?"

His personnel officer spoke. "We're doing good, so far. About twenty per cent casualties, mostly in the Third. They soaked up the brunt when we came in."

The operations officer spoke. "This looks like the time to go after that mother ship, but we have some raiders to get through, first. That last wave of landing barges is on the ground, I'd say about five hundred plus of the Wareegans are massing for a counterattack."

"Who's facing them?" Corona asked.

"Second Cohort. First is moving to support, along with the remnants of the Third and the bulk of the First. Athan's men have driven in their swords. They won't be moved from there, that's certain."

"He ought to keep enough of their attention to allow us to break through," Corona said with somber satisfaction. "Well, let's get to it. Where are the sleds?"

"I have them, Tribune-Commander," a young officer, the Command Security Guard Section Leader, said. "There are six, with enough men to ride them and a qualified barge-rated pilot. We'll get you there."

"I know you will," Corona smiled. "Let's go get that mother ship."

He turned to his staff. "Gentlemen, this will be our last staff call."

They all smiled savagely and left for the fighting line on the edge of town.

Corona turned back to the small group of troopers clustered around the young officer. "Mount up! Let's finish this thing!"

As the sleds trembled into the air on their anti-gravs, one of the men began a high, warbling yell, taken up almost immediately by the others. As the first sled began to move forward, thirty-six throats bellowed out in a yell that echoed from the surrounding buildings. "NIR YALLAH!!"

The six sleds flew out of the city streets and across the dug-in Gladius line, headed for the grounded landing barges. One was blasted to fragments moments after leaving the protection of the buildings, but the others began to interweave and bob, dodging the incoming alien fire. Blasts began to erupt around the raiders, covering fire from the units still in the city. The sleds blasted through the alien lines like a ton of bricks, the troopers on board firing as they passed.

Each dead alien was one less to reach his troops, Corona thought with savage satisfaction.

The landing barges seemed to leap up in front of them, growing bigger almost instantly. Corona chose his target, then triggered his throat mike. "Stand by to release . . . RELEASE!"

Instantly, the surviving thirty hit their harness release buttons and were thrown free. The five sleds continued on to strike and explode five of the landing barges, the five closest to the one chosen. Before all of the men touched ground, two were up and into the airlock of the barge. One folded, hit by an alien blast, but the other laid down a steady fire, covering for the others.

"Up there!" Corona yelled. "Get into that ship!"

Several more died on the way in, but they made it. Once inside, they all scattered, clearing the barge and headed for designated tasks. One came pelting back to the Tribune-Commander. "Sir, Ensign Evoy reports the barge has no autopilot! There's no installation for one, either. Apparently this model never carried one."

"Can he fly it?"

"Yes sir."

Corona triggered his mike. "All hands, give me your attention. We can no longer set this ship to ram and detonate. It will have to be flown in. I will remain and insure it reaches its target. The remainder of you will eject out the escape ports as soon as we have taken off."

"Negative!" The voice on the mike circuit was that of the young officer leading the section. The chorus of agreement from the other voices made it plain the feeling was unanimous. "Tribune-Commander, you're going to need men to man the barge defenses and the guns if you're going to make it. We're coming with you!"

"Only volunteers!" Corona injected.

"Tribune-Commander," the young voice replied, "we volunteered when we were born."

Corona cut his mike and turned to walk up to the control room. "I know you did," he muttered sadly. "I know you did."

While he was en route, the barge lurched as it sprang up from the ground and leaped screaming up into the sky. When he reached the control room, the pilot turned to him. "The anti-matter drive is rigged, sir. When this thing hits, it'll be like a small sun, just off Cauldwell's surface."

"Very good," he replied quietly, "just make sure it impacts. There's a lot of innocent people down there that won't live past that damned mothership's next visit if we don't."

"They will not see the dawn," the pilot's traditional reply was spoken just as quietly, but with hardened conviction.

They shot into the fighter screen surrounding the mothership with guns blazing, burning a way through. They were taking constant hits, but Corona somehow kept his feet and stared into the screen where the gigantic Wareegan ship continued to grow. As he watched, he drew his ax and began to finger the haft.

He suddenly realized he was quietly singing the words to an old, soft melody.

It had been a favorite of his wife's, he recalled.

The blast was bright enough to bathe the whole quarter of Caulfield in a stark, actinic glare.

"He did it! He rammed the mothership!" Etrranty found himself on his feet, yelling.

"He did it," Athan breathed. Then he set his face to the oncoming horde of the raiders, and the expression was terrible to see. "Nir Yallah!"

From the hundreds of throats around him, the battle cry began to well up. "Nir Yallah! Nir Yallah! NIR-R-RYAALLLAH-H-H!!!"

From the safety of the buildings, Shana leaned around the wall and watched. By ones and twos, then tens and dozens, the Gladii rose up and moved into the oncoming aliens, their axes rising and falling in a steady motion, their weapons steadily blasting. She realized she was watching another act in the million-year-old drama of the protector and the predator, both locked in a final great deathgrip, like two huge beasts.

The Gladii moved among their foe, killing with terrible abandon before they fell.

But, when each Gladius fell, no other stepped

forward to take his place.

The Narsima sailed through the hospital ward like a huge ship, trailing the Changaree like a tender in his wake. "Simply amazing!" he proclaimed. "All of the Wareegans destroyed. Not just some, mind you, but all. Granted, only a handful of wounded survived, but the whole thing does credit to their record as fighting men. I must write this up for the militaria collector's journal.

"Ah, Shana, my dear," he said as she came into the ward. She was wearing hospital dress. She was freshly scrubbed, but still looked worn and haggard. She was still carrying the burshara.

"I'm happy to see you survived," he continued. "And you saved one of their brusharas. Hold on to it. It's very valuable."

Imin moved up next to her. "I'm sorry for what you went through," he said softly. "I'm glad you're still alive. Is there anything I can do?"

She looked at him. "Only leave me alone for awhile," she said quietly. "Really, Imin, I have to think things out."

"I understand," he said, moving back away from her.

She heard a low moan from one of the beds. It was one of the Gladii, and he gestured weakly in her direction. She moved past Imin like he wasn't there, and walked over to the trooper's bedside.

The man's face, what was left of it, was familiar to her. It was the same soldier that had grabbed her in the Lower Ranks Club, the day she'd first come to the regimental compound.

She sat down in the chair next to the bed. The Narsima looked at her with a musing expression for a moment, shrugged at Imin, then took his arm and left the room. She sat staring at the ruined face of the young soldier, then took his hand and held it gently.

"Sim Etrranty," the quiet voice of a nurse broke into her absorbtion with the man. "This was left for you by the Gladius Commander. It was only just delivered to the hospital."

It was a small letter. She absently thanked the nurse as she tore open the envelope and began to read.

"Sim Etrranty," it began. "The fact that you are reading this means that I am dead, but the regiment was able to fulfill its mission. You, and many others like you, are alive because of that. I am glad.

"You may have wondered why you were the first person to see as much of our lives as you saw. Simply, I had carefully chosen you for that task.

"My reasoning was simple. You are a well-known personality in the public's eye, with access to your father's political contacts. You also possess great depth of personality and ability.

"There was one other consideration. You are a woman. As I told you, the women among us are the ones that maintain our tradition and our stability.

"I chose you to continue that mission. We have no one else.

"Another mission, far more important, must take precedence, however. In the bag of my personal effects, left with the transport commander, is an Imperial survey tape of Cauldwell. It indicates that this world has both the raw materials and manufacturing capability to build starships. With the technical library on the transport, and the transport itself as a guide, Cauldwell will be able to create an interstellar fleet.

"That means that this world could be the one to rebuild human culture, after the Empire completely destroys itself. You are far enough away from the Empire's current span of control to be unaffected in the final debacle, whenever that comes.

"Your only stumbling block is the total corruption of your social system. My original intention was to use my regiment to control the government and destroy that corruption. I know now that I was wrong. A military dictatorship would not only be worse than the venal government you now have, it would destroy all of the ideals and beliefs that made the Gladius what he is. That is intolerable.

"I now feel there will be no further need for us after the destruction of the Wareegans. In fact, our continued presence might still lead to the very military dictatorship I fear. Instead, we will do our duty to the best of our ability and take what comes.

"You have, then, two missions. You must work with body and soul to revitalize your social system, to prepare it for the future it must one day face. You are not alone. You have your personal resources, and you have the remaining men and resources of the Victrix. From the day of their recovery or survival, all of my men that return from this battle are under instructions to support your every action. As I said before, you have the depth of character to be a good leader and the public connections to accomplish your ends. With my men behind you, you will not fail. You must not fail.

"The human race depends on it.

"The second mission I have for you is simple, but one I ask from the bottom of my heart. Do not let us be forgotten.

"As time goes on, you will need a military force. Raise them from your people and train them well, but do not make them in our image. The Gladius was created by uncaring men with clinical efficiency. We are the best soldiers in history, but we paid a terrible price. We lost a portion of our humanity. Do not let that happen again.

"You have every scrap of information about the regiment I can give you, including a record of this, our last battle. Use it well, and teach people the good and bad of what we were.

"The Victrix has fought for humankind for a hundred generations. It is little enough to ask, that someone keep alive the memory of what we were, but I ask it of you.

"Please do not let us die."

It was signed, "Corona, Tribune-Commander of the Victrix."

Matic Etrranty was holding forth in a small lounge in the hospital. "I tell you, it was the greatest experience of my life, watching those men in battle."

Imin replied, "I'm glad they were able to save Harborview."

The Narsima waved the thought aside as trivial. "It would have been rebuilt, eventually."

"There was some good come of this, though," he continued. "Corona's dead. The man wasn't entirely trustworthy. I will even say he was dangerous."

In the ward, the soldier was stirring under Shana's hand. "Were they all killed?" he asked in a weak, shaky voice.

"No," she said softly, "a few survived."

She gently placed the brushara under the young

soldier's feebly groping hand. As he felt it, he began to smile.

"A brushara. Then we still exist."

"Yes," she said, and her eyes began to fill with tears, "you still exist. And you always will."

FRED SABERHAGEN

☐ 49548	**LOVE CONQUERS ALL**	$1.95
☐ 52077	**THE MASK OF THE SUN**	$1.95
☐ 86064	**THE VEILS OF AZLAROC**	$2.25
☐ 20563	**EMPIRE OF THE EAST**	$2.95
☐ 77766	**A SPADEFUL OF SPACETIME**	$2.50

BERSERKER SERIES

Humanity struggles against inhuman death machines whose mission is to destroy life wherever they find it:

☐ 05462	**BERSERKER**	$2.25
☐ 05407	**BERSERKER MAN**	$1.95
☐ 05408	**BERSERKER'S PLANET**	$2.25
☐ 08215	**BROTHER ASSASSIN**	$1.95
☐ 84315	**THE ULTIMATE ENEMY**	$1.95

THE NEW DRACULA

The *real* story—as told by the dread Count himself!

☐ 34245	**THE HOLMES DRACULA FILE**	$1.95
☐ 16600	**THE DRACULA TAPE**	$1.95
☐ 62160	**AN OLD FRIEND OF THE FAMILY**	$1.95
☐ 80744	**THORN**	$2.75

H. BEAM PIPER

☐ 24890	**FOUR DAY PLANET/LONE STAR PLANET**	$2.25
☐ 26192	**FUZZY SAPIENS**	$1.95
☐ 48492	**LITTLE FUZZY**	$1.95
☐ 26193	**FUZZY PAPERS**	$2.75
☐ 49053	**LORD KALVAN OF OTHERWHEN**	$2.25
☐ 77779	**SPACE VIKING**	$2.25
☐ 23188	**FEDERATION** (5¼" x 8¼")	$5.95

MORE TRADE SCIENCE FICTION

Ace Books is proud to publish these latest works by major SF authors in deluxe large format collectors' editions. Many are illustrated by top artists such as Alicia Austin, Esteban Maroto and Fernando.

Robert A. Heinlein	Expanded Universe	21883	$8.95
Frederik Pohl	Science Fiction: Studies in Film (illustrated)	75437	$6.95
Frank Herbert	Direct Descent (illustrated)	14897	$6.95
Harry G. Stine	The Space Enterprise (illustrated)	77742	$6.95
Ursula K. LeGuin and Virginia Kidd	Interfaces	37092	$5.95
Marion Zimmer Bradley	Survey Ship (illustrated)	79110	$6.95
Hal Clement	The Nitrogen Fix	58116	$6.95
Andre Norton	Voorloper	86609	$6.95
Orson Scott Card	Dragons of Light (illustrated)	16660	$7.95

Available wherever paperbacks are sold or use this coupon.

Gordon R. Dickson

☐	16015	Dorsai! 1.95
☐	34256	Home From The Shore 2.25
☐	56010	Naked To The Stars 1.95
☐	63160	On The Run 1.95
☐	68023	Pro 1.95
☐	77417	Soldier, Ask Not 1.95
☐	77765	The Space Swimmers 1.95
☐	77749	Spacial Deliver 1.95
☐	77803	The Spirit Of Dorsai 2.50

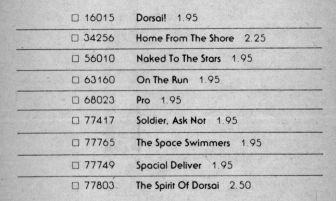

Available wherever paperbacks are sold or use this coupon.

ACE SCIENCE FICTION
P.O. Box 400, Kirkwood, N.Y. 13795

Please send me the titles checked above. I enclose _____.
Include 75¢ for postage and handling if one book is ordered; 50¢ per book for two to five. If six or more are ordered, postage is free. California, Illinois, New York and Tennessee residents please add sales tax.

NAME_____

ADDRESS_____

CITY_____STATE_____ZIP_____